Home Again

By Julie Campbell

Contents

Prologue – August 1938 – Barcelona

Tom had gone out to pursue a potential story in another part of the city. There were rumours of a dispute between different Republican factions at the Plaza de Espana and he thought it could be worth a picture or even a story. It had turned out to be something and nothing, as so often happened and he cursed himself for going. When he returned to the port area building where he shared an apartment with his wife and child, he knew immediately that something was wrong. The proprietor of the bar on the ground floor, Senor Garcia gave him a look of distress in between serving his customers. Tom ran upstairs to their rooms to find his sister-in-law Pilar trying to sort out washing while two young children, Maria and Luis, played with some wooden toys on the floor. She looked at him with eyes red from crying.

'Oh Tom, thank goodness you are back, sit down. I'm so sorry. It was Teresa's turn to queue for bread. It could so easily have been mine. It should have been me!' she wailed. The children both looked alarmed.

'What's happened. Tell me!'

'A plane was dropping bombs along the quayside. One fell on the queue by the baker's shop.

4

It must have been over in an instant. Five people are gone, including our Teresa. One of the neighbours came to tell us as his daughter is missing too. We are all heartbroken. I'm so sorry.'

Tom ran over to the scene by the baker's shop. There was nothing left of the shop except a smoking pile of rubble surrounding the mangled metal remains of the ovens. There was a foul burning odour still heavy in the air. Oddly, he was reminded of the smells of fireworks night. He picked up a woman's shoe from the mess, sat down in the middle of the street and howled. Yet another random act of violence: he had seen so many in the last few years. But this time, it wasn't a stranger but his beautiful young wife and unborn child who had paid the price. All his hopes for the future had gone in an instant. Teresa had been his anchor and the love of his life. Now, he was numb and senseless with loss. Neighbours came out to check that he wasn't hurt and took him back to Senor Garcia and his daughter Pilar.

Pilar was married to Teresa's brother Antonio and she reminded him that the family needed to be told. Post and transport were both unreliable now that the war was reaching a turning point and, before they had settled on a plan to do something, Teresa's elder brother Xavier turned up at the bar. Pilar and Antonio had met because Teresa's brothers supplemented the family income

5

bringing fish to sell in the Barcelona fish market. Xavier had braved the dangers on the coast to bring in another catch and to visit his sister Teresa. It fell to Tom and Pilar to tell Xavier what had happened. He had come seeking news of his brother but instead had to take back more anguish to his parents.

There was no funeral as there was no body. They could not tell her beloved brother Antonio the news as he was out of reach in a Nationalist jail. Tom went around in a daze but eventually focussed on the need to get his young daughter away to safety. He now saw Barcelona, the city he had once loved, as a cursed place that he needed to get out of. They left two weeks later thanks to help from his friend Martin, who worked in the British Consulate. He worried about leaving Pilar and little Luis behind in a city that would inevitably fall to the Nationalists. But he saw no other choice and doubted that he or his daughter would ever want to return.

Chapter 1 – September 1938 – South East England

As they boarded the train at Dover, Tom was surprised that he felt relieved to be back on English soil. There had been a delay at immigration when, as well as his own passport, he had to present all the papers obtained from the authorities in Barcelona. These had explained the presence of his companion: a bewildered, motherless girl of five who kept as close to him as their bags would allow. Explanations were still hard for him. His daughter, Maria, wore the flowered dress that he had bought her in France. After a while, the customs official waved them through, and they made their way to the train station.

The clackety-clack of the train stopped for a while at a signal, his fair head turned towards Maria and he couldn't help smiling. She was swinging her legs backwards and forwards, so engrossed in her drawing that she stuck out her tongue to help her concentration. He had bought her some pencils and an exercise book in a shop near the Gard du Nord the previous evening. Her black hair, brown eyes and olive skin would always remind him of her mother: she even used some of the same facial expressions. When he had struggled to brush her thick hair that morning, he could see in the mirror that she was frowning up at him with the same exasperated expression that her mother often wore. He still felt broken from the terrible loss of his beloved young wife and the weight of responsibility for Maria. His little girl had drawn a crude picture of a small person holding the hand of a larger female figure with a huge shining sun in the top right-hand corner. You could tell that they were female by the triangular skirts they both wore. She passed it to him to see if he liked it and he smiled.

'Muy bien, very good' he said.

'Very good' she repeated looking out at the alien landscape. Her Papa had told her that they were on an adventure but she wanted the journey to be over and to see her mother waiting to meet her at the other end. They said that her mother had gone. But where had she gone?

He turned from the carriage to the patchwork of shades of green outside the window: unseen for several years but at the same time so familiar to him. There were fields of grazing sheep, deeper greens of the hedgerows and more fields of crops, golden in the gentle afternoon sun. He noted how the colours here were muted: the earth's brown was tinged with grey not red like the earth in Spain and the sky was a paler shade of blue yet the grass was a deeper, fresher green. The fields were divided by a haphazard hand: neither regimented in the endless straight rows of French vines nor following the rocky outcrops and mountains so common in Catalonia.

Tom Lambert was going home but all too aware that the carefree young man who had left England was gone. He still had the same light brown hair, grey eyes and slim build but his skin was now tanned, his ever-observant eyes had seen too much cruelty and he ached from grief. He had left his rural home in Sussex seven years previously: full of curiosity and ambition. His education and his camera had been his passport to adventure. He wasn't sure if England was home any more or how he would manage on his own without Teresa. But he was the only family that his daughter Maria knew now and had to find a way through for her sake, as well as his own. He opened the water flask that he always carried and offered it to his companion while they waited for the train to start moving again.

'Cuidado! Be careful, my dear. Have a drink. Tienes hambre, are you hungry?' Tom pointed to his shoulder bag which contained some food as well the case of his Leica camera. The tools of his trade as a photographer and journalist were never far away. Maria took a drink, passed the flask back to him with a shrug. He secured the top and put it on the seat next to them. For several years, he had been covering the political situation in France and Spain for an English newspaper but even now, his Spanish was not the best. He had to make frequent use of the battered English-Spanish dictionary he had picked up on the Charing Cross road before leaving years earlier. Even then it did not always help as most of the people in Barcelona, where he had been based, spoke Catalan. He found that the Spanish people he met were generally generous with help if he made an effort to speak their language. In contrast, when he summoned up some French to speak to the waiter the previous evening in Paris, the man had sneered and replied back in English.

Tom had written to his mother explaining that he was bringing Maria home with him but had not received an answer. He was sure that the girl would be given a warm welcome but he felt apprehensive about the task that lay ahead of them. Maria barely spoke any English and she had lost her mother, just a month ago. He had started planning to take his family back to England for safety a while back when it seemed likely that the Republican side would lose the war. But before they were ready to leave, Teresa had been killed.

At only twenty-eight, he was already a widower and his young face carried a careworn look. Neither he nor his daughter had really taken in what had happened yet.

He thought about Antonio, Teresa's brother and Pilar's husband. He would now find himself, like so many others, on the losing side. As he and Maria had made their way from Catalonia to Northern France, the feeling of unease about the future only grew. They had to change trains along the way and, with the school French that had given him a passport to European assignments, he could make out parts of conversations around him. Some of their fellow travellers talked about everyday concerns but others mentioned the threat posed by Germany and the likelihood of another war in Europe. He knew that France, like Britain, was still very much under the spell of the Great War losses: they wanted to avoid another war at almost any cost. Tom's own uncle Jim had come back scarred from his time in France and another uncle had not returned at all. He had visited Germany briefly a couple of years previously and could feel the threat of nationalism even then.

Tom got out the sandwiches and apples that he had bought at Dover station and offered some to Maria for a late lunch.

'Apple' he said as he held one out to Maria.

'Apple' she said taking the apple and when he smiled, she said 'I speak English Papa.'

'Very good. Muy Bien. Very good' he said. He wondered how well his mother would cope with her new charge and if the local school would be able to help her. He was unlikely to be around much if he needed to return to his work at The News Chronicle.

They stopped overnight in London so that he could drop off some pictures and copy with his editor and run some other errands that afternoon. He changed his remaining francs and pesetas into pounds keeping the coins for Maria. He rang a few colleagues to check on possible new assignments and also rang his friend Martin at the British Consulate in Barcelona. Martin confirmed that the Nationalists were closing in on the city and the International Brigades were planning to leave. Tom had left just in time as the border was now closed. Martin thought that he himself may get re-assigned and they promised to keep in touch as regularly as they could.

Tom sent a postcard back to Aunt Pilar in Barcelona to say that they had arrived safely. Maria struggled to keep up with his walking pace, but she did not like to complain. He bought her some new clothes along with a doll in a red dress that she chose in Hamleys' toy shop on Regent Street.

She had stared open-mouthed with wonder on the shopping trip. Everything was available in London: there didn't seem to be any shortages like in Barcelona and there were no long queues for bread. The people looked well fed and content and

Tom felt safe for the first time in years. In Barcelona, you could never tell when uneasy alliances between anarchists, socialists and the Russian backed Communists would disintegrate into factional fighting. London was calm and easy going in comparison. They went out for a meal at Lyons Corner House and stayed overnight in a cheap hotel near Victoria station. Tom was keen to get home after such a long absence but he wanted to stick to the date that he had given his parents for his return. Also, he wanted Maria to see her new home at its best when it was still light.

The next morning, they took the train from Victoria to Lewes and as they emerged from the station, Tom observed a familiar, heavy old bay horse attached to a cart drawn up outside. The horse was drinking from a wooden bucket and at its side, a shabby looking man in a flat cap turned towards the sound of their footsteps, raised his cap and shouted:

'Aye, aye Tom. Over here!' as he moved towards them. Maria stopped in her tracks when she noticed the man's scarred face and the mangled remains of an ear on one side of his head. However, Tom dropped one of his bags and put an encouraging hand on her back. His uncle's war injuries were so familiar to him that he often forgot the effect they had on strangers.

'This is Uncle Jim. Say Hello Maria or he may just leave us here.' Tom joked as he greeted his uncle with a clap on the back. They exchanged looks that said more than words ever could.

'Good to see you, Tom. Hello there, young lady' he said as he turned the good side of his weather- beaten ruddy face towards the girl and held out a leathery hand in greeting.

'Hello Uncle Jim' said the girl struggling with the unfamiliar 'J' sound.

'It was good of you to come when you didn't know what time we would arrive,' Tom said as he took the largest bag over to the cart and put it in the back.

'Ah, it was no bother. I picked up one or two bits of business while I was hanging about here.' Jim replied as he put his cap back on his greying head and loaded up the smaller leather holdall along with the horse's bucket in back of the cart. He didn't tell Tom that he had also come the previous afternoon and ended up having a couple of drinks in the town before he went home. Uncle Jim was a blacksmith and also took on odd jobs around the town. He was well known especially at the local pubs. They climbed up onto the seat and Jim drove the horse through the town.

'I daresay it's a relief to be home then?' Jim asked.

'Yes, although I'd forgotten about the cold.'

'Your mother will be that pleased to see you and the littl'un.'

'How is she? How are things at the farm?'

'All fine, no big changes here. You'll be well looked after.' Jim patted Tom on the shoulder.

Jim then took a right turn up a gradual incline to the village of Haldenhurst. There was very little sound as the horse trotted along and even after a gap of several years, Jim did not feel the need to fill it with conversation. He was never one for talking and would not trouble his nephew with meaningless words of sympathy. He'd been on the Somme twenty years earlier and was no stranger to the shadows cast by war.

At a break in the low flint wall that ran along the road on their left, Tom gazed across the wide flat expanse of fields towards the hills in the distance and felt the pull again of this gentle countryside he called home. His England was not the wild crags and dark towns of the north nor the bleak moors of the west. This was his home: green valleys and gently sloping hills. When he spotted a kestrel hovering silently in the sky, he pointed it out to Maria. They could hear some sheep calling to

15

each other in a distant field. After a while, they turned down a lane and came to a stop at a row of three adjoining flint and brick cottages. One of these was his parent's home, Blackthorn Farmhouse where he had been raised, another now belonged to his brother's family and the third, a smaller house, was the blacksmith's cottage where his uncle lived alone. A black weather-vane showed that the wind was coming from the west across the valley that lay among the South Downs of Sussex. Tom saw his mother waiting by the gate: she had emerged at the sound of Jim calling the horse to a halt.

Vera was a short, neat woman in her early fifties with light brown hair pinned back in a bun and the same grey eyes as Tom. She wore a blue dress with a floral apron and opened her arms in a smiling welcome to the travellers.

'This is your new home' he said to Maria as he helped her down. 'And this is my mother. You can call her Granny.. Abuelita... Granny'. Maria tried out the word as Tom turned to his mother 'Mother, this is Maria' and he turned to pick up their bags before Jim nodded, walked the horse through a gate and disappeared.

'You're a sight for sore eyes. Come here Maria. Let me look at you.' She stooped to hug the girl and then stood straight to reach up to Tom.

'How are you son, really?' she asked holding on to the embrace for some time. After a few minutes, Tom released his mother's grip.

'Good to be home again, mother. Maria doesn't speak much English as you know but if you speak slowly, she will soon learn.' Tom looked at Maria and smiled. He was trying to deflect his mother's searching question.

'I speak English little… Granny' Maria said looking up at the kindly face.

'Oh, bless you' replied Vera with a reassuring smile as she took Maria's hand and led them into the house. A comforting smell of lamb stew permeated the warm house from the kitchen as Vera showed them to the upstairs room she had prepared. An additional bed had been squeezed into the corner of Tom's old room in the place where his desk used to be. Now the room contained just two beds, a chest of drawers and an embroidered sampler on the wall. There was a shelf above his old bed with a collection of books and an old teddy bear that had clearly been loved. The beds had candlewick covers and Tom noticed that his mother had put a newly knitted rabbit toy on Maria's bed. Vera squatted down to speak to Maria eye to eye:

'This is your new bedroom if you like it, yes?' she said leading her to one of the beds.

Maria smiled in thanks and put her bag down on the bed. She put her new doll on the pillow along with a wooden horse that she had bought from Spain. Vera touched her shoulder and turned to Tom.

'I thought she may want to be close to you to start with or she can go on her own in David's old room. What do you think?'

'This will be fine for now. Thanks mother.' Tom put their other bags down on the larger bed and looked through the small window to the yard below and the familiar fields beyond the gate.

'Now, let's have some tea and you can tell me about your journey.' Vera was anxious about her son but wouldn't push him yet.

Maria found a big tabby cat asleep on a chair in the kitchen and started to stroke it.

'The Cat's name is Tip' said Vera as she poured a glass of milk and put it on the table for Maria.

'Thank you,' said Maria.

Vera cut them each a thick slice of bread, spread it with butter and homemade strawberry jam and placed them on blue and white striped plates. She poured herself a cup of tea and smiled at Tom:

'Water bewitched..'

'And tea begrudged,' he completed her saying as she poured a cup for him from an old brown teapot with a knitted cosy. 'Tea is something I had to learn to do without in Spain. They mainly drink coffee or wine.'

'Really? I hope you will stay for a while this time. You're not planning on going away again, are you?' Vera put the teapot back on its stand. She had never spent much time thinking about the world outside her corner of Sussex, let alone another country. In truth, Vera considered a trip to Brighton to be an unnecessary extravagance.

'No. The Editor agreed that I can stay in England for a while. But I will need to be away on assignments, especially in London. Will that be alright?' Tom's boss had offered to give him some work closer to home for a while although another trip to Germany had been suggested. Picture Post also had plans to cover the changing situation in Europe and had suggested some freelance work might be available. However, Tom was reluctant to go far away so soon after his return home. He had been away for most of the last seven years, mostly in France and Spain, and he had not been back at all for the last three of those.

He noticed that very little had changed in the cosy room. The same odd set of ornaments were placed around the room: aside from family photographs, there was a Toby Jug and a brightly coloured pottery cottage on the dresser and an old ram's horn on the windowsill. On the wall, there was a watercolour of Ditchling Beacon that his father had won in a raffle.

'Of course, it's fine. But surely you will be taking some time off to recover from everything that's happened ? You have suffered such a terrible loss. It can't be easy for you.'

'I find it best to keep busy rather than sit around moping. That either makes me angry or sad. And it won't help my little girl make a home here, will it?' Tom looked shattered but forced a smile.

'You both need time my lad. We'll all look out for the poor mite. And you need to take things easy.'

'Really mother, don't fuss. I need to keep myself occupied.'

'Well, I thought we could take Maria down to see the school later today and pick up your nephew. Perhaps we can have a chat with Mr Harris the headmaster? Or is it too soon? Are you tired from all that travelling?'

'Oh, yes, let's do that,' replied Tom who turned at the sound of voices at the back door. It was his brother's wife Sue and their youngest Georgina who was only three.

'Come in, come in, hello there, sweet pea' Vera said getting to her feet to scoop up a fair-haired girl who was wearing a green pinafore dress over a home knitted red jumper.

'Granny!' said the little girl who turned to look at Tom and Maria suspiciously.

'Hello Tom, lovely to see you. Here is our little Georgie.' Sue greeted her brother-in-law with a hug and Tom introduced Maria to her Auntie Sue and cousin. Both Sue and Georgie had fair hair and blue eyes although Georgie's hair was a much lighter shade and seemed to form a halo around her head. Sue was tall but did not look as strong as her mother-in-law: her face was pale and drawn. Hugs and greetings were tentatively exchanged.

'I was so sad to hear your news, Tom. It must be so terrible for you. If there is anything I can do?' Sue said as she held onto Tom.

'Thanks Sue. You are very kind. People keep telling me it will get better with time,' he replied. He knew people meant well but what could they do? Nobody could turn back time or make the pain go away. All they could do was be there while he got through each hour and each day.

They went outside to feed the hens and to show some of the other animals to Maria. When the wooden clock on the sideboard chimed three, they made their way down to the village school to pick up Teddy: Tom's six- year-old nephew. Vera and Sue joined in the chatter in the playground outside the school while Tom took Maria's hand to look for the school's head teacher. Tom found Mr Harris, a balding man with spectacles talking to one of the other teachers in the school office.

'Good afternoon, Mr Harris, do you have time for a word please?' Tom asked when Mr Harris had turned towards him with an enquiring look.

'Yes, of course, Mr ??'

'Lambert. The name is Tom Lambert. I am Teddy Lambert's uncle… from Blackthorn Farm …but I have been away for quite some time. And this is my daughter Maria. We have come from Spain in the last few days. She is five years old, and she speaks very little English. Can we register her to start school? She will be living here now.'

'Ah. Well, hello there Maria' said Mr Harris looking towards the girl.

'Good Afternoon. I speak English little. My name is Maria.' Maria smiled at Mr Harris hopefully.

'Mmm. Very good. We can start her off in Class One with Teddy and see how she gets on. Miss Houseman takes that class and is an excellent teacher. How about starting on Monday?'

'Ah yes, I know of Miss Houseman.' He remembered that Miss Houseman had been a maid up at the local landowner's house, Ringmer Hall and she had been encouraged to pick up her education again. So, she had then gone on to do so well that she became a teacher at the school. 'Will the lack of English be a problem do you think?'

'It will be difficult for her to start with. But don't worry, I taught at a school in London years ago where some of the children had come from Russia. They don't even use the same alphabet as us and those children soon got the hang of things. I am sure we can manage with Maria.' Mr Harrison was beaming with confidence. 'In the meantime, I'm sure it would help if you tried to teach her some simple words by repetition.'

'Thank you so much. My mother or I will bring her in on Monday morning then. Thank you, Mr Harris.' Tom took Maria out to the playground and they all walked back to the cottage.

Later that afternoon, Tom's father Ted walked into the yard at the back of the house with two black and white sheepdogs. He sat down heavily on a wooden seat and took off his large boots before entering the house. The dogs remained outside panting after their day's work. He put the boots down and hung his jacket and cap on a peg by the back door before turning to greet his wife as normal. Then he caught sight of his younger son.

'Ah Tom. It's so good to see you son' he said holding out a hand to Tom. But they were soon slapping each other on the back by way of a greeting.

'We were all so sad to hear about your Teresa. But who do we have here?' Ted turned his dark eyes to Maria and pinched her cheek affectionately which only drew a quiet 'hello' in reply.

'This is Maria, dad. She may be tired now from all the travelling we have done. How are you doing yourself?'

'Ah, fair to middling. I'll not grumble. Not much has changed here.' He finished washing his hands in the kitchen sink and sat down in a chair just as Vera placed a mug of tea in front of him.

'Tom, can you set the table for nine please as we'll all be sitting down together for dinner tonight.' Vera was busy with the pots and pans on the range and her son pulled the table out to its full size and then went to a dresser for the cutlery.

Ted went to retrieve a wooden bench which he put down one side of the table to accommodate the youngsters. Then he took a wooden dice out of his pocked and tossed it towards Maria with a wink.

The girl shot him a conspiratorial smile and they played with the dice while Ted finished his tea. They were disturbed by the noisy arrival of Tom's older brother David along with Sue and the children and the house filled up with several conversations. Shortly afterwards Uncle Jim arrived unobtrusively: his movements were as quiet and careful as a deer.

They all sat down while Vera handed out hot plates of lamb stew and vegetables. David was as tall as Tom but was much heavier and darker: more like their father. He spoke in a loud voice so that he tended to dominate the room from one end of the table. He greeted his brother and directed his wife and children to their places while his mother passed out the plates.

'Welcome home Tom and Maria' said Ted once they all had a portion

'Go on, tuck in everyone,' added Vera.

After a few mouthfuls, David waved a fork towards his brother and asked:

'Good to see you made it back safe and sound. So, what was the news on your way home, Tom? Will it be peace or are we heading for another war would you say?' but before he could answer, Vera stepped in:

'Oh goodness, can you at least leave this kind of talk until after the children have gone to bed, David'

Her request was granted and as they carried on with the meal, they talked of Maria's schooling, who was helping with the harvest and various bits of gossip until first the stew and then the rice pudding was finished. Sue took her two youngsters back next door and Tom carried Maria up to their bedroom. She looked very tired and he tried to sing the lullaby that her mother always sang her, tucked his old teddy bear, the new doll and the knitted rabbit in bed with her. Maria was pleased that her new granny had also come to kiss her goodnight and must have been exhausted as she had closed her eyes before they both left her.

Tom's father was outside feeding scraps to the dogs and his mother set about tidying the kitchen. David and Uncle Jim were pouring out tankards of beer from a huge earthenware container that Jim had bought back from Lewes the previous day.

'One for you, Tom? I bet you couldn't get any decent beer over there could you.' At a nod from Tom, Jim poured out another and handed it to him. Tom took several large gulps and wiped his mouth in satisfaction.

'No, they certainly don't have anything like this. The beer is lighter but most people in Spain drink wine. It's an acquired taste.' Tom answered taking another gulp.

'And I suppose you managed to acquire it?' David nudged his brother to encourage him to enjoy the joke but only got a grin in response. These Lambert men did not seem to waste their breath on too many words. 'So, what is your opinion on the intentions of Germany then? Should we be making peace with Mr Hitler?' David did not always agree with his brother, but he knew that Tom kept up with world events and was interested in his opinions. Tom thought carefully for a while before answering.

'I hope rather than believe that Germany wants to keep the peace. They and the Italians certainly were not keeping out of the war in Spain as you must know. The bastards...sorry mother...dropped bombs on innocent civilians wherever they chose. And no country in Europe tried to stop them. All Britain did was take in a boatload of orphans.'

'It seems like most of our politicians will do anything rather than start another Great War' David said looking over at his father for confirmation but Tom's anger spurred him to continue: 'Chamberlain needs to make it clear that Britain will not stand by and let Germany and her allies expand anywhere they like. They have already absorbed Austria and now seem to have their eye on Sudetenland.' Tom was not hiding his anger now.

'I don't even know where those places are. Do you think there could be another war then?' asked Ted before taking a few more gulps.

'It's hard to say. It depends on what Germany do next and how the other countries respond. I wouldn't rule it out. If there is another war, it won't be confined to the battlefield: they see legitimate targets everywhere and if civilians get in the way, so be it.'

'Let's hope not. Nobody wants another war surely?' said Ted looking over at Jim who still bore the scars of the last war in Europe. The man that came back from France was so different to the boy he had grown up with. The same was true of himself but they rarely spoke of it.

'So many lives lost' said Jim thinking of his comrades who never made it home. These included his own brother, his best friend and also, Ted's younger brother. 'To absent friends and to family returned' he said as he finished his drink. Tom raised his glass and finished his drink before turning towards the door.

'I'll check on Maria' he said as he left the room so that they could not see him blinking back the tears. He knew that they came easily at any mention of loss but he could not show his grief openly, even with family.

Vera turned on the radio so that they could hear the BBC news and all the talk was of Prime Minister Chamberlain and the Berlin Conference. Tom was back downstairs fairly quickly and when the news had finished, Vera asked him if Maria was still asleep.

'Yes, she must have been tired and like me is probably glad to have stopped travelling. We have been on the road for nearly a week now'

'I hope she'll be happy here poor mite.' Vera replied trying to keep things light.

'I'm sure she will be spoilt rotten if you have anything to do with it.' David joked.

'Children need to know that they are safe and loved, that's all.' Vera replied.

'That is why I bought her here. I was sure she would be well cared for.' Vera's answer to Tom's words was to place her hand on his to reassure him.

'Well, we will be on an early start tomorrow. Young Billy and Mr Granger, the land agent, are due with the threshing machine. Tom, can you lend a hand?' David asked. Young Billy was one of their cousins.

'Of course. I know you will enjoy telling your ignorant little brother what do.'

'Hah, those soft hands aren't used to hard graft are they?' David held out his large, hardened hands that carried several injuries against his brother's soft, elegant hands and they both laughed. David had always been destined to take over the farm and Tom had been happy to take another path in life. Their father was a tenant farmer with a particular talent for looking after the animals. David had taken over the arable side of the farm and they were confident that the tenancy would remain in the family. The landowner, the Earl of Arundel who lived in Ringmer Hall, had been fairly decent over the years and the land agent would be checking that everything was as it should be when he came over the next day. There were rumours that the Earl was planning some changes to avoid the estate being lost to Death Duties like so many others. The Lambert family had been farm labourers and tenant farmers since the Doomsday Book and never thought to change that. Tom had been the first one to look outside of that world.

David and Uncle Jim took their leave, thanking Vera for the meal and praying for dry weather the following day. Tom asked his mother if everything was alright with Sue as he thought she had looked pale and unwell. His mother was surprised that he had noticed.

'Oh, that's just because she's expecting again. She'll be fine once she stops feeling queasy. If you've got everything you need, I'll be off to bed.'

'Goodnight mother' and Vera reached up to stroke her son's cheek and look into the grey eyes that were so like her own.

'Goodnight, Tom. It *will* get easier with time you know.' She smiled at him and went up to bed. She had seen the sadness of grief in her son's eyes.

Tom thought back to his arrival in Spain in late April 1931 when he was still a naïve teenager. He had only got the role as a photographer/journalist due to his benefactor Imogen's connections and had expected to stay for a couple of weeks covering the birth of the Second Spanish republic.

Tom had fallen into photography by an unlikely twist of luck. He had always enjoyed sketching as a child and had been encouraged by his mother who saw that he had some talent. On one of those long, light summer evenings when he was about ten years old, he had managed to escape from farm chores and was sitting by a gate sketching when a couple of aristocratic ladies from Ringmer Hall had ridden by on their horses. One of them, Imogen Clements stopped in surprise when she saw one of the local farm boys drawing. She had asked to look at his work and was so impressed with his artistic eye that she found out where he lived and sent over a box brownie camera and some paints as a gift.

Imogen was the Earl of Arundel's daughter and was one of those 'surplus women' from the generation of the Great War: having so few men around to marry, they had time, and in her case money, to spare. Tom was to become one of her many causes and it had opened up a new world of possibilities for him. He had secured a place at the local Grammar School and she encouraged him to stay on to take School Certificate. Imogen had then helped him to apply for an apprenticeship with the Brighton Argos newspaper. She had given assistance to several other local people and was on the board of a number of local charities. The Earldom and Ringmer Hall had passed to a cousin when her father had died.

She was now a middle-aged spinster but still kept in touch with Tom in spite of the social chasm between them: she had grown up as the local landowner's daughter and he was the son of one of their many tenants. There had never been anything romantic in their connection: she had no family of her own and enjoyed spending time with other intelligent and thoughtful people. She didn't pay much attention to the conventions of polite society and Tom thought that she actually took pleasure in her quiet rebellions. Her mother had been a suffragist and this may have shaped her outlook and opinions. He had certainly benefitted from the connection.

Tom crept into the bed next to his daughter and tried to sleep, Tom also thought of Barcelona. He had met his friend Martin on his first visit to the British consulate and it was on his advice that he had rented a room at Senor Garcia's bar and hotel. There he had met Senor Garcia's daughter Pilar, her husband Antonio and his sister, Teresa.

He remembered how they had all been caught up in the greed for change in Barcelona. In Senor Garcia's bar, the men and the women discussed how life would change under the new socialist government. The traditions of the monarchy and the church were being rejected. Maybe this was one of the reasons why Teresa had looked twice at the young foreigner she could see was looking at her with interest. Her brother Antonio had noticed the looks that they exchanged and had warned them both off. That was back in the early days of his stay when he struggled to communicate with the people around him. The paper had sent him to Madrid for a while that summer but he returned to Barcelona for the winter. He found himself spending more and more time with Teresa: they lived in the same building and she helped him to learn Spanish as well as discussing the changing political situation. They discovered a mutual love of Gaudi's architecture and also of music. Over a year later, in May 1932, the paper asked him to cover the aftermath of the assassination of the French President Paul Doumer. He was away only a couple of weeks but during that time, he had realised that he was in love and was going to ask Teresa to marry him. He was shocked and pleased when he found out that she felt the same way and agreed to his proposal.

There were objections from both families that they were too young and hadn't known each other long enough but perhaps their youth gave them additional determination. They had married in the small fishing village South of Barcelona where Teresa had been born and Maria had come along the following year. They had over six happy and eventful years together. So many strange twists of fate had led him to this point. Why did she have to go out to that particular place at that exact time. 'Why' was the question he kept coming back to. But it was no good going over and over the same thing as he would drive himself crazy. What's done is done and he had to carry on. There were so many happy memories and he had to hang on to those. And there was Maria.

Eventually, he did get to sleep that night but he was woken early by the excited clucking of a chicken outside. The family were all up early that morning to eat breakfast and get all the chores that did not relate to the day's harvesting out of the way. Ted milked the few cows and fed the pigs while Vera prepared some lunch. Tom fed the hens with Maria as Sue had not appeared again. Vera guessed that she was probably unwell that morning and was relieved that Tom and Maria were happy to take her place. Maria stuck to her father like glue throughout that first day.

David went with Uncle Jim to get as much wheat cut, bundled and loaded onto the cart as they could before the machine arrived. When Mr Granger, cousin Harry and Young Billy arrived, they all trooped down the first field and got going. Maria and Georgie ran round the field having fun while Sue took a reluctant Teddy to school. Ted, Uncle Jim, David, Tom, Harry and Billy loaded the bundles into the machine while Mr Granger supervised. Harry was Vera's sister Peg's eldest and Billy was the youngest child. They were both outdoor staff up at the Hall but were able to help on the farm at really busy times.

After a while, the machine was moved on and Uncle Jim loaded the sacks of grain onto the cart to take it up to the barn. Maria and Georgie wanted a ride on the cart. Tom asked Maria if she could retrieve his camera bag from their room and bring it back with her. Maria glowed with pride that her father had trusted her with the precious bag and both girls squealed as the cart bumped along. They carried on working all morning but stopped at 12:30 for lunch. Mr Granger sat down with Ted and David to discuss business while the others gossiped about what was planned for the Lewes fireworks that year. Tom spent most of the break taking pictures of the family groups as they sat and ate. He loved to catch these moments in time as he knew such opportunities could pass all too easily. Maria had bought him his small Leica not the heavy Graphlex that he used for most of his professional work.

Later that week, Vera and Tom took Maria and Georgie for a morning stroll down by the river to pick the blackberries that were ripening along the hedgerows. Vera had wanted to give Sue a break from Georgie and also to talk to Tom. She found comfort in always being attentive to the needs of others. The children were picking some lower hanging fruit further along the bank but still within sight. It was doubtful whether much of it was making it as far as the basket they had been given. Vera looked towards her son:

'We used to come to this spot when you were little. Do you remember?'

'Of course. The river seems lazier than ever. I am guessing you haven't had much rain recently.'

'Not for a couple of weeks. Will you be going back up to London next week?' she asked moving closer to where he was reaching up for a particularly plump group of berries.

'Yes, I told my editor I would be back in on Monday to talk about what he wants me to do next. I may need to be away from time to time. Are you sure you will be alright with Maria?'

'Of course, although it does seem too soon. You know I will do anything I can to help. It must be very hard for her coming to a strange place without her mother. You won't be away that much will you? She is going to miss you.'

'You know, I was often away for weeks at a time in Spain. She is used to me going away but she knows I always come back.'

'But then she had her mother didn't she. And how about you son? You must be missing Teresa too. I wish I had got to meet her' Vera pronounced Tom's wife's name in the English way which always made Tom smile.

'I miss Teresa every day and probably always will. Everyone tells me that it get easier with time. But I still feel so… empty inside.' He struggled to articulate his feelings.

'Yes, you'll just have to believe me that the burden you are carrying will get lighter. You don't ever forget them, you just get used to the fact that someone precious has gone.' Vera was thinking about the child she had lost to influenza as well as her brother and the other men she knew who hadn't come back from the Great War.

'You know, the worst thing is that she was expecting again. So, there were two lives lost that day.' Tom's words had clearly taken a toll on him and he had to summon up a bucketload of self-control to stop himself crumbling. Even so, he had to brush away some tears.

'I know love, it's so sad and I'm so sorry. At least you have Maria to bring you joy and you will always have your memories to treasure.' They both turned to watch Maria and Georgie giggling over a small blue butterfly that they were trying to catch. The spell was broken and they both couldn't help smiling.

'Have we picked enough yet do you think?' asked Tom after swallowing hard.

'This is enough to make a couple of pies for tonight. The season isn't over yet as you can see. Let's just go back by the chestnut in Four Wents Field to see if those are ready yet. Come on girls, we are going that way now.' Vera pointed up the incline to where a stile was visible in the corner of the field. When they got to it, Tom went over first and composed a picture of the two girls sitting on the top step with his mother standing behind them. Maria smiled broadly at the camera.

Maria loved to have her papa take her picture and had learned to pose from an early age. To start with, she hated for him to leave the farm but she would gradually transfer more and more of her affection for him to Vera and Vera in her turn enjoyed the company of the girl. She had lost a daughter, Lily to the flu epidemic of 1919 when the child was only four years old. She often thought about Lily, who could never be replaced, but this little girl seemed like an unexpected gift. Vera understood the power of grief and encouraged the child to talk about her mother. She found a beautiful walnut frame for the picture of her mother and father that Maria kept by her bed.

The first night that Tom stayed away, Maria had woken up and wandered into Vera and Ted's bedroom asking for her Mama and Papa. Vera took her back to her own bed and cuddled up with her until she was asleep again. She hadn't wanted to disturb Ted. The same thing happened several more times until Maria settled. Vera discovered that it happened less often if she let Maria sleep with her mother's shawl as a comforter. Maria would often call Vera 'Mama' in the night as she went off to sleep and she accepted this without correcting her: it seemed to help the little girl to settle. She would love her like her mother would have.

The family were all looking forward to the fireworks in Lewes as they did every year. Bonfire Societies were a key part of social life throughout Sussex and although the village did not have its own bonfire, they were so close to Lewes that they usually joined in with those celebrations. There were several small fireworks factories in the area to supply the needs of the festivities. Tom, like all local children, was told of the historical connection to some notorious Sixteenth century Protestant martyrs in the town but he felt that there must also be a strong but lost link back to pagan Halloween and Samhain. The festival was so full of ritual and tradition, particularly in Lewes where most people belonged to a Bonfire Society.

On the evening of November 5th, the whole family went by horse and cart to Lewes. The town was packed out with many townspeople colourfully dressed up either in the stripey tops of the various Bonfire Societies or in fancy dress. Some dressed as pirates, some as Vikings, English Civil War soldiers, Roman Centurions and other themes associated with the Societies. They paraded through the town with marching bands thumping out a beat on drums: there was a festival feel with an undercurrent of menace coming from the chanting crowd with their flaming torches. Tom took his heavy Graflex professional camera as he hoped to get some atmospheric pictures that he could sell. Maria was fascinated by the whole event, and he saw her eyes were shining with excitement as she hung onto Vera's hand. She sought out her father as he moved through the raucous crowd taking pictures. She had little understanding of the chanting that was going on but parades with people shouting slogans and playing music had been a familiar part of growing up in 1930's Barcelona and she felt strangely drawn in.

Tom saw several of his old school friends amongst the crowds. He wanted to stop to talk to Imogen Clements but she was with her cousin Alexander, Earl of Uckfield and his wife the Countess, Beatrice. They were surrounded by all the important people of the town so were beyond his reach. She was dressed in a fur lined grey coat with a fur hat and signalled towards him before making her way over. She wanted to know what he had been doing and what his plans were. The noisy parade was underway and the crowds were cheering them on. Since it was proving difficult to have a conversation without raised voices, she had asked him to join her for tea at a convenient date in the future.

Later on, he saw the unmistakeable moustache and beard of his friend from the photographic course he had taken years earlier. George Fletcher was older than Tom and he was one of the local doctors based in Brighton and also a Quaker. Photography was just a hobby for George but he was incredibly well-read and knowledgeable on many subjects. This made him fascinating company for Tom and they chatted over a pint outside one of the pubs. Tom was glad to reconnect with old friends and he promised George that he would keep in touch now that he was back in Sussex.

The family had all gone home late that evening with the smell of gunpowder and burning still fresh on the air. No doubt the following morning would be a foggy one. Vera asked Ted to take the reins from her brother as she could detect that Jim had had a few too many drinks to get them all home safely.

Chapter Two – London February 1939

Tom bought a pint in a pub along The Strand and waited for Martin to appear. He had received a letter from his friend in the New Year to say he was coming back to London in a few weeks and they should meet up for lunch. Tom was keen to meet him but was apprehensive as to what news he would bring. Martin worked as a diplomat in the British Consulate in Barcelona and had been really helpful to Tom from the day he arrived until the time he was arranging to leave Spain. He was fluent in several languages having been born to a Swiss mother and studying at the Sorbonne as well as Oxford. They had agreed to meet one evening in between Whitehall and Fleet Street where they each worked.

Martin looked immaculate in a dark lounge suit, his hair was slicked back without a strand out of place. He exuded an air of amused superiority that Tom had at first found off-putting and intimidating. However, after discovering a mutual liking for both politics and chess, Tom had realised that underneath his film star looks and public-school confidence, Martin was a likeable and decent man who was a great source of local information. They had been friends for long enough to speak openly without any need for ceremony.

'Good to see you again, Martin. I see you are sporting the Clark Gable look now.' Tom held out a hand in greeting. They shook hands and Martin smiled touching his newly grown thin moustache as they sat down at the table Tom had managed to secure in the busy pub.

'Not bad is it. Would you like another drink here? I was just going to have a quick G 'n T and then we could eat at the Savoy – my treat. I've got some news and would rather we had some peace and quiet to chat. What do you say? Maybe fit in a game too?'

'Yes, that's fine with me. I'll stick with this' Tom replied holding up his nearly full pint of beer. Martin put his hat on the table, hung his coat and umbrella on the stand by the door and went to order a drink at the bar.

Tom recalled how they had struck up this unlikely friendship. Martin was an avid chess player and Tom was one of the few people in Barcelona who could occasionally beat him. Tom had started playing at the Grammar School chess club and he had continued playing with some of his fellow students at night school. Martin soon returned to the table with his drink.

'So, how are you finding being back in Blighty? And how is little Maria settling in?'

'Oh, she is doing well. My mother is taking charge of her and she has started at school with her cousin. But what brings you back here? Were you summoned back for a family Christmas?'

'Yes, but I didn't make it back for Christmas day as the border kept closing. I've been here for a couple of weeks and went back to my parent's place near Stroud for a while. It's tundra cold in that house in winter. My mother opens the windows expecting alpine air to come in. I'll be glad to get back to Spain next week.'

'Ah, so they are not moving you on yet?'

'I may get moved to Paris or Berne later in the year but nothing is certain. Who knows how things will go will considering what is currently brewing in Germany. We could be living in interesting times.' They both took another drink before Tom replied.

'That's one way of putting it. A colleague of mine was in Berlin last November. He was taking pictures of a gang vandalising shops owned by Jews. He had his camera smashed and the thugs beat him up for good measure. I think he was lucky to get away in one piece. I'd like to get another look at Germany myself.'

'You still want to go after what happened to your colleague?'

'Well, maybe not but then Spain wasn't exactly quiet was it? I don't think anyone like Hitler or Franco would ever be able to take charge here, do you?'

'I should hope not. I'm not sure I have much confidence in Chamberlain though.' At this Martin finished his drink and, noting that Tom had finished, he nodded to his companion: 'Shall we make tracks?'

Tom got to his feet by way of a reply. They both put on their coats and hats and went out into the cold evening making their way down The Strand to the entrance of The Savoy. Martin gave his name and they were shown to a table which was immaculately laid out with silver cutlery, crystal wine glasses and white serviettes bound in silver rings on a crisp, white cloth. The place was very quiet in comparison to the bustling pub. It was a familiar haunt for Martin and he ordered Beef Wellington after a quick glance of the menu and Tom followed suit. Martin chose a claret and once this was served, he got straight down to delivering his news.

'So, I'm sure you already know that Barcelona finally fell to the nationalists who will, in all likelihood, take the whole of Spain in due course. I think the writing was on the wall when the International Brigades left back in October. Only

Madrid and a few southern areas are holding out. Reprisals against the Republicans have started all over Spain and even in France. I heard that the bar 'Las Llanternes' was taken over and' Martin paused 'I'm sorry to say that the proprietor Senor Garcia was shot on the spot by Nationalists.'

'Good God, no!' Tom was shocked. He had spent so much time in Pilar's father's hotel and bar. This was where he had met Teresa. When Pilar and Teresa's brother Antonio had married, Teresa had come to Barcelona for the wedding and had stayed on to work as a chambermaid in the hotel. She and her brother had republican sympathies and wanted to be close to where the action was. Ironically, Pilar's father had never been particularly political but the bar became known as a meeting place for Republicans.

'The reason I am telling you this is to warn you off if you are thinking of sending letters to Pilar. You could be opening her up to suspicion and possibly even danger.' Martin looked very concerned as he gave this advice.

'I sent her a postcard when we first got home and a letter just before Christmas. She may not have got them. I know that she had talked about going to Antonio and Teresa's family home south of Barcelona. I have the address but perhaps you are right... I don't want to add to her troubles...

Antonio was taken prisoner after Ebro as you know. Last I heard, she didn't know where he was being held.'

'Yes. I remember. I hear life in Franco's prison camps is pretty grim. We are currently trying to get a Brit out of one near Leon: perhaps you remember Jimmy McAuley formerly of the International Brigade? They should have let him go as only Spanish nationals should be kept as prisoners. I knew him up at Oxford but that's another story. Just be aware that a letter from England could spell trouble for the family no matter how well meant.'

'Yes, I see. Things must be worse than I imagined. It seems you were right when you advised us to leave. For that you have my thanks, Martin. I hope you can help Jimmy too. I met him a couple of years back in Barcelona. He was drinking with some other International Brigaders who were complaining about the lack of decent guns and ammunition...' Tom broke off as their food arrived and the waiter topped up their glasses before leaving them to their conversation.

'Is there anything I can do to help when I go back? Take a letter or something? I expect to leave next week.' Martin said just before he took a mouthful.

'Can you get a letter and some money to Pilar safely? And if there is a way to find out where Antonio is being held, can you let her know?' Tom felt that he owed so much to Pilar and to Teresa's family. He hadn't been able to keep her safe but he had to try to do something for them. He didn't want to do anything that would put them at risk though and Martin would be best placed to make a judgement on that.

'Of course, I'd be happy to. Drop the information at my office or call me before next Thursday. This really is delicious, isn't it? No food shortages here, thank goodness. Tell me, what have you been up to since you got back?' Martin didn't like to dwell on bad news and could not help noticing that a very attractive woman of his acquaintance had looked over at him from a nearby table. He nodded at her in acknowledgment as he waited for Tom to answer.

'I managed to sell some pictures of the Lewes Fireworks to Picture Post. It's quite a unique event and I was really pleased with them. Maria is doing well learning English and I've been glad to spend time at home with her as well as catching up with family and friends after such a long time away.'

'Yes, it is always good to get home. And your work here is not too dull after Spain, is it?'

49

'I took some pictures of Jewish children arriving in London: they are calling it the Kindertransport. Some of them were as young as Maria and most only carried a small suitcase of all they owned in the world. I felt so sorry for them. It's so shameful.'

'Yes. Things must be getting unbearable over there if their parents choose to send them away like that. It seems to me that this Herr Hitler could be even worse than Franco. Thanks God we were born British eh Tom? Cheers!' he said as he finished his wine and refilled their glasses.

After the meal, they went into one of the lounges to play a game of chess.

'Who was that beautiful girl in the colourful dress and diamonds who was watching you leave the restaurant then? You nodded at her. How do you know each other?' asked Tom. The woman had flashed a bright red smile at Martin as they left the restaurant.

'Oh, that's Judit Steiner, certainly a looker: her family arrived from central Europe – Hungary I think, a couple of years back. The diamonds are probably either borrowed or fake. She is looking for a well-connected husband but won't find it in this direction. Her mother's family is somehow distantly related to mine. Her father plays a good game of chess though and she is a passable player. It sometimes amuses me to see her try her luck. She is very attractive so I daresay someone will fall for her charms eventually,' Martin replied as he took a white and a black pawn in his hands and shuffled them behind his back.

'Good grief. You are a cool one sometimes Martin!' Tom admired the self-assurance of his friend and wondered if he would ever acquire some for himself. In losing Teresa, he thought that he had lost the better part of himself. He chose the pawn in Martin's right hand and went on to play white. The game had gone on for about an hour and eventually Martin had won. Tom resisted the offer of another game and made his way south of the river to where he was staying in Waterloo. He wondered if Martin would be seeking more glamorous company back at the Savoy. His friend moved in such different circles to his own but it occurred to him it was quite possible that he knew Imogen Clements. Maybe he should ask him next time they met.

The next day, before calling into the news office, Tom took some money out of his bank. He took a walk down to Whitehall and dropped off an envelope containing the money along with a letter for Pilar at Martin's office. It also contained a picture he had taken of Maria, standing with his mother next to the old carthorse while they had all been helping with the harvest. His thoughts often turned to Teresa and the life that was lost. He told himself that he had to make a new life now forced himself into the distractions of work and family life. He wasn't sure if he had it in him.

Before he left, Martin invited Tom to a party and he had decided to go on a whim. It was in one of those huge Georgian town houses on a square in Kensington and as he checked the number on the door, he could see Martin standing by the huge bay window waving him in. The front door was open and Martin guided him to a huge reception room and made straight for a waiter holding a tray of filled wine glasses.

'Help yourself to a glass Tom. I have some people I want you to meet.' They went over to a group of three men standing by the window that Martin had just left. 'This is my friend Tom who works for the 'News Chron' and has recently come back from Spain. This is George Thompson from 'The Times' Foreign Desk and this is Marcus Osbourne from the FO. We were just chatting about whether our friend General Franco will throw in his lot with the Germans now.'

'I can't see it myself. I think Franco has enough on his plate with problems in his own country.' George chipped in.

'Both Mussolini and Hitler helped Franco to win so they will be expecting something in return, won't they?' Tom put in and the debate continued.

A while later, Tom looked across the room and recognised the striking but familiar blue eyes and high cheekbones of Imogen Clements. She wore a silk tea dress with stylised leaves in shades of green, gold, red and brown on a black background. She was talking to a much older man with a grey moustache. Tom was going to make his way over but she moved towards his group instead.

'Darling Tom, I needed rescuing from a rather tedious gentleman. How are you? Are you going to introduce me then...' Imogen addressed him alone before they re-joined his group. Tom made the introductions stressing that he had met Martin in Spain.

'I've always wanted to meet a diplomat. I suppose it's all very hush hush. Are you still based in Spain or will you be moving on do you think? Tom tells me that Barcelona has fallen to the fascists.' Imogen addressed Martin and the others in the group were drawn elsewhere leaving the three together.

'I have some unfinished business in Spain but it is probably time they moved me on as I do not have many friends inside the new regime.' Martin then changed with subject with perfect ease: 'Tom told me about his lady benefactor and I had pictured a grey-haired old dowager in tweeds. He neglected to mention how young and beautiful you are.'

'How very charming of you. I am grateful that you were able to help Tom when he needed to get out of Spain and come home. So, is this General Franco as bad as the radicals say do you think?'

'The British government will continue to take a neutral line of course. But I have heard several sorry tales from some of those who have been taken prisoner by the Nationalist side.'

'Oh, weren't there atrocities on both sides? Tom said the Republicans spent too much energy fighting with each other.'

'Things are never black and white are they. Best not to take sides don't you find?'

'That's the diplomatic way I suppose but not mine. I am fortunate to be able to use my influence to help people and so I often **do** take sides.' Imogen said emphatically and Tom was fascinated to see his two friends seeming to enjoy a clash of ideas.

'Yes, well I can see that Tom was lucky to have you on his side.' Martin said as he took another drink from a passing waiter. Imogen waved him away to indicate that she did not want another glass.

'Tom is very talented and it gives me great pleasure to see him succeed. Perhaps I should spare his blushes. And so, when do you think that you will return to Spain Mr Lascelles?'

'I will be going back next Thursday but it may be a brief stay. Things are moving quickly across Europe. Here is my card if you need to contact me again.'

'Thank you. Perhaps we might be able to help each other in the future. I have some contacts that could potentially be of use to you.' Imogen put the card in her small handbag and handed her own card to Martin before continuing: 'Tom, I have another engagement this evening but I would like to catch up with you properly. I'm in town for the next few days. Could we meet for lunch or tea on Friday before you go back to Sussex?'

'Yes, let's do that. I'll give you a call on Friday morning. Enjoy your evening.'

'It was a pleasure to meet you Miss Clements' Martin said with a nod. Tom wondered for a minute if his friend was flirting with Imogen but then Martin was universally charming and that was how he seemed to make so many connections.

'Likewise. I must take my leave gentlemen,' Imogen said as she turned to leave the room. Several of the other people in the room turned their heads to watch her leave.

'Phew! That is one impressive lady, Tom, curious that she never married.'

'Her fiancé was killed in Flanders in the war: he was heir to a title and fortune. She lost two brothers as well which is how she came to inherit part of her family's fortune I believe. She told me all the good men in her generation were killed and so she got used to an independent life. As you may find, she is a very bright, well-travelled and unusual woman. Her mother was a campaigner for women's rights and insisted that she had an education. I think that was fairly unusual at the time. And you are right, I am lucky to have met her.'

'I wonder if my folks have heard of the Clements – it could be a French name. Does she spend most of her time down in Sussex then? I suppose the family own a huge pile down there, do they?' asked Martin.

'The estate passed to a cousin along with the title after her father died. She stays down there some of the time but she also has a house of her own in Mayfair. Her sister lives in the South of France and she has another place down there. I wonder how she thinks she can help you.'

'I haven't the foggiest but she seems like a good person to know. Are you going to stick around here? How about a game of chess at my club?'

'We could have a farewell game. I suppose it may be a long time before we meet again.'

Tom and Martin played a game, which went on for some time and Tom finally won, before saying their goodbyes. Martin promised to do all he could to contact Pilar and let Tom know how things were back in Spain.

On Friday, Tom met Imogen for afternoon tea at Fortnum and Masons in Piccadilly before going back to Sussex by train. He was slightly late and Imogen was already being seated at a table and waved her copy of The Times at him as he arrived. She was wearing a rather plain navy coloured blouse and skirt.

'Lovely to see you Tom dear. I'm famished so was thinking of the full afternoon tea. Will that suit you?'

'That's fine although I daresay mother will have prepared a substantial dinner for me when I get home.' Tom was aware that this was all too true. His father joked that he could judge when Tom was due back by the volume of baking Vera did during the day.

'Yes, well I've been in a committee meeting for hours and the sandwich lunch was barely edible, so please indulge me.' She smiled at the waiter who took the order along Tom's coat and hat.

'I see that Chamberlain has formally recognised Franco's regime,' she said pointing at the story in the newspaper and stuffing it into her bag. 'Now, tell me all your news,' Imogen said as she tucked the satchel of papers under the table by the wall. 'And don't let me forget that lot,' she added smiling.

'Well, I am back working for the New Chronicle over here and have a couple of other irons in the fire that may come to something. Things are going well, although I do feel a bit guilty about leaving Maria with my mother. Naturally, she doesn't complain and Maria is doing well. She is learning English quickly and competes with her cousin Teddy at school.'

'Ah that's good so she's a bright little thing then?'

'It seems so. She updates me on her progress with great enthusiasm. I really am proud of how she is coping. Mother tells me that she follows my father around after school to help check on the animals and he tells me that she helps my mother around the house and in the kitchen garden. I rather think that they both enjoy having her around.'

'You know, she is probably a tonic for them. I suppose she misses her mother though so perhaps she doesn't want to be left alone?'

The appearance of the waiter with teapots and plates of tiny sandwiches and cakes saved Tom from having to answer that straight away.

'Of course, we both miss her,' Tom answered as he held his cup up for Imogen to pour. 'But tell me, what have you been busy with since we last met?' He asked as a rather obvious deflection. Imogen took in his need to move the conversation on. She could see that he was still struggling and obliged him. He reminded her of the men who came back from the Great War with haunted looks in their eyes. She hoped that he would come to terms with his loss before long, just as she had. She believed in looking forward and making the best of things.

'I was down at Ringmer Hall for a week or so, as you know and had to spend some time in the company of my cousins, the Earl and Countess. Beatrice has been putting a great deal of effort into the gardens there. They took a trip to Italy and she seems to have decided to build an Italian garden in Sussex: fountains, statues, hedged walkways. At least it will give some work to some of the local gardeners and builders. It may look lovely when it's finished and gives her something to do I suppose. Some of the other ideas she bought back were not so palatable. They seem to have fallen under of the spell of Mussolini.' Imogen gave Tom a meaningful look.

'Seriously? I didn't realise your cousins were that way inclined. He seems to be a good landlord or perhaps he leaves that side to the Agent? Mr Grainger is a decent man and my father gets on well with him.'

'Let me know if that ever changes. I still have some influence there you know.'

'Thank you. So, what else have you been up to in London?'

'Well, yesterday I went to a rather sad funeral of an old suffragist friend of ours. There are less and less of us left to attend such things now. I got out my mother's old purple and green sash for the occasion and it was nice to see some of the familiar faces. Of course, there are new causes to fight now. Goodness knows what the world is coming to.' Imogen paused to sip her tea and take some more sandwiches before continuing: 'I read that the border between Spain and France is closed. How long did it take you to get back home?' Imogen turned to Tom to listen to his reply while she ate.

'Martin helped us get the papers we needed. The journey itself took five days and four nights as we got stuck at the border, changed trains in Lyon, and then we stayed in Paris and London overnight. We had to sleep in a train station at the border as there were so many people trying to get out and there were armed patrols. It's easy to forget what a big country France is and the atmosphere there seemed tense compared to last time I was there. Even Paris seemed subdued.'

Tom broke off and watched Imogen demolish another sandwich. He remembered how scarce food had been towards the end of their time in Spain but dismissed the thought.

'Have you heard from your sister in France recently?'

'Yes, all seems well there. She does not appear to be concerned with what is happening in Germany. She is looking forward to the birth of her first grandchild. Her son Jean-Paul and his wife are expecting a new arrival soon. You must join me in trying one of these cakes, Tom' Imogen said passing the double-layered cake plate towards him. He took a small iced cake and wondered how someone who clearly enjoyed good food managed to remain so slim. But then he remembered how busy her life was.

So, what was your committee about this time?' he asked out of genuine curiosity.

'This morning was just a routine hospital committee. I don't know if my contribution is particularly valuable there. I am more interested in the British Committee for Refugees and of course I still serve on the committee for the Women's Home.' Tom was aware of the work she did for women and children in the East End. She spent years trying to co-ordinate the efforts of a number of charities and religious organisations there. The Refugee work was a new thing.

'Is it mainly Jewish children who are coming here as refugees now?' He was thinking of the Kindertransport.

'Yes, there are quite a few Jewish children coming out of Czechoslovakia at the moment. And there are arrivals from several other countries in the region. The Quakers are quite heavily involved you know. There are plenty of people on the move around Europe and North Africa. British people are returning from various places that no longer feel so comfortable: Italy, Egypt, Cyprus and Portugal. There seems to be a general desire to look for safety. Of course, you felt that too. I am pleased you are back and that I have a new young person to look out for in the shape of your daughter. As always, do let me know if there is anything I can do to help you. And keep me up to date with how you are getting on won't you. I worry about you, you know. It's such a pity I never met Maria's mother.'

'You certainly don't need to worry.' Tom scoffed. 'It is a shame that nobody here knew her – apart from Maria and Martin of course. We'll be

fine. Do you have plans for my friend Martin?'
Imogen was surprised.

'Not right now. But you never know, it
doesn't hurt to make a new contact here and there
does it?' She said giving nothing away.

'He was quite taken with you.'

'Was he indeed?' Imogen fixed Tom with a
look of unflappability. 'And now I think you are
trying to tease me and it won't work. You forget
that I grew up with two brothers. Don't you have a
train to catch?' She smiled at him before asking the
waiter to bring the bill.

'Now that you are back, I expect to see you
regularly, Tom. Promise?'

'Of course. It was good to see you again.
And you are right, I should be making tracks.' Tom
had given up arguing with Imogen over the fact that
she always paid the bill. He occasionally had to put
up with strange looks from waiters who made the
wrong assumption about their relationship but he
didn't mind. He often thought that it was a pity she
had no children of her own. He picked up the
Evening paper to read at the station and made his
way home.

Tom slipped into a regular routine of
travelling up to London for work. Occasionally he
had to stay overnight in town and on these nights,

Maria would sometimes be difficult to settle. Gradually, Maria got to rely on Vera as she was the new constant in her life. She hated the cold of her new home but she seemed to cheer as the weather warmed and she thought of her mother less and less. One evening in April, Tom returned home in reflective mood and as he walked along the road from the bus stop to the farmhouse, he noticed a row of wallflowers in red, yellow and purple. He did a double-take as he realised that the colour combination had reminded him of Spain, of the Republican flag and therefore of Teresa. He was surprised to find that he hadn't thought about her all day. This was unusual and he suddenly felt guilty about the lapse: a tear rolled down his face at the thought of his motherless daughter.

Later that evening, when he took Maria upstairs to bed. She said to him:

'Papa, you look sad today. Do you miss Mama?'

'Yes, Maria. I miss your Mama. I probably always will and I know it must be hard for you too. But I love you very much, don't ever forget that. Your Granny and Grandad love you too. Here's Granny coming up the stairs to say Goodnight.' He tucked the blankets around her and kissed her forehead.

Vera sang some Nursery Rhymes to Maria. Her favourite was 'Sing a Song of Sixpence' and Vera had to repeat it several times. Tom took down an old book of stories and read the story of the Three Billy Goats Gruff until she fell asleep. It would have been Teresa's 27th birthday the following day and, as it was Saturday, he took Maria up Cliffe Beacon to where they could see the sea.

Tom had found a picture he had taken of Teresa and Maria in Parc Guell in Barcelona. It was a lovely picture of the quirky fountain designed by Gaudi in the Parc which was high up in the city. They had spent a sunny day there during one of his days off a couple of years previously. He showed it to Maria and they spoke of Barcelona, of her mother and the good times they had spent together. Tom wanted his daughter to treasure the memories they shared of the past as well as looking forward to a new future. When they got back home, he had put the picture in his wallet.

Maria found that she was not the only child in the school who did not go home to a mother: one of the other girls had lost her mother to a sudden illness and they became friends for a short time. Her English had improved considerably and her cousin Teddy made sure that she was not teased for being a 'foreigner' at school.

'Ok my friends, this is Les Trois Chemins where you can all rest for a while. It belongs to friends of mine,' said Martin in Spanish and then English. He turned the black car into the drive of a house that appeared to stand on its own within extensive grounds. 'But don't let anyone hear you speak Spanish when you are outside the house. Franco's spies are everywhere, even in France.' At this, he got out of the car, retrieved his bag from the boot, pulled a key from under a plant pot and opened the front door. Antonio, Nicholas and Jimmy, who had all recently escaped from a Spanish jail thanks to Martin, all followed him inside. Martin was the only one who had any luggage as the others only possessed the clothes that they stood up in and these were the ill-fitting clothes of working mariners. Martin dropped his bag in the hallway and led them into a large kitchen where he turned on the light to reveal a wooden table and chairs standing on a tiled floor. There was a cooking range on one side and the delicious smell became more intense when Martin took a cloth and opened the oven door. There was a huge pot of stew inside which had been left for them.

Antonio took off the beret he was wearing and scratched his head where the hair was starting to grow back and felt itchy. The Captain of the boat had ordered them all to shave the hair off their heads and faces several days earlier to make sure that they did not bring lice onto his vessel. They had then washed in the sea and rinsed themselves at fresh water tap before putting on the clothes that Martin had provided for them. It had taken them eight days to get from the coast of Valencia to the harbour at Marseille. They had French papers and the boat carried a load of Spanish olive oil and fish giving a valid reason for their presence to the customs. Once the formalities and the sales were complete, the Captain, a short wiry man from Corsica had wished them well and turned back to his boat thrusting the notes that Martin had given him into his pocket. Martin broke the silence:

'Can someone get some plates and cutlery from that cupboard over there. Also, there should be glasses and some wine left out for us,' he had taken charge quite naturally. They had forgotten about eating in a civilised manner.

Antonio, the older of the two olive-skinned Spaniards took the plates over to the range while Nicholas placed cutlery and glasses in front of four of the chairs. Then, Nicholas opened the bottle of wine that had been left on the table, savoured the aroma and poured some into each glass. He was younger and taller than his comrade but shuffled along quietly: still in pain from the many beatings he had taken from the prison guards.

'Oh god, it feels like the floor is moving…I think I am going to be sick.' Jimmy rushed over to the sink and vomited. Jimmy had joined the International Brigade from University in spite of the opposition from his family. He had gained a school scholarship in his home town of Dundee followed by a place at Oxford University: he was the first in his family to gain such an education. At University, he had joined the Communist party and left for Spain before finishing his degree. Martin had not known him very well at University but nevertheless had volunteered to help with his rescue. Spain was not supposed to imprison foreign combatants but somehow Jimmy had found himself still locked up after all the other International Brigaders had been sent home. A sympathetic guard had let the British Embassy know where he was.

'I don't think our English friend likes travelling by boat.' Antonio laughed.

'How many times do I have to say, I am not English, I am a Scot, from Scotland. And no, I do not like boats. Eight whole days of bobbing up and down on that blasted thing and it feels like I am still on it: never again.' Jimmy said as he turned a very pale face towards the others. He had the kind of freckled fair skin that never tanned and his reddish hair was starting to grow back on his head. He turned the tap on to clean up.

'Do you want anything to eat Jimmy? It may settle your stomach,' asked Martin in English.

'Perhaps some bread, but let me wait a while so I'm sure the floor has stopped moving around,' Jimmy replied before taking a drink of water from the tap.

'This looks really good. Who cooked the food: surely it wasn't you was it Martin?' asked Antonio staring into the pot. He hadn't smelled food that good in months.

Martin took a ladle from a hook on the wall and started to share out the stew from the pot, 'No. The owner of this house has a sister who lives with her French husband and their two children in the neighbouring house. Her name is Ermine Bernard and she, or her housekeeper Francoise, will have left this for us. Mme Bernard is going to come to help you learn French but don't expect her to cook for you after this. You will probably have to fend for yourselves. I will stay a couple of days here but, once Jimmy is feeling better, I will take him to Marseille and put him on a train back home.' Martin had only met Ermine Bernard and her husband Claude briefly a couple of weeks previously but had been reassured that the estate would offer a safe haven for the men. He had been surprised how Ermine, who had been born in England as Hermione Clements but had lived in France for two decades, had transformed herself from an English aristocrat to a French country-woman. Only a double row of pearls gave a clue of her past life as Imogen's sister.

'What about us? Will Pilar and my son be coming to join me soon?' asked Antonio as he handed out the plates of stew.

'Please be patient. Your best chance of survival is to learn French and become Antoine as soon as possible. There are many Spanish Republicans in camps in France and some of the men have been sent back to Franco's detention centres. The French government are officially neutral but are helping Franco's forces to round up so-called troublemakers. Do you want to go back to jail and starve to death or get shot?' Martin put the lid back on the pot and took the bread to the table.

'Do you suppose my family are safe in Spain now?' Antonio asked angrily as he sat down.

'Last I heard, your wife and son were well and being sheltered by your older brother Xavier. Pilar wanted me to make sure your got out of that prison alive. You should be happy about that and concentrate on getting to look and sound like a healthy Frenchman. Then you can make whatever plans you want. At this moment, you look like an ex-prisoner that hasn't eaten properly for months and has taken a serious beating or two.' Martin ripped the baguette into two and passed the bigger half of it to Nicholas.

'Well, I can't tell you how grateful I am that you all let me come along too.' Nicholas said taking a piece of bread and passing the rest over to Antonio.

'It wasn't in the original plan but I managed to get French papers for you too as you know. Nicholas is a name used throughout France so we thought you could keep that. You will both need to work on the estate as a cover and to pay back the family for letting you stay. This will also help you to learn French without drawing attention to yourselves.'

'That's fine with me. I don't have anywhere or anyone to go back to. I am not afraid of hard work. I think the bruises are getting better already. Antonio, sorry Antoine, still has a bad cough though.' Nicholas said.

'I got that from working down the mine at the prison near Leon. It isn't so bad now. I don't know why they moved most of us out of that jail but it was lucky for me. And lucky that the guard Rodrigo and his cousin could be trusted' Antonio said looking at Jimmy. 'Ah, so you are feeling a bit better are you, Diego my friend?' Jimmy, known in the prison as Diego, had started to eat some of the bread. Martin had been able to locate a guard at the prison who was willing to help with the escape in return for some money. He was very pleased with the outcome and was aware that it had given him a taste for a more adventurous life. He had lost interest in working his way up the ladder at the British Consular service. Martin raised his glass.

'To freedom!' he said and they all joined the toast:

'To freedom.'

The three ex-prisoners slept well that night in the first truly comfortable beds they had seen for months.

Claude and Ermine Bernard came over the following morning to welcome them. Claude was not a tall man and had the typical dark colouring of a Frenchman from the South. He had only inherited the house, the land and the work because his older brother had been killed in the trenches near Ypres. They were hoping that these men might help, if only for a short while, to set things straight on the estate: ever since the war, there had been a shortage of labour in the countryside. Ermine was an attractive woman in her forties: she still had a good figure with noticeably large blue/grey eyes and a weathered face. She wore a well-fitted blue dress with cream coloured polka dots. She welcomed them all in French and then spoke to Martin quietly in English.

Claude set the men to work with his son Jean-Paul: they chopped wood for the winter, cut the grass in the orchards, mended fences and weeded around the vines. Nic volunteered that he could use a gun and so he was despatched to shoot rabbits. Antoine could drive and knew a bit about engines: he found some tools in the barn and fixed the tractor. After a couple of days, Martin and Jimmy said farewell and left the house. Jimmy was returning home to Scotland and Martin went back to his work at the British Consulate in Marseille.

Martin returned a week or so later bringing extra clothing, a gift of a guitar for Nicholas and a set of carpentry tools for Antoine. Ermine and her daughter Marianne were spending time helping them to learn French. Marianne at around twenty looked like a younger version of her mother: Nic and Antoine had first seen her in the yard behind the large old house, more like a little chateau than a farmhouse with its blue shutters and columns outside the enormous double fronted doors. The main house was a good way away from 'Les Trois Chemins' where the men were staying. Marianne had obviously just wrung the necks of two chickens and was sitting down plucking the feathers from one while the other was hanging up on the fence next to her. There was a knife covered in blood by her feet. She looked up and nodded at them in recognition but wasn't to be distracted from her task. They unloaded their barrows of chopped wood onto a pile that was being stacked up in an outhouse and went back to their work. Antoine did not pay her any attention but Nic had to force his gaze away from her pretty face framed by a headscarf before she noticed. Jean-Paul was not so welcoming and seemed to confine himself to giving orders to the newcomers.

For Antoine and Nic, the next few weeks were almost like being back in school: they learned basic conversation, numbers, how to tell the time, the names of various animals, parts of the body and a typical basket of food items. They would be tested for speaking and writing and gradually got on to verbs and more advanced vocabulary. Marianne seemed to bring endless patience and imagination to the task of teaching them her language.

One evening, Claude came over to bring some wine after the day's work was over. Antoine got out three glasses and offered one to 'Le Patron'. Claude accepted the drink, sat down and thanked them for working so hard that day.

'No problem. I enjoy it,' Nic replied.

'Marianne says that the French lessons are going well'

'Marianne is a good teacher. But we are not French. Is it safe to leave, perhaps visit the town?'

Antoine asked as he was the one who was most anxious to leave.

'You are learning classic French. Perhaps in a few weeks. You can say that you come from Perpignan or Beziers. Wait a minute,' here Claude went over to a book case and got out an atlas. He turned to a page showing the southern part of France. 'We are here' he said pointing to the nearby town of Pezenas. Then he pointed to a large area with a sweep of his finger. 'This is Langedoc-Rousillon. Many people here do not speak classic French at home, you understand? They learn French in school. At home they speak a local dialect, especially the older people: here some Occitan, here some Catalan.'

'Catalan? But I speak Catalan' Antoine said excitedly.

'Perhaps not the same Catalan. But similar. It may help you. You don't need to speak perfect classic French.'

'This is a good idea. Thank you so much. I can't stay here forever. You understand?'

'Yes. I understand. You are welcome to stay but you are free to go if you must.' Claude looked at the two men. Antoine and Nic exchanged glances.

'I want to stay to work.' Nic confirmed what Claude had already thought. Nic was likely to stay for some time but Antoine was only staying until he felt he had the means to leave. He wished them goodnight and returned to his own house.

The work and the lessons continued. In the evenings, Nic would play guitar and Antoine would whittle away at pieces of wood to fashion small animals to pass the time. He made a rabbit, a cat and a dog which he left on a shelf in the kitchen. They took turns to cook or sometimes took what was offered by the Bernard family.

Nic soon settled into his new life: he worked hard with Jean-Paul and a young man who came in from the village called Joelle. There was always plenty of work to do: weeding around the rows of tomatoes, peppers and aubergines; picking fruit; feeding and clearing out the muck from the pigs, chopping wood. They would also go out shooting rabbits and in Autumn, they all went out into the woods to collect wild mushrooms. The women were left with the tasks of bottling, drying and preserving the harvests. The grapes were transported to the local co-operative and they would receive their quota of wine back each year. The cellars were full of wine, preserved fruit, dried herbs, cured meats. There was plenty of food to go round.

Antoine helped too but his heart was not in it and he never stopped talking about his wish to see his wife and son again. Shortly after another visit from Martin, Antoine told Nic that as he now had papers for his family and he was going to bring them back to France. He assured Nic that he would come back one day to check up on his old comrade.

Chapter Four – late September 1940 - London W1

Martin walked the short distance from Whitehall to Mayfair and noticed new banks of sandbags being built up but no bomb damage in his immediate sight. It was quite a different story to the widespread destruction in the East of the city. He was sharing a flat with a family friend on Great Portland Street and day after day had heard the terrible noise of the bombing raids and had felt the fear of Londoners for weeks now. Tom had told him that bombs had even fallen in Brighton. He wasn't able to shed any light on the invitation Martin had received from Imogen Clements.

'Ah, Good Evening, Martin. Can I introduce you to my good friend Dorothy Napier and her husband, Charles.' Imogen said as Martin entered her drawing room. Martin was dressed for dinner and held out a hand to the older man. He had asked a colleague and found out that Sir Charles Napier had been a war hero in 1914-18 and was now in the thick of things at the War Office. His hairline was receding, and his moustache had flecks of grey.

'Pleased to meet you Sir Charles.'

His wife also exchanged greetings. She was a petite blonde lady in her forties dressed in a well-cut mustard and rust dress.

'This is Martin Lascelles who recently returned from Marseille and, is I think, at something of a crossroads.' Imogen said as they helped themselves to drinks served by Imogen's butler.

'I suppose all the French embassy staff are up for re-assignment. Do you have something to go to yet? I hear you were in Spain before France.' Dorothy asked as she sat down.

'Some of my colleagues have already been dispersed around the world. I don't think I could go back to Spain as I left under a bit of a cloud and it is doubtful that I would do well under the new Ambassador. They are keeping me busy with translation work and there is talk of Lisbon or South America. To be honest, I'm not sure if the diplomatic service is where I belong now. Of course, I'm not too old to volunteer.'

'From what Imogen told me, you would be far too useful here to sign up as an ordinary soldier. I should wait a while longer to see how the land lies.' Sir Charles put in.

'Martin is fluent in French and Spanish and can also speak some German you know. His mother is Swiss.' Imogen added.

'Ah, that explains it.' Dorothy replied. 'It's not a talent shared by many of us English. I blame the school system you know. Why do they teach a dead language like Latin at so many schools when modern languages would be far more useful? I had a French governess for a while, but it just wasn't something I was any good at. I envy you. It must be marvellous to be able to switch to another language.'

The butler reappeared and announced that dinner was served so they moved into the dining room. Martin noticed that there was a stunning painting of a French landscape on one of the walls and a portrait of an Edwardian beauty adorned one of the other walls. He looked at his hostess and back at the portrait.

'Ah, I see you are admiring the painting of my mother. Do sit next to me Martin. You can compare our likenesses.'

'I can see that you have the same bone structure and eyes. It really is a beautiful painting!' exclaimed Martin as he gave Imogen one of the charming smiles she had seen before.

'Imogen's mother was quite a character, you know. She was a suffragist and never lost an opportunity to argue her case. She was quite an inspiration to us and we all miss her terribly.' Dorothy addressed Martin from across the table as they began to eat the starter of salmon mousse.

'That's kind of you to say, my dear,' said Imogen. Feeling the need turn the conversation to the present, she continued: 'Dorothy works alongside me at the Auxiliary Territorial Service. We are currently organising the evacuation and billeting of children with the Air Raid Precautions services. The bombing has been brutal around the docks this month.'

'We sent the Luftwaffe a message in return though. We are a harder nut to crack than the French. It isn't all going Germany's way now.' Sir Charles said waving a knife as he spoke. His words hit home hard with Imogen, who worried for her sister in France, but she concealed her feelings well.

'Yes. The RAF gave them a bloody nose, didn't they? So, do you think Churchill will take the war back to Europe soon? I know you can't tell us anything specific... Careless talk and all that.' Martin answered hoping for some hint of the mood in government. He was thoroughly disillusioned with life on the sidelines.

'I think we have more reason to be optimistic now than a few month's back. If only the Americans could be persuaded to join the fight.' Sir Charles answered.

'Yes, that could really change things. But FDR does not have much support for such a move within his own party does he? I'd love to get more involved in the action somehow.' Martin continued the conversation eagerly after swallowing another mouthful of the excellent wine.

'We lost so many good men last time round. Surely America won't leave us to fight Germany alone, will they?' Imogen asked.

'It seems that the president has his hands tied right now.'

The conversation continued through dinner and when the two women went into the drawing room, Sir Charles took the opportunity to ask Martin what he wanted to do next.

'As I said earlier, I'd like to test myself and make a real contribution. In Spain, I organised getting a Brit out of a Spanish jail. All a bit hush hush and definitely not strictly according to the rules. I enjoyed planning it and seeing it through. There must be some department where I could be more useful.' Martin had a feeling that Sir Charles could help him and was rewarded.

'Are you married or do you have someone special?'

'No. I have no ties.'

'I think that I know of an opportunity that you would be interested in.' He took a small diary out of his pocket. 'Can you come to my office next

Tuesday at 11:30. Don't tell anyone about it. Just say it's a medical appointment. Does that suit you?'

'Yes, I can do that.' Martin was intrigued. They shook hands on it and then got up to join the ladies.

Martin went to meet Sir Charles at the appointed time having kept the whole thing to himself. Sir Charles greeted him promptly and lost no time getting straight to the point.

'Would you be interested in serving in undercover operations in France?' Sir Charles noted the smile with which the question was received.

'Yes, I would. When can I start?' So, it was as Martin had suspected and secretly hoped. They took a bus to Baker Street where Sir Charles took him to a house and introduced him to another man.

'Martin, this is Paul, he is going to test your language skills in a way that I can't. I'll leave you here and be in touch again soon.'

Evidently, he passed the test and by December, Martin was at a large estate in Oxfordshire with several others being trained in things such as personal combat and sending signals in code. He was joining a new covert organisation, later known as SOE. He left England by plane in early 1941.

* * *

Meanwhile, Imogen received news from her family in France sporadically. Letters from her sister came via a cousin in Switzerland and gave her very little sense of how their lives had been changed by the war. Ermine obviously felt the need to be careful about what she said and this made Imogen very anxious about life in Vichy France. She was able to pass on plenty of family news though. Claude Bernard had been shocked to the core to see the newspaper pictures of the German flag flying in Paris that June 1940. His health had been deteriorating but he died suddenly two months later.

After the funeral, Jean-Paul and Marianne had had several heated disagreements. Marianne had to accept that her father had left everything to Jean-Paul. Imogen had already known from her sister that Marianne would not inherit and had signed 'Les Trois Chemins' over to her niece to give her some independence once she came of age. When they married later in the year, in spite of opposition from Jean-Paul, Nicolas and Marianne moved into the house she now owned. They all continued to work together but things were never the same between them.

Imogen was desperate to see her sister and her family again but she had no idea when that might happen. They were the only close family she

85

had left and seemed so far away. She kept herself busy in London working for the ATS at the War Office.

Chapter Five - July 1942 — near Lewes

Maria and her grandfather came back from the fields and into the house leaving the dogs outside in the yard. They left their boots in the porch and hung up their wet coats and hats. The rain had started ten minutes earlier but was only a light drizzle.

'Come and have a warm cup of tea both of you. It's a good job you came back when you did otherwise you'd have got soaked.'

'Thanks love,' said Ted taking the cup. 'Young missy must take after our Tom. She's been telling me how she is top of the class again in spelling.' Maria had overtaken her cousin Teddy at school some time ago.

'If you carry on the way you are, you may end up going to the grammar school in Lewes like your father.' Vera said as she sat down at the table after refilling the teapot. They all heard the bus pass the house and then come to a halt at the bus-stop a few yards up the road.

'I wonder if my papa is on that bus. Can I go and look?'

'Of course you can, my dear' answered Vera. As Maria ran to the front room window, Vera spoke to Ted in a low voice: 'A letter came for Tom today. It's from the War Office.'

'No, surely not' replied Ted full of concern.

'It is Papa!' Maria yelled as she opened the front door to let her father in from the rain.

'Hello there my poppet. Let me get out of these wet things first.' Tom put his bags down, taking off his coat and hat as he went into the kitchen to the coat hooks. He had been away since Monday on assignments for work.

'Hello all. Horrible weather out there now.' Tom leaned down to give Maria a hug. He picked her up and sat down in one of the chairs with his daughter on his lap. Vera poured him a tea and pushed it towards him

'How was your week son?' asked Vera. She always tried to draw him out although she saw how adept he was at hiding himself away. 'So like a man' she often thought.

'London has been relatively quiet again. There seems to be good news coming from both Egypt and Stalingrad though. How are things here?' Tom had got into a habit of giving political updates rather than telling her about his own experiences. He didn't want his mother to worry unnecessarily.

'All ticking along here. David's been haymaking, Uncle Jim's horse has not been so good. That new dog Bess is coming on well. And Maria has some news.' Ted nodded over at Maria.

'Another tooth has fallen out here' and she showed him the gap. 'And I beat Graham Tucker in the arithmetic and writing tests this week. That means that I came top of the class.'

'Well done, Maria. You are such a clever girl. I really am so proud of you.' He hugged his daughter again. 'Now what is it that smells so good?'

'Everyone can go wash their hands while I finish things off.' Vera was always in command in the kitchen and they all followed her instructions.

After dinner, Vera and Ted listened to the radio while Tom and Maria played a game of draughts. When she was ready, they would move on to chess. He hoped that she would take to it just as he had. Tom no longer let his daughter win as he wanted her to both improve her skills and learn to lose. After the game, father and daughter went upstairs to get ready for bed and read for a while. Maria was reading 'The Secret Garden' and they took turns to read pages before he left her to go to sleep. She loved the story maybe because the girl protagonist had also lived in a different country and lost her mother. When Tom went downstairs, Vera handed him the post nervously. He sat down, opened the brown envelope and read the contents before announcing:

'This might not be what you were dreading. I am being called up but only to serve in something called the Army Film and Photographic Unit. I have to report to Pinewood Studios in a couple of weeks.' Tom said drawing a sigh of relief from his father.

'That sounds relatively safe. Do you think you will get to stay there or be sent abroad?' asked Vera.

'I'm not sure, I've heard that some of the unit are already in North Africa but it isn't clear what they want me to do. I'll have to wait to find out. You can be sure you will be the first to know.' Tom put his hand on his mother's hand knowing that she would be worried about him. She worried all the way through the bombings of London, Bristol and Liverpool that he had photographed for newspapers and then filmed for the Crown Film Unit. She had never stopped worrying about him just as he now worried about Maria: he understood that now. Yet a part of him was pleased by this posting: he was feeling so confined in England and wanted to take a more active part in the war.

'Young Billy has been called up to serve in the navy. Our Peg is so worried for him. She also told me that her granddaughter Cath has started working up at the Hall with her father. She's going to be looking after the horses as there are no grooms left to do it. It doesn't seem right for a girl to be doing that sort of work but she seems happy with it. I don't suppose it's any different from the Land Girls is it. You know that they have a load of Canadian soldiers billeted up at the Hall now don't you. And there are more around the village and in Lewes so my nephew Harry says.'

'Yes, you said. They've been down here a while though haven't they?' Tom seemed to remember his mother telling him this already.

'Yes, but more of them arrived recently. It seems that they are helping to man the coastal defences in Sussex now. Have you heard any other news this week?' his father asked.

'Our boys are gaining ground in North Africa.' replied Tom after some thought.

'Did you ever hear from that friend of yours from Spain, Matthew was it?' Vera asked.

'Do you mean Martin? He was working in Marseille in some capacity. I haven't heard from him for a while but don't really expect to.' In fact, Tom knew from Imogen that his friend Martin was doing some dangerous and secret work in France but he didn't know much about it and shouldn't mention what he did know to anyone. 'Have David and Sue decided what to do with the Forge cottage yet?' He asked to change the subject. Uncle Jim had died from liver and heart failure some months previously and, as there was nobody left to take over as blacksmith, David had gained permission from the landowner to use the forge as a store and absorb the cottage into theirs.

'They say they are going to let Georgie have a bigger bedroom and put a bathroom in her old bedroom. Goodness know when and how they'll get that done.' Vera struggled to understand why her children both seemed to want to change everything. The wartime attitude of 'make do and mend' suited her down to the ground.

'Is there anything you need me to help you with while I'm here, dad?' Tom asked.

'Oh no, son. You spend some time with Maria while you can.' Vera shot him a worried glance and he added. 'She will enjoy that. I'll need to turn in now and see you in the morning.'

A couple of weeks later, they all heard the sound of many aeroplanes droning overhead and explosions out at sea. There was an unsuccessful raid on Dieppe where many British and Canadians lost their lives. Tom found himself training new recruits to his unit to use the camera and film equipment that they had at their disposal. He remained in London for the following few months but then was stationed with the unit in North Africa. When he told Maria that he was going abroad for a while and would be back soon, she believed him. Although an intelligent girl with a logical mind, she carried an unerring belief all through the war and beyond that her father would always be there and nothing bad would happen to him. This was surprising given what had happened to her mother but anything else was unthinkable. She relied on her grandparents more and more and was driven to succeed at school. Vera took great care to conceal from her granddaughter the fears that she herself harboured every time Tom left the house.

****

Martin worked throughout the Languedoc region: Narbonne, Beziers, Montpelier. Things had been difficult enough what with the food shortages caused by the farmers having to give up a huge portion of their produce to the Nazis. Also, as he was far away from any accessible safe air drop zones, he was reliant on other groups for money and other supplies. But now, the Nazis had taken control in the so-called unoccupied zone. He had heard that the London team were working on a way to pull him out but he had another assignment planned before that could happen: they were going to set off a series of explosions on key road and rail routes.

He dressed in warm clothes as the wind was cold that Sunday morning and he needed to cycle to a drop zone in a disused pigsty. Antoine had recently concealed money and explosives that he had picked up further north in one of their hiding places near Narbonne. The news had been passed to him by one of his contacts at the local bar. Antoine had built a number of hidden compartments in the lorry that he drove. He and Martin, now known as Auguste, had not actually met for several weeks now but then they didn't need to risk that. He picked up the bag of cash and divided it up placing some in his inside pocket, some in a belt around his waist and the rest in his shoulder bag along with the explosives. He had detonators ready in another location.

The radio operator had provided the information on their target for the following Tuesday. He checked the location out with one of the local men once the contents of the shoulder bag were hidden close by. He liked to work with Benoit as he was quiet and methodical. He was an older man and unlikely to raise suspicion. They walked across the bridge and on to the church where they pretended to look at some of the graves and then walked back across the bridge to the town. There did not seem to be any guards on duty close to the bridge. Benoit went back to his home and Martin returned to his room in the local hotel. He was posing as an antique dealer and had a small warehouse building where he kept furniture, old clocks and pottery. He would generally buy from locals and sell to the occupiers who wanted souvenirs to take home. He often went fishing: this was allegedly to eat his catch but it was a great way to watch what was going on in a town or village.

The next day, Martin and Benoit made their way to a wooded area down by the bridge. They retrieved the explosives and started planting their device but before they were ready to light the fuse, several trucks of Germans arrived. Benoit and Martin ran off in different directions but Benoit was shot in the back and Auguste was captured and bundled into a truck with an armed guard. Back at local SS headquarters he was searched and beaten.

They were referring to him as 'The Swiss' and Martin knew enough German to understand that he was being kept alive as a prize for the SS Command in Lyon. They had taken his cyanide supply so there seemed to be no way out. He suspected that someone had betrayed him and hoped that he would be strong enough to die without giving away any helpful information.

Antoine did not receive any more instructions from his friend Martin. He made discreet enquiries and learned rumours of his fate. He felt lucky to have escaped yet again. However, rather discouraging him, his friend's death only gave him more reasons to carry on with the fight.

****

Maria put on her best dress to catch the bus into Lewes with her father: she was pleased to be spending time with him again. He was back home for a short break after spending three months in Southern Italy. They made their way to the train station to meet Imogen coming in on the London train.

'I expect Imogen has asked to see you to congratulate you on getting to the Grammar School.' Tom said as they waited for the train to arrive. Maria beamed and could hear the loud noise of the engine in the distance. That was soon followed by the smell and sight of the steam.

'There's the train now,' she said tugging at her father's raincoat sleeve. There were several soldiers and civilians waiting on the station concourse as the train made its way in.

'Brighton train arriving from London' shouted a stout woman dressed in a British Rail uniform. Quite a number of passengers were leaving the train including the tall familiar figure of Imogen who emerged from a first-class carriage, carrying a leather bag that was half way between a handbag and a case.

'Imogen, over here,' Tom said as he waved over and then walked towards her to take the bag. They embraced in the European style as they often did.

'Good morning, Tom, so lovely to see you. Can we walk up to the White Hart Hotel. I am being met there in a couple of hours. Be a dear and take my bag for me, would you?'

Tom was happy to take the case and gestured with his hand to Maria.

'Goodness me, is this young Maria?' she said as they walked over to the young, dark-haired girl who had stood back from the encounter.

'Lovely to see you. My, you have shot up. Just like an asparagus spear in June while I wasn't watching.' Imogen laughed at the thought but Maria looked puzzled. Vera didn't grow asparagus in their kitchen garden. As Maria embraced Imogen, she took in a flowery scent with a hint of lavender. The lady was dressed in a light blue skirt and jacket with a dark blue silk blouse. It was slightly old-fashioned hinting at its pre-war origin. Maria was conscious of the home-made dress that she herself was wearing. Imogen continued as she glanced at the station clock:

'Well done, Maria, I hear congratulations are in order. You will be going to the Grammar School like your father before you.'

'Yes, Miss Clements. I am looking forward to it.'

'Yes, now let's go shall we. I have a proposal to make once we get up to the High Street.' Imogen looked over at Tom and he tried to hide a smile. He knew there was some reason why Imogen had asked to see them that morning. Imogen put her arm through Tom's free arm leaving Maria to run on ahead.

'How long did you say you were home for Tom?'

'I have two weeks here on leave before I go back to Italy. Progress is incredibly slow there as the Germans mined all over the countryside and the towns as they left.' Tom couldn't tell her too much about the horrors that he had seen as the allies had advanced. He had witnessed one of his colleagues and some other men being blown up by an explosion only yards ahead of him. There were so many things that were best left unsaid. He was going to see the man's widow in London before he went back. They had made an agreement to look out for each other's families should anything happen to either one of them.

'I do hope that the allies will look towards France soon. I have a feeling that things are far worse than I am being told by my sister and her family.' Imogen said as they continued along the pavement.

'Oh, are you still hearing from them?'

'Yes, very occasionally, via a connection in Switzerland. Ermine talks of some shortages but I am sure it is much worse than that. Many of the young men were sent to work in Germany. Both of her children have married and had children in my absence and I can't wait to see them. Surely the allies will try to take France back soon.' Imogen looked over at Tom.

'I daresay that there will be moves to invade on another front at some point. So much progress has been made on the Eastern Front that it seems inevitable that the allies will make a move there soon. I've seen quite a lot of troops moving around the place. Isn't there a new army camp outside Brighton in Stanmer Park?' Tom said as they made their way along the pavement.

'Is there really? I hope it comes soon, even though it is bound to be at such a cost. I didn't think I would see another war in my lifetime. But enough of this, I happen to have some spare clothing coupons and Maria will be needing uniform for the school...' Tom didn't usually interrupt Imogen but blurted out in shock.

'Imogen, are you of all people getting involved in the black market?'

'Certainly not!' Imogen stopped walking and turned to her companion. 'These are my coupons which I do not need as I have more than enough clothes already. Really Tom, I am surprised at you. And rather insulted. But I will not withdraw my offer to Maria just because her father seems to have become cynical like so many other journalists.'

Tom held up his hand in his defence. 'I'm sorry Imogen. You must be the only person left in England who doesn't bend the rules. And thank you.' He turned back towards Maria, who was walking behind them. She gave him a questioning look in response but he smiled and turned back to Imogen. 'I am sure that Maria will be glad to accept your offer. And it will no doubt save my mother from wrestling with her old treadle Singer in an attempt to make something out of nothing. Even mother's talents have limits and we had all saved some coupons up for her. Any contribution you would like to make will be gratefully received.'

'So, I am being picked up by car from the hotel in about an hour. We can leave my bag in the hotel reception while we take some tea and continue our talk. Does that suit you my dears?' Imogen said as Maria joined them to cross the road to the hotel.

'Right, it's clear now' Tom said as he guided them both across the road. They went into the hotel where the lady on reception clearly knew Imogen and took her bag from her. They made their way into an informal dining area and sat at a small table. A young lady took their order for two teas and a Dandelion and Burdock drink for Maria. As they waited for their order to arrive, Imogen reached into her handbag and took out the coupons.

'So, Maria, I've discussed this with your father. I have twelve coupons here for you to help with the school uniform.

'Thank you so much, Miss Clements. Granny says that there is a second-hand Uniform exchange being run over the Summer but I will still need coupons to get some of the things that I need.'

'There you are, I knew Granny would already be on the case.' Tom said.

'I expect that the Women's Royal Voluntary Service run the clothing exchange down here just like up in London. They do such invaluable work in so many areas.' Imogen said but broke off as the waitress arrived with a tray.

'Another thought that I had was that I have an extensive library that you could draw on. I know that there is a public library here in Lewes but, if you let me know of any books you would like to have long term: particularly novels, French dictionaries and history books, please let me know. What books are you reading at the moment?' Imogen looked at the girl expectantly. Maria was a bit shy to answer at first as she found Imogen a bit intimidating but eventually found her courage.

'I've recently finished Jane Eyre which I borrowed from the library and I have just started a new one called Swallows and Amazons which my teacher recommended to me.' Maria said looking over to her father.

'She's a good reader, you know. She can play chess and she's picked up a lot about animals and plants from my parents.' Tom put in.

'That's good: formal education isn't everything. But what did you think of Jane Eyre? Who was your favourite character in it?' Imogen asked and Maria thought carefully before answering...

'Well, I liked Jane but I thought she should have stayed teaching in the school rather than going back to look for Mr Rochester. He didn't seem like a very good person to me.' Maria started with enthusiasm but then stopped to look to the adults for reassurance. Her father smiled as he was used to her ready opinions. Imogen raised her eyebrows and replied:

'That's a perfectly valid opinion and I am pleased to see that you have a lively mind. It is always curious to see what choices people make in life. You know, I would be very pleased if you would write to me to tell me how you are getting on at the new school. You will find it very different from going to the village school as you will be meeting girls whose families come from all walks of life. Is there anyone else from your school going on to the Grammar with you?' She remembered that Tom had found starting at the Grammar difficult and having friends always seemed more important to girls.

'Yes, the daughter of the Methodist minister is going but we are the only ones. It will be good to have someone to share the bus ride with. My father has warned me that I may have to get used to not being the top of the class and a lot of the girls will come from the town but I won't let that put me off. I am looking forward to starting new subjects.

'Oh yes?'

'We will be learning Science subjects and also French.'

'Ah yes, I may be able to help you there as I speak and write French quite well.'

Tom nodded in agreement: 'Imogen helped me with French as nobody at home knew any. Perhaps Maria would be interested to know how your sister came to be living in France.' The adults both looked at Maria.

'Oh, yes please,' she had answered.

'So, where should I begin? Tom already knows that my mother was a suffragette and insisted that her daughters had some sort of an education. My father joked that he should never have agreed to it given what happened. Anyway, my older sister Hermione was sent to a school in Switzerland for a couple of years before the first war. Shortly before her eighteenth birthday when she was due to return home, she ran away with one of her teachers: a Monsieur Bernard.' Maria opened her eyes in surprise and looked at her father while Imogen continued: 'My father went to Switzerland to look for her but came home empty handed just like Mr Bennet in Pride and Prejudice. We all feared a scandal. A few weeks later, we received a letter to say that she and the teacher had been married in France and intended to stay there. She was to be known as Ermine Bernard.' Imogen stopped for a minute to catch her breath.

'It turned out that this Claude Bernard was not as penniless as my parents had assumed and in fact, his family owned land in the South of France near Montpelier. Being a second son, he had sought out a profession so became a teacher. Ermine and Claude were going to come to England for a reconciliation with our parents but she fell pregnant and then the war broke out. So, my nephew Jean-Paul was born in early 1915 and none of us could visit. As the war progressed, both my brothers, Claude's brother and then my fiancée were killed.

But you already know that part.' Imogen looked at Tom and then took a drink before continuing.

'Later on, in the summer of 1919, my mother and I went to visit them. This was when my niece Marianne was born. We stayed there for a while as the weather was good for my mother's health. My father was able to buy a house 'Les Trois Chemins' with some land close to my brother-in-law's place. This house now belongs to my niece Marianne and her husband Nic. So there you are: that is how I come to have family in France and I can't wait for this war to end so that I can see them all again.' Imogen smiled and could see that Maria had been fascinated by the story.

At that point, they noticed that a group of Canadian soldiers were sitting down at the next table and talking quite loudly.

'I wonder if any of those boys are billeted up at the Hall. They have had to make a lot of changes to accommodate them but we all have to do our bit don't we.'

'One of my cousins is engaged to a Canadian rifleman who is billeted in the village.' Tom said, looking over at the men in uniform.

'Was there any news of your other cousin. I know that your mother worried about him doing the Atlantic run.' Imogen asked.

'Unfortunately, he was on a ship that took a u-boat hit and is now missing.'

'Oh no. His poor family. He was very young, wasn't he?'

'Yes, Billy was only eighteen. He used to work up at the Hall you know. His father still does.'

'I'll make sure that we send them something.'

'That's very kind, Imogen.'

'It's the least we can do. I just hope that the tide is really turning now and we can get some normality back. I feel for the youngsters like Maria who can barely remember anything different. Now, is there anything else I can help you with? Any books or equipment that you might need? So many things are scarce and I may be able to help my dears.'

Imogen got Maria to promise to write to her and it was started off when Maria needed to thank her for some books that she had sent over. There was a set of Observer's books that covered British Birds, Wild Flowers and Wild Animals along with some more novels and a French/English dictionary. It was such a generous and thoughtful gift.

The girls at the new school were mainly the daughters of the town's professional men and they were all bright. Some of the town girls teased her for being a country bumpkin. But Maria was driven to show them that she could keep up with them: she loved to read and enjoyed learning new things. She became particularly friendly with Sarah Katz whose family had arrived from Vienna a few years before. She was anchored by the home that Vera had made for her at Blackthorn Farm and loved to tell her granny about all her enthusiasms. Occasionally Imogen Clements, who spent most of her time in London, would visit and bring her gifts of books and clothing.

It was a crisp, autumn day as Tom and Imogen, both dressed in black, walked to the church in Cheltenham. A couple of weeks earlier, Martin's mother had let Tom know that they had received notification of his death in Lyon, France from the War Office. This confirmed what he had already been surmised by those close to Martin. Tom was back in England for a short time and was pleased to be able to attend in person to pay his respects. The memorial service was fairly short and gave only vague details about the circumstances of his death. There were few attendees due to the practical difficulties of getting around and the fact that loss seemed to be so commonplace now. The only people that Tom had any connection with were Martin's parents.

When it was over, Tom took his turn in giving his condolences to Mr and Mrs Lascelles outside the church. 'I owe an enormous debt of gratitude to Martin. He was a good friend to me when I first went to Spain and he was tireless in helping me and my daughter to escape. He was a credit to both of you and will be sorely missed.' He then turned to Imogen to introduce her.

'I didn't know your son as well as Tom, but am so sorry for your loss,' she said. 'I'm afraid I feel partly responsible for putting him on the path to more dangerous work. I hope you can forgive that. He wanted to put his language talents to good use and I introduced him to someone who might help him.' In truth Imogen did feel guilty both about offering her house to be used for his Spanish prisoners and for introducing Martin to Sir Charles.

'Please believe me, nothing would have stopped Martin from doing what he wanted to do. He was a wonderful son. You are welcome to join us for tea if you can.' Mrs Lascelles replied with shining eyes.

'We are proud of him. Now the tide is turning in Europe and surely that is due to many brave people like our boy.' Mr Lascelles added shaking both their hands as they moved on to make way for other mourners.

They had decided to go straight back to the train station rather than go for tea as it was a long journey back to London and a train was due in about an hour. Now that the blackout restrictions had been lifted, at least they didn't have to worry about curfews.

'The atmosphere in London has completely changed since the invasion of France, don't you find?' Imogen asked as they settled into an empty carriage.

'Oh yes, the tide is really turning now. No more running to air raid shelters but the food situation is no better. Everyone seems more optimistic now that the end is in sight.' Tom took his coat off and the Order of Service fell out of the pocket. He bent to pick it up and looked though it as he sat down.

'It's so sad to attend another service for a man who had a bright future ahead of him. He really was a charmer too, wasn't he?' Imogen was making herself comfortable in the seat opposite.

'Oh yes. But so many families across so many countries have suffered loss of some kind, haven't they? Sometimes it is hard not to feel guilty for being alive. It makes me want to make the most of whatever time I have left.'

'What do you have in mind Tom? Is some change in direction on the horizon?' Imogen held onto the armrest as the train started to leave the station.

'Well once the war is over, a change of work will be necessary as my unit will be disbanded. I must join the scramble back to civilian life. I need to decide if I want to continue with moving pictures or go back to still photography, which is my real forte.'

'Do you think the war will be over soon?'
Imogen asked hopefully.

'It seems inevitable that the Allies will push
for victory now. The Soviets are moving faster than
we are. The question is what will it take to get a
surrender from both Germany and Japan. I would
guess it won't take more than a few months. What's
your view?'

'Some say that Germany already knows it is
beaten on both fronts but that the Japanese will take
much longer to contemplate defeat.' Imogen read
the news voraciously.

'I haven't followed the war in Asia so
closely. You may be right but I hope not. It would
be so good to see things get back to some kind of
normality. You must have enjoyed the sight of Paris
and Marseille being liberated.'

'Oh yes. But I haven't heard from my sister
for months now. I just want to know that they are all
alright. My sister has two grandchildren now and I
will be going over there as soon as I know that it's
safe.'

'I can see you are determined.'

'I am. But I shall need to be patient too. So,
you will go back in Italy next week. Are you going
down to Sussex for the rest of the time?'

'I'll be in London for a day or two and then down to Sussex to see the family. Did I tell you I was looking out for the widow of my colleague Bert Chisolm? I was there when he and some others were killed in Italy.' Tom paused to wipe away the picture he held in his mind. It had been pretty gruesome. 'Anyway, her name is Grace and she's good company and, before you ask, we are just friends. But we do seem to have a lot in common: she has been left to bring up a young boy without his father.' Tom paused as he tried to find the right words, 'I used to think it would be a betrayal of Maria and her mother to move on but life is too short to stay frozen in one place and time. The war is changing all of us.'

'Well, I'm glad for you, Tom. You deserve some happiness. Do send my best wishes to your family. Your daughter writes to me occasionally you know. I love to hear from the young, they give me so much hope for the future.'

Tom went back to filming in Italy for a while. In the following year, they spent some time in conquered Germany before his Unit was disbanded. After the war, he started to work as a freelance photographer with close ties to the Observer newspaper. Imogen found herself busy working for refugee organisations such as the Red Cross. She was able to get to see her sister in France eventually in the Autumn of 1945.

Chapter Seven – 1946 near Lewes

'Maria, how about a walk up Cliffe Beacon? I need to clear the cobwebs out of my head.' It was Saturday morning and Tom had only just had his breakfast and was finishing yet another cup of tea but he still looked tired. His mother was upstairs tending to his father. The doctor had come the previous day but had offered no clarity as to whether Ted would get better or not. He had suffered a stroke and been taken to hospital the week before and had been sent home to recuperate. They all took turns to sit with him until he had whispered to Vera that they should all get on with their lives and stop hovering over him. Tom was keen to get back to work in London the following Monday but was unsure if that was fair on his mother and his daughter.

'Yes, of course dad. We could take the dogs out for some exercise if Uncle David or Teddy aren't working them.' Maria replied. She was now thirteen and still a girl in his eyes although he could see that she had grown in confidence since going to the grammar school in Lewes. It had taken her out of village life and she was mixing with other bright young girls like her friend Sarah.

'Ask them if there is anything useful we can do will you? I may only be here today and tomorrow' Tom said as Maria ran outside. She saw that the two black and white dogs were both hanging about the yard and she went next door to see if anyone was there.

'Morning Auntie Sue, Georgie.' Maria saw that Sue was drying up the breakfast things and her daughter Georgie was helping.

'How is grandad today?' Georgie asked as she emptied the tealeaves into a pail of scraps and swilled out the pot. Maria's cousin had grown into a pretty girl with her fair hair kept in place with a pink Alice band. They saw less of each other now that they went to different schools but they were still close.

'No change. I was going to take the dogs out for some exercise with my dad. Does Uncle David need them today?' Maria asked.

'No, I don't think so. He's out turning the field up by Bell Lane. Teddy took them with him when he moved the sheep earlier but then he brought them back. Now he is out clearing the ditches at Lower Field. Those dogs wont object to another run out though.'

'Dad said to ask you if there is anything we can do to help. I think he may be going back to work on Monday.' Maria asked.

'I'll ask David when he comes back for some lunch. We'll let you know if there is. And you can check if you see anything amiss on your way. Without your grandfather, they struggle to keep up with everything. Just make sure that Vera is getting some rest although I'm sure you are already doing what you can to help her.' Auntie Sue gave Maria a reassuring smile.

'Ok, I'll see you later then.' Maria went back to Vera's kitchen to find it empty. Then she heard heavy footsteps coming down the stairs.

'Everything ok there?' Tom asked.

'Yes. Sue said we should take the dogs and they will let us know if they need any help.'

'Hmm. I'll pop round to see David later. We should be back in time to catch him having lunch. Let's get our coats on then. Mum says she will stay here.' Tom went to the pegs at the back door, saw his father's cap on the door and quickly picked up his own coat. Maria caught his look as she put on her own coat and they headed out into the windy September day. Maria whistled to the dogs who ran out of the back gate in front of them.

'Those dogs never seem to run out of energy, do they?' Tom said with a grin.

'No. They'd keep going all day if you asked them to.' Maria replied as her father took the path next to the hedge.

'It's such a shock to see the change in your grandfather. He could walk for miles beside those dogs every day and not seem to be tired. He looks like a shadow of himself lying in that bed. It must be worse for you seeing him every day as you do.' He turned to his daughter briefly: he didn't want to scare her but she had to be prepared for what might happen. They walked up the slight incline of the field, sheltered by the hedgerow, side by side.

'Yes, it is sad to see. Granny is putting on a brave face: just like she did when you went away in the war. Somehow, I always knew that you would come back. But I've heard what the doctor says and I understand that grandad might not get better.'

'It is possible that he will get better. But it is as well if we prepare for the worst. My mother is going to need us to help her although it is unlikely that she will ever ask for it. Us Lamberts are a stubborn lot as you know.' Tom winked at his daughter. He was relieved that she seemed to already understand the situation.

'Yes, I know. I'm happy to help out you know. And you can go back to work if you need to. I'm not a little girl anymore and I enjoy spending time with Grandad, making sure he is as comfortable as he can be.' The wind was getting colder as they walked across the open field and Maria pulled her hand-knitted green striped hat over her ears to keep warm.

'I know that. I'm very proud of you, you know.' Maria glowed with pleasure to hear this from her father. She still looked up to him although he had spent so much time away from home.

'Race you to the top!' she said as she got a head start on her father.

'You're on' he shouted from behind her. They ran up the hill and were both puffed out by the time they reached the top together. She ran towards the flat stone at the top and touched it shouting:

'I won!' Tom was still trying to catch his breath. He wasn't used to much physical exercise these days and held up his hands in defeat. Maria, on the other hand, was used to cross-country running and other sports at school as well as physical work on the farm.

'Ok. You won. Now let this old man sit down for a minute and enjoy a rest.' The dogs came back to check why they had stopped and lay down panting for a while.

'I always loved this view. Your dad used to bring me up here you know.' Maria said as she sat down on the grass.

'I'm not surprised, he used to bring David and I up here too. Probably his dad brought him up here before that.' Tom said.

'So even grandad's dad lived here?'

'Oh yes. I don't know how many generations. But people didn't have so many choices back then.' Tom looked down towards Brighton and the sea but could not make much out. There were too many clouds today in spite of the wind moving them along towards the east.

'Why was it that Uncle David has the farm and you had to leave? Was it just because he was the oldest?' asked Maria, curious as ever.

'Maybe. We just always assumed that he would be the farmer and I would find something else. Maybe Imogen helped me realise there were other possibilities. Speaking of whom, Imogen took off for France again in Summer to see that sister of hers. She has been so busy lately helping refugees from Europe, she needs to do something for herself for a change.' Tom gazed into the distance and was silent for a moment as if deep in thought. Maria looked down at Lewes seeking out her school but it was hidden behind the huge clump of trees in the park. Her father wasn't usually this serious and she wondered if grandad's illness had put him in this strange mood. In truth, he was thinking about his colleague's widow, Grace. He had promised his friend that he would look out for her but the relationship was taking an unexpectedly romantic turn. He wasn't about to share this news with his daughter yet as he wasn't sure how serious it was going to be. He wanted to protect her from any hurt wherever it came from but he was also keen for her to have the confidence to look outside of the small world she currently inhabited, just as he had.

'You need to consider your choices, Maria. You are a smart girl and I think you have the same spark that made me want to see something of the world and choose a different life. Perhaps it is the same spark that your mother had too: she wasn't going to let being a woman stand in her way. You can stay in the same place and let life happen to you or you reach out for new opportunities. Don't let anything hold you back from where you want to go.' This speech took them both by surprise: Tom rarely mentioned Maria's mother and she had guessed that her father found talking about her difficult. Maria had nobody else to ask about her and sometimes she was curious as to what sort of person her mother was.

'What did my mother do? You never really told me much about her.' Tom was slightly taken aback by the question and was thoughtful for a while before answering. He realised that he hadn't thought about his wife for a while. Teresa had possessed a fierce intelligence and an outgoing, impulsive nature.

'Your mother was very bright. But we married in very different and difficult times. She was working in a hotel when I met her. And she was soon busy looking after you. If she had lived, I am sure she would have found some way of making her mark.' Tom reached for Maria's hand and drifted off into a reverie of memories but then, some movement in the vista drew his mind back to the present. 'Look at all those houses in Lewes and Brighton full of people doing all different things. There is a whole world of new possibilities that you can grab hold of if you want to. Do you understand what I mean?'

'Sort of.' Maria's thoughts turned to her Granny, who was like a mother to her now. It was her Granny who had waited with the other mothers to pick her up from the village school and made sure she was fed and clothed. It was Granny who cuddled her when she was sad and congratulated her when she did well. But she did want something more than the life that her Granny had.

'I don't see anything wrong with being content and working on the farm like Granny and Grandad. But I don't want to let being a girl hold me back and I want to do something useful. I enjoy English and Biology at school and I have been thinking about training to be a teacher or a nurse. Aunt Imogen gave me some books and one of them was about a girl who was a nursing assistant in the

First World War. It was called 'A Testament of Youth' and I really enjoyed it.' Tom loved to see his daughter so animated. He considered how different Grace was from Maria and her mother both in looks and temperament. Grace had the fair colouring of an English rose and was dependable but quietly determined. He thought it likely that he would have a much more settled life with Grace than the one he would have had with Teresa.

Maria had talked about the future careers with her friends but hadn't mentioned any of these thoughts to her granny. It occurred to her that her dad would be better placed to offer advice but could see that he was miles away in his own thoughts: 'Have you got your puff back now dad?' This question bought him back to the present with a jolt.

'Yes, I was just taking in the view. So, Imogen has been giving you ideas, has she? Good old Imogen! A nurse or a teacher? Both of those are good choices and I'm glad you are thinking about it. You don't have any boys to distract you from doing well at school either.' Tom looked over at his daughter: he wanted to give her time to continue talking but she did not take the chance and so he continued: 'I suppose we had better get back and see if there is anything that needs to be done. Otherwise, I might have to challenge you to game of chess. Or is there anything else you would like to do?'

'I think we should ask Granny and Uncle David first: there is always something that needs to be done. We could check if there are still blackberries to gather down by the river or there may be apples ready to pick, Granny always has plenty for me to do.'

There were in fact a number of harvesting tasks that kept them all busy that weekend but Tom went back to London on the Monday as Vera had assured him that there was no reason for him not to. His father remained an invalid for several months. Maria spent a great deal of time helping Vera to care for him until he died from another stroke just after Christmas.

The two months that followed were quite literally freezing cold with snow and minus temperatures for most of that time throughout the country. It was the coldest winter in anyone's memory. Sometimes, it was too cold for the bus to run into Lewes or the train to get from London so Maria spent many days at home alone with her granny. They relied on each other and on the radio for company. Thankfully, that long winter ended eventually and Maria worked hard at school with renewed determination.

Chapter Eight – September 1949 near Lewes

Maria teased her thick hair off her face with some hair grips, packed her new uniform into a bag and kissed Granny Vera before making her way to the bus stop with her father.

'Good Luck my dear. Enjoy yourself,' Vera added as she waved from the front passage. She closed the door before Maria and Tom could see her sadness. 'They are all growing up so fast.' She said to the dog as she sat down to finish her tea. There was nobody else left in the house to listen to her now that Ted had passed away. After tidying the kitchen, she picked up her knitting and gazed out the window.

It was nearly seven on a bright, late summer morning and it was Maria's first day of nurse training at the Royal Sussex in Brighton: a big day that made her both excited and apprehensive. She saw Auntie Sue and cousin Georgie waving to her from their front room window and waved back with a nervous smile. Georgie was a very pretty girl who would shortly be leaving for school in Lewes. Her uncle David and cousin Teddy were no doubt already working on the farm. Thankfully, the bus was on time and she met her friend Sarah Katz on the platform at Lewes Station. The dark-haired girls greeted each other excitedly.

'Look at you two: you are so grown up' said Tom as they bought their tickets. Maria kissed her father goodbye before he walked over the bridge to take the train to London. He stayed up in town more and more now that he had his own flat in Clerkenwell. Tom's family now owned the farm as the landowner, the Earl of Uckfield had wanted to avoid paying so much in Death Duties when the old Earl died. They had gifted some of their land to their best tenants and that had included the Lamberts. When their father had died, they had sold some land for housing and Tom had taken most of this in lieu of his share of the farm. Tom had bought a flat and was now quite well set up with a good salary. He enjoyed his work in spite of some of the distant places and horrific sights it had led him to.

On the journey up to the city, he thought about how well Maria was doing and how she did not need him there to guide and protect her as much. His mother was always there when she needed it and he felt that her lively enthusiasm would help build the confidence that she sometimes lacked. He knew that at 35, he was a bit old to start a new family but he wanted to propose to Grace and thought that she would accept. They had been seeing each other for several years now. He would be a father to her son Peter and to any other children who may come along. Grace was still in her twenties after all. He wondered how his mother would take to the news. But he was getting ahead of himself, he had to propose first and supposed it was possible that she would not accept him. It hadn't occurred to him that Grace had been expecting the proposal for several months and was starting to get impatient.

The girls caught the train south to Brighton. They had met at school in Lewes where they had both gained their School Certificates with high marks.

'I wonder what we'll be doing today,' Sarah said as they sat down in the carriage.

'I tried on my uniform last night. I just love it, especially the cape, don't you? I don't know about the shoes though. I suppose they need to be comfortable.' Maria had had so few new clothes over the last few years due to the rationing that had been in force until earlier that year.

'I don't think we'll need it today though. Surely, we will have to learn much more before we're allowed onto the wards? They told us to report to the reception at the College not the hospital' Sarah reasoned.

'Are your uncle and aunt any happier about all this?'

'Not really. They still think nursing isn't a suitable profession for me. I think they expect me to wait around until I am married. They are quite old-fashioned but I love them just the same.' Sarah had been bought up by her aunt and uncle after her parents sent her to England from Rotterdam. She had found out a couple of years previously that her mother and father had died in Bergen-Belsen. Both girls had had their share of tragedy but both had been driven to succeed: perhaps they wanted to make their absent parents proud of them. They were only too aware that many people had suffered loss over the last decade and that they were lucky to have people left who cared for them.

'You know, I think my dad may have a girlfriend in London. He seems happier these days and he stays up there more often,' Maria said thoughtfully.

'Would you mind if he married again. I suppose he is still young enough,' answered Sarah slightly embarrassed at the thought.

'I used to think how romantic it was that my dad didn't want anyone but me and the memory of my mother. But now I am thinking that he of all people deserves to find happiness even if that is with somebody else. I just hope she is good enough for him. He has always made sure that he was there for me and I also had Granny and Grandad. Like your aunt and uncle have been there for you.' Maria was always very open about her feelings and Sarah was used to that.

The experience of nursing her grandfather had made her think seriously of nursing as a profession. She was encouraged by the doctor who had called in on a few occasions to check how Ted was doing. The doctor had explained the nurse training courses to herself and Vera. They had decided that she would take the two-year State Enrolled Nurse training course at the Royal Sussex. There was an option to take another year for the State Registered Nurse qualification. That same year Maria broke up with the boy that she had been seeing in the last years of school. Stephen Dixon was going to train as a draughtsman with his uncle's firm in Horsham and, as she would be spending a lot of time in Brighton, they agreed to bring their relationship to an end. Sarah had never really thought that he was good enough for her friend and had told her so.

It was a short train ride into Brighton but then there was a long walk uphill to the Technical College and even longer up to the hospital.

'I suppose we will have to get used to this hill' said Sarah as they started to get puffed out.

'There are a few buses that come up this way. Maybe if it's raining?' Maria said in between puffing for air.

'Maybe,' Sarah said without much conviction. It seemed like she was determined to walk whatever the weather.

At last, they arrived at the college reception where they were told to go upstairs to room Two. There they saw five rows of bench-like tables with wooden stools behind them. Some were already occupied by other girls. Most of them looked as young as they were but there were a few who looked older. At the front of the room was a tallish woman in uniform with grey hair tied back in some kind of a bun.

'Do come in, please take a seat,' the woman said with a gesture of welcome, waving to the empty stools. Maria and Sarah took two stools together in the second row and watched as other girls arrived. The woman consulted her watch and at nine o'clock precisely, she went to close the door.

'Good morning! My name is Miss Bateman and I will be leading the Nursing Studies Course this year. Firstly, let us check who is here..' She proceeded to call out names and make notes on a sheet before taking them through the timetable that she had chalked up on the board. They were asked to note this down in the front of their books while she explained what the lessons were, where they would take place and who would be taking them. For the first term, they would be spending four days a week at the college with Wednesday spent in the hospital. They would need to pass some tests at the end of term and then would spend more time in the hospital. There seemed to be a great many rules that had to be followed. At 10:30, there was a break for tea and a large trolley full of cups and a tea urn was wheeled in. Maria took her turn to fill her cup and turned to the tall girl standing close to her:

'How are you finding it? My name is Maria by the way and this is my friend Sarah'

'Nice to meet you. My name is Lizzie. I'm so looking forward to working in the hospital. I think it's in my blood: my father is a GP and my brother is training here too.' Lizzie was the tallest of the three girls. She had brown hair, blue eyes and rosy cheeks.

'You have a head start on us then.' Sarah said. 'I expect you will be able to get loads of help with the homework.'

'I doubt it. My father is very keen for me to do this but he will leave the work to me. And my brother works far too hard to spare any time for me.'

'Do you live in town?' asked Maria.

'Yes. We live above my dad's practice in Regency Square. I can either cycle up the hill or catch the bus. How about you?' replied Lizzie.

'We both have to come on the train from Lewes. But hang on, our fathers may know each other. Your name was called out as Elizabeth Fletcher wasn't it? Your dad isn't Dr George Fletcher is he?' Maria asked emphasizing the 'George'.

'Why yes. So how do they know each other?'

'My father is Tom Lambert. He is a photographer and cameraman and I think he met your father at evening classes years ago. He says that your dad is incredibly clever. You ask him when you go home tonight. Isn't that such a wondrous coincidence.'

'Yes, I suppose it is. I'm so glad I've met you two. I don't know anyone here as nobody else from my school came here, 'replied Lizzie.

'I think we need to go back in now,' Sarah said as she returned her teacup to the trolley. The three girls made their way back to their seats with Lizzie moving her things to the gap that Sarah had indicated next to her. They spent the rest of the day together and then Sarah and Maria made their way to the station while Lizzie rode her bicycle along the seafront back to her home in Regency Square.

A couple of evenings later, Tom appeared just as Vera was clearing away the dinner plates and Maria jumped up to greet him.

'Lovely to see you, son. I wasn't sure if you were coming back tonight but there's some shepherd's pie that I can warm for you.' Vera said as she greeted Tom with a hug.

'Yes, please mum. If it isn't too much trouble.'

'No trouble at all.'

'So how is the nurse training going Maria?' Tom asked as he could see she was fit to burst with her news.

'Well, Miss Bateman is quite strict but we have learned so much. Sarah and I are having a great time and we have a new friend called Lizzie. And she is the daughter of your friend from Brighton - Dr George Fletcher.' Maria emphasised each syllable of the name and received a nod of surprise and recognition from her father. 'And tomorrow we are actually going on a ward to work. I really think I am going to love it.'

'I haven't seen George for quite a while. And so, his daughter is going to be a nurse: I suppose it runs in the family as I seem to remember that his son was training to be a doctor. I am so glad you are enjoying it. And I know myself how good it is to have a skill that leads on to work you enjoy. Keep at it my dear.' And he gave her another hug while Vera was busy getting his dinner ready. They would delay having their apple and blackberry crumble until he had finished. So, Maria was quite happy to fill that time with more news about her training. When Tom had finished and thanked his mother, he cleared his throat to start talking.

'So, I have some news too. Sit down please mother, the crumble can wait. I think you both know that I have been seeing a lot of my friend's widow Grace.' Here he stopped to gauge their reaction. Finding no great surprise on either face, he continued. 'Yesterday, I asked her to marry me and she agreed.' Here he couldn't help smiling with joy and looked at Maria.

'This is really good news. Congratulations! son, I hope you will be very happy together.' Vera got up to kiss Tom and they both waited for Maria.

'Dad, I am really happy for you, I promise. But when can we meet her?' asked Maria smiling.

'I would like to bring her down here at the weekend. She does have a young son Peter so he would be coming too. Would that be alright? It would be a squeeze I suppose...'

'Oh, that won't be a problem. We can easily work something out. So, have you talked about when will you get married? I suppose you will live in London, will you?' asked Vera.

'You won't forget about us, will you?' asked Maria

'I could never forget my first and best girl.' Tom said looking straight into Maria's eyes so that she could be in no doubt. 'As to the wedding, we haven't finalised it yet but we were thinking Springtime in London. Gracie grew up in Islington so it makes sense. I've met her father but her mother died a few years ago.'

'Poor girl, she's lost her husband and her mother. I'd love to meet her Tom. Tell her they will both be really welcome.'

'Thank you, mother. I knew I could count on you. Now, what else have you been up to since Monday Maria? Perhaps you would like to get the chess out after dinner so that we can play while we talk about it.' Tom was pleased that Maria had taken to chess. He had found it a great leveller and had played it around the world with such a variety of people.

Vera's baking went into overdrive in anticipation of the arrival of the visitors that weekend. Maria had offered to sleep with her cousin next door so that Vera had her room while Grace and her son stayed in the main bedroom.

133

They arrived on the bus around dinnertime on the Friday and once the introductions were made and Tom took the small suitcases up to the bedroom, the five of them settled down to dinner. Maria noticed that her father seemed unusually nervous, fussing around making sure that Grace was warm enough. She introduced the ginger cat, who had been stretched out by the fire but he had taken himself off to hide as soon as Peter had tried to pick him up.

Vera handed round plates of cottage pie and vegetables while Tom filled glasses of water.

'What's this?' asked Peter poking the mashed swede with his fork.

'It's swede Peter. You don't have to eat it if you don't want to.' Grace said. Maria noticed that the diamond solitaire on her finger flashed in the light. She also noticed that she wore red lipstick. This was something that Maria only did when she was going somewhere special like a dance.

'This is lovely Mrs Lambert. But Peter never wants to eat his vegetables. Lots of children are like that, aren't they?' Grace asked.

'I can't say. Our children were never fussy eaters.' Vera replied thinking that she would never have given them the luxury of choice in the matter. Luckily, the Bakewell tart and custard was received more enthusiastically by Peter although Grace only wanted a small piece as she was 'watching her figure'.

They carried on chatting about the children and various other trivial matters after dinner until it was time for Peter's bedtime. Tom left Grace to it while he caught up with Maria and his mother. The following day, they took Peter round the farm to see the animals. He was quite fascinated as he had never seen chickens or sheep or pigs before. Maria was confused when he said.

'It all pen and inks a bit, doesn't it?' His mother laughed but Tom had to explain that this was London slang that meant that the farm smells a bit. Vera raised her eyebrows but Maria was puzzled. Plenty of her schoolfriends were townies but they hadn't grown up as ignorant as this boy had.

They carried on with a walk down to the stream where Maria and her Granny gathered some blackberries. Tom got them to all to stand together to take a picture. Grace asked him to wait until she had checked her face in the mirror that she kept in a handbag. She told Peter to hold his blackberry-stained hands behind his back. Maria was amused but then swapped with her father so that she could take a picture with him in the frame for once. They had intended to walk up to the top of Cliffe Beacon but Peter had complained that it was too far so they had turned round half way up. They had left on Sunday morning. It had been expected that they would stay for Sunday lunch but Grace had asked Tom if they could go earlier as Peter was bored and wanted to go home. He acquiesced to her wishes as he didn't want the visit to end badly. Vera kept her disappointment to herself.

All in all, Tom knew that the visit had shown up the difference between the life that he had grown up with and the life that he would be living in the middle of London. He had achieved his ambition of working with a respected national newspaper and it made sense for him to live there after the wedding. He hoped to find a new happiness with Grace and was looking forward to being a father again. He told Maria that she was welcome to visit them in London as often as she wanted and he would return to the Farm frequently. Grace was obviously not at home in the country but Vera could see from the looks of admiration she gave him that she did love Tom.

Chapter Nine London – September 1949

Tom waited in the foyer and glanced at the evening paper as he waited for Imogen to arrive for their dinner appointment at Claridges. She had issued the invitation and he felt obliged to accept especially as he had news to share with her. He had had to dig out his old dinner jacket as he knew that although she pretended not to care these days, she still thought that people should stick to pre-war dress codes. She arrived in a cab wearing a beautiful lilac silk outfit. He thought it was the sort of thing that was called a gown rather than a dress but such things did not really interest him.

'Tom, darling, how lovely to see you' she said as she walked up the stairs towards him. He kissed her on the cheek as he would an elderly relative. One of the waiters appeared instantly to show them to the table she had reserved. Imogen was happy to work hard for the WRVS or one of her other organisations during the day but also liked to be seen out in the best places, preferably accompanied by interesting people. The truth was that she missed the excitement and usefulness that she had enjoyed in wartime when she had worked as a translator at the Ministry of War. She nodded to a few acquaintances on her way to the table.

'Now Tom, I can see that you are well and, before you ask, I am also in perfect health. I gather you have some news' she said as they glanced at the menus.

'Well, yes, I do. You remember that I have been seeing Grace, a friend's widow?'

'Yes. Have you finally asked her to marry you?' Tom was amused that she had guessed his intention.

'Yes, and luckily she has agreed.'

'I thought that would be it. You know, I think I will plump for the Turbot. So, when is the wedding, is it decided yet?' she asked.

'Not yet but it will be here in London and probably next Spring. You will be one of the first to know of course.'

'Congratulations Tom, I hope you will be happy together. We all need something to cheer us up I think. Perhaps you could bring Grace with you next time we arrange to meet?'

'Yes, let's do that.'

'Now have you made up your mind on what you will order? I always like an excuse for some champagne. Would that suit you? My treat as I invited you.'

'If you would like, I'm happy to join you. I think I am ready to order if you are?' Imogen looked over at a waiter and he came over to take their order.

'I assume that you have introduced Grace to your family?'

'Yes, they came down last weekend. It went as well as I expected. Mother and Maria were both welcoming and I think that they both liked Grace. She and her son are real townies so I don't think they felt much at home in the countryside.'

'Yes, well I suppose they have led such different lives.'

'Was there something else you wanted to talk about Imogen?' Tom asked knowing that there almost certainly was something else on her mind.

'Well, I had an idea I wanted to run past you and this news means that it makes even more sense. Now that she is of an age to appreciate it, I thought that I could take your daughter on a trip to France with me. It would bring her out I think and she probably needs cheering up what with nurse training and now you will be setting up home with Grace. What do you think?' This took Tom by surprise but then they were both distracted by the whole performance of the glasses being changed and the champagne opened and poured.

'Your continuing good health.' Tom clinked his glass with Imogen's.

'Congratulations to you both.' Imogen replied as she took a sip. 'About my idea? Do you need time to think it over?'

'Are you sure it won't be too much for you? She hasn't been abroad at all since …'

'It certainly isn't too much trouble as I will be going anyway and I always enjoy the company of young people. They haven't had a chance to get stuck in their ways and have so much 'joie de vivre'. And if she hasn't been abroad since she came here all those years ago, isn't it time she did broaden her horizons? She must be bright to have done so well at Grammar School. I thought she might have sights on taking her education further, maybe even University. But, if nursing is what she has chosen, then it can be a good career. Travel is good for young people of course, as you yourself know.'

'I agree that going to France with you would be a good opportunity for her but haven't you done enough for us?' Tom asked as their first course arrived: potted shrimps for him and a terrine for Imogen.

'Oh nonsense. You know it gives me pleasure to offer a helping hand here and there. I have to do something with my time. I can't just go shopping and stay home embroidering like some other women. During the war, I had a purpose and now things seem..' Imogen waved her glass around as she searched for the right word. 'Things seem somehow flat and I need a change of scene. Do you have any other concerns?'

'I assume that you would you be going to your house in the South of France: the one where Martin took Antonio and the other men he got out of that Spanish camp?' Tom lowered his voice as if he didn't want anyone to hear them. He was concerned for Maria and his face showed it.

'Yes, of course I will be going to see my sister and her family. Her husband died in the war you know. I'm pretty sure that only Martin knew that one of those men was Maria's uncle. I seem to recall that he left soon afterwards and there would have been no reason to discuss it with my sister's family. I can check if that is what you are worrying about.'

'Yes. I suppose I am a bit concerned. Maria has had enough to cope with what with losing her mother and then having to go to another country and learn a new language. Then more recently, there was the loss of my father and my marriage. I never heard anything from Martin about Antonio other than that he left to go back to look for his wife and son. I recall from news coming out of Spain at the time that the chances of them surviving were incredibly low. I wouldn't want Maria to start looking for an uncle who also turned out to have died in tragic circumstances. Don't you agree?'

'Yes, I can see why you might see it that way. I think you are being a little over cautious. But I will write to my sister and check before I take it any further. Apart from that are you in broad agreement that it would be a good thing?'

'Yes, I am. She is a bright girl and it is very kind of you to think of it. Perhaps you could speak to my mother about it next time you are down our way. After all, she spends more time with Maria now,' Tom replied as he ate the last piece of bread and shrimps.

'Of course. I still think that you and Martin were right to give those men the choice about their future. The other one, Nicholas, is married to my niece as you probably remember. They have two lovely children now. It was so sad about Martin though: I really enjoyed meeting him. Like so many others, we lost him too soon.' Imogen stopped talking while the waiter took their empty plates away.

'Martin was a good friend and, by all accounts was extraordinarily brave during the war. I would never have guessed he had it in him.' Tom felt that he had got off very lightly in the war compared to so many of the men he knew.

'He was quite a charmer. I'm surprised that he was never snapped up.'

'I seem to recall he said the same thing about you.'

'If only I had been a lot younger!' Imogen laughed and blushed slightly: perhaps it was the champagne.

'So, tell me, what other causes are taking up your time these days? Are you still involved in Victor Gollancz's refugee organisation?' Tom asked and that started a whole new conversation about the committee she was on to help unmarried mothers in the East End. They then turned to the issue of capital punishment which Imogen was campaigning against with their mutual acquaintance, Peggy Duff.

The following day, Imogen wrote to her sister to let her know that she was planning to visit with a young friend. She told her sister that it had been confirmed that Martin had died in France during the war. She asked if they knew anything about what happened to Martin and if they had ever heard from the men who had arrived from Spain with Nic before the war. She soon received a reply to say that she didn't know much about them apart from that one was a friend of Martin's and had gone back to Scotland. The other one had left to return to Spain and they hadn't heard from him or even thought about him since before the war. She had no idea what made Martin rescue those particular men but assumed that he was acting under instruction from someone else. She had not seen Martin or heard anything about him since around 1943. Imogen was pleased with this response as it meant that she could act on her idea.

Chapter Ten - October 1949 near Lewes

It had been a cool, windy but dry day at Blackthorn Farm and Vera had been busy making raspberry jam and apple chutney. She thought they were both good enough to enter in the village produce show that was coming up in a fortnight's time. She would also enter some pies and cakes she thought as she washed up the pans she had used. There was an apple crumble and a lamb hotpot ready for dinner that night.

Her little dog Trixie started to bark and wag her tail just before there was a knock on the front door. Vera dried her hands, took her apron off before shutting the dog in the kitchen and going to answer it. She opened the door and was surprised to see Imogen Clements dressed in warm outdoor clothes and stout walking shoes.

'Good afternoon, Mrs Lambert.'

'Oh, good afternoon Miss Clements.' Vera said reaching up to check that her hair wasn't in a mess.

'I hope I have called at a convenient hour. I thought perhaps this was around the time that you take that lovely little dog of yours for a walk. So perhaps I could join you? Roberts is coming to collect me in an hour or so.' Roberts was the chauffeur up at Ringmer Hall where Imogen was still an occasional visitor.

'Ah yes, that would be lovely. I just need to tidy a few things up. Would you like a cup of tea while I do that? I'm afraid there is nobody else here but me until Maria and Tom get back later on.' Vera led the way to the front parlour but Imogen laughed.

'Oh, please, Vera, no need to stand on ceremony on my account. Unless you are hiding something in the kitchen? Perhaps something that smells rather wonderful...' Imogen smiled at Vera. They were both in their mid-fifties and the huge social gulf between them seemed to have narrowed over the years. David now owned the farm, Tom and Imogen were friends and since the war, it felt like deference to the aristocracy was no longer taken for granted.

'I've just been making some raspberry jam and I am quite pleased with it. Perhaps you shouldn't see in case you are judging the entries?' This year she had added some redcurrants to the raspberries and was very pleased with the result. Imogen was sometimes a judge at the Autumn Produce Show in the village.

'I don't think anyone could accuse me of being anything other than scrupulously fair would they?'

'Probably not,' Vera answered as she finished her washing up and wiped down the surfaces. Meanwhile, Imogen was making friends with Trixie who was enjoying the fuss.

'I usually take her across the fields to the river and back. Will that suit you?' asked Vera as she hung her floral apron on a hook by the back door.

'Lovely. Actually, I do have an idea that I wanted to discuss with you.'

'Ah. I did wonder if there was something. I just need to go and change into my shoes. I won't be a tick.' Vera disappeared to the cupboard under the stairs where she changed out of her slippers and picked up the dog's lead. At this Trixie got very excited and started running between the back door and the cupboard until they left.

'You lead the way' Imogen said as they went through the back gate to the field behind the houses. The crop had been harvested and they walked along the side following the little terrier who wagged her tail and sniffed at everything along the way.

'So how are all the family? And how is Maria getting on with her nurse training?' Imogen asked.

'Oh, she is really enjoying it. Sometimes I think she might just burst with enthusiasm.'

'Ah yes. It's so nice to see the young being able to enjoy themselves again. I have just had a letter from my sister in France. It seems like the war has been forgotten there too thank goodness.'

'How are they all?' Vera asked with genuine interest. In spite of the fact that she had never met these relatives of Imogen's, she felt like she knew them from what Tom and Imogen had told her over the years. She knew that Imogen's brother-in-law had died from natural causes during the war.

'I went over for le vendage -the grape harvest you know. The estate is now being run by my nephew Jean-Paul and my niece Marianne and it all seems to be going quite well for them. They went through some terrible times while France was occupied as you can imagine. Marianne was married during the war and has two young children now: a boy and a girl. It was so good to see them again after so many years. Thank goodness they have all come through it relatively unscathed.'

'Yes. I will always be grateful that David didn't get called up and Tom came home safe and sound. Not every family was so lucky. My sister's son Billy was killed in the Atlantic in a U-boat attack you know.' Vera checked across the stile to the next field and seeing that there were no sheep there, she climbed over and called Trixie to do the same. They walked down towards the river which was flowing slowly due to lack of rain in recent days.

'Tom told me that you met Grace a couple of week ago. How did you find her?' asked Imogen.

'I suppose you have already met her in London?'

'Yes. We went for tea with her little boy. She seems very pleasant but perhaps not a country girl.'

'No. I think you are right there. I think they will make a home in London close to Tom's work. She seemed very nice: perhaps younger than I had expected.' Vera replied tactfully. In truth, she had not really taken to Grace although she could see that Tom and she were happy with each other.

'I wondered how Maria would feel about the changes?' asked Imogen.

'I think she is happy for her father but she will miss seeing him so often especially if they have children of their own. She is growing up so fast.'

'That is exactly what I was thinking. How would you feel if I offered to take Maria with me another time when I go to France? She must get time off over Summer doesn't she. Maybe it will do her good to see a bit more of the world. What do you think?' Imogen couldn't disguise the fact that she thought that this was a good idea and she hoped that Vera would be in favour.

'You have done so much for this family over the years. You've been so kind.'

'Well, you know, I never do anything that I don't want to do. I would enjoy taking her and perhaps she could bring one of her friends. We would go to Paris first. I do so enjoy the company of the young. Unfortunately, I wasn't able to have any children of my own. Would it be alright with you if I at least asked Maria if she would like to go?'

'Have you asked Tom?'

'Oh yes. Tom said that he was in favour but that I should ask you as you spend more time with his daughter than he does.'

'Well, he always made sure he was there for her and I am sure you are both right. She may well enjoy it. I know that she learned French at school but I am not sure how well she speaks it as I myself don't speak a word. Her friend Sarah used to help her as she speaks several languages. She grew up in

Holland, poor girl and lost both her parents in the war. She and Maria are thick as thieves.'

'It's so important for her to have a good friend. So, do I have your permission. I won't mention it again if you are not happy with it.'

'Is it close to Spain? You wouldn't be going there, would you? I know little about the country and neither does Maria. I fear a visit there may upset her.'

'It may look close on a map but it is actually a long way away from where we will be staying. I have never been to Spain as I understand it is not a country that welcomes visitors.' Imogen replied to try to put Vera's mind at rest.

'Yes, I see,' replied Vera. Tom had never told her much about his wife Teresa's family and she had never wanted to open old wounds by asking about them. She saw her role as giving Maria so much love that she wouldn't feel the loss of her other family too much and thus far, it seemed to have worked.

'Of course, I will contact her friend's family as well if they would both like to come. I will pay their fares and if Tom could provide her with some spending money, that would be helpful.'

'Yes, of course. I don't want to hold her back. I've always been happy to stay here in Sussex but I know that isn't the modern way. Tom loves to travel. I don't know where he got that from but perhaps Maria will be the same. Who knows?' Vera turned back up towards the big chestnut tree in the direction home. It was a Sweet Chestnut with incredibly prickly seedcases which she stopped to check. She thought they would be ready in the next week or so. Vera had a lifetime of training in storing up food for winter just like the squirrels.

'I'll need to keep an eye on this tree' she said. 'Otherwise, the greedy squirrels will have the lot before I get a chance. I love to roast them on the fire on a cold autumn evening, don't you?' Imogen had no idea what Vera was talking about as she did not connect that particular tree with the roast chestnuts she had seen for sale on the street during the Fireworks Festival in Lewes. Perhaps she wasn't much of a country girl either: Imogen switched the subject back to the one that interested her.

'I'm so glad you have agreed to my plan. When do you think would be a convenient time to ask her? I am staying down here for a few days this time.'

'Maria leaves early in the morning during the week and doesn't get back until around 6:30. She should be here most of the weekend though. Unless she is going somewhere with Sarah that she hasn't told me about yet. They sometimes go to films together on a Saturday afternoon.'

'Perhaps I could call in tomorrow morning then. Around 11 o'clock?' asked Imogen.

'Oh yes. That would be fine. I'll tell her that you are coming.'

'Thank you. So how are the rest of your family? David's children are Teddy and Georgina aren't they?'

Vera told her about the rest of the family but she thought that Imogen had already got what she had come for and was only asking out of politeness.

That evening, the family all had dinner together. When David and his family left, Vera told Maria that Imogen Clements would be coming to see them the following morning. Maria wanted to know what it was about but in spite of using all her pleading wiles, Vera refused to tell her. Maria went up to bed with a mixture of annoyance and excitement. Her father was staying up in town that weekend so she had very little to look forward to apart from this visit and the trip to the cinema she had arranged with Sarah in the afternoon.

Maria spent the morning helping Vera with the household chores until Imogen arrived just after eleven o'clock. She ran towards the door and welcomed their guest into the front parlour according to the instructions issued earlier by Vera. Imogen was beautifully dressed in a dark blue fitted dress with a matching jacket and hat. Maria assumed that the outfit must be from pre-war as there was so much fabric in it. She was also wearing a floral scent that smelled expensive. She accepted the offer of a cup of tea and Vera came in with a tray laden with their best tea things as well as scones and jam. Imogen took her tea black which Maria found very odd. When they all had a cup, Imogen addressed Maria:

'I spoke to your grandma yesterday and she has kindly given permission for me to ask you something. You may know that my family have a house in the South of France which I often go to. I wondered if during the summer, you would like to accompany me there for a week or so. You could also bring a friend if you would like to. It's a farm like yours but they have grapes, peaches and pears there as well as few animals. They have a young family so it won't be just old people like me. What do you think? Would you like to go?'

'Really? Are you sure? My dad said that we travelled though France on our way to England when I was young but I don't remember much about it. Would I need to speak French? That would be so good as I have hardly used what I learned in school. Can I really go?' Maria clapped her hands with the excitement of a child.

'Can you let me know when your course closes for summer so we can plan when to go. No hurry. Also, let me know if you would like to bring a friend and I will speak to her parents.' Maria only needed a moment.

'I'd love for my friend Sarah to come. But her aunt and uncle may be too worried to let her go. I'll ask her later. Her family came from Vienna originally. We are going to the cinema to see Orson Welles in The Third Man.'

'I've heard that picture is very good. Won't it be upsetting for her to see a film set in Vienna?'

'It was her idea. Anyway, she never lived there. She was born in Rotterdam in Holland.'

'Ah, I see. So, you would like to come to France and you will let me know about your friend?' asked Imogen.

'Where will we be going? I can look it up in the atlas. Has my dad been there?'

'No, your father has not been there. It is near a place called Montpelier.'

'Montpelier.' Maria tried out the word and thought it sounded very exotic. She went to get the atlas that her father had bought her out of the bookcase and Imogen helped her to find it.

'It is in the South and not far from the Mediterranean coast. It is a long way from here so we would need to stop over in Paris. As you know, you went through there with your father on your way to England. I'm so pleased that you want to come. I'm sure you will find it very interesting: I always think that travel widens one's horizons. We will be staying with my niece, Marianne and her family. Would you like to know anything else?'

'What will I need to take? Is it like England?' Maria had also noticed that it looked quite close to Barcelona where she had been born. She didn't mention this out loud. She never asked much about her Spanish mother as she didn't want to offend her granny. Vera had done everything for her that a mother would have done.

'It is usually much warmer near the Mediterranean than it is here. Of course, you will need to help out with chores while we are there. Don't worry, I can assist you with what you need to pack once we know when we are going and for how long. I may need to take you shopping.' At this, Maria's eyes widened and Imogen smiled at Vera. They could both see how excited she was about the trip. Imogen left shortly afterwards: there was a chauffeured car waiting for her at the front of the house. She thanked Vera for the tea and said that she would keep in touch.

Vera was worried that Imogen was going to give Maria a taste for expensive things but she had been pleased to hear her mention that there would be chores to be done. She imagined that Imogen was used to having everything done for her. She knew how many staff they still had up at Ringmer Hall but perhaps things were different in France.

Maria could not wait to tell Sarah her news as they waited in the cinema queue. Sarah was more guarded in her response as although she loved the idea of going to Paris, she thought that her aunt and uncle would not be inclined to sanction such a trip. The girls really enjoyed the film and Maria found herself humming the theme tune to herself on the way home.

Chapter Eleven Easter 1950 Islington, London

Tom and Grace were married at St Marks, Islington. This was close to where she had grown up and also to the house that they had bought. Vera had visited once before the wedding and decided that she never wanted to spend the night in London as it was too dirty and noisy. She felt the same about the city as Grace had evidently felt about being in the country.

Maria was really excited about the day and was grateful when Imogen offered to accommodate her overnight: she wasn't sure she could cope with being surrounded by Grace's family. Imogen had made the offer partly so that Grace's relatives had more room but she also wanted to get to know Tom's daughter better. The two bridesmaids were Maria and Grace's younger sister Enid. Maria hadn't really liked the yellow dresses that had been chosen and complained about them to her granny. Vera advised her to keep her opinion on this to herself as it was Grace and Tom's day.

Vera, Maria, David and all the Lambert family took the train up to London in the morning having left their cousin Harry in charge of the farm.

David and Teddy both fidgeted around feeling uncomfortable dressed in their Sunday best but Sue had been pleased to have the opportunity to dress up.

Tom was dressed in a dark blue suit and tie and Grace wore a cream dress with a matching jacket. She carried yellow spring flowers to match the bridesmaid's dresses. The service was relatively simple and thankfully the weather was good enough to take the pictures outside. The poor photographer had to put up with Tom's frequent advice on angles and shutter speeds. Before four o'clock, they were sitting down to a wedding breakfast of steak pie and mash in the function room of a nearby pub.

It was about 6 o'clock in the evening when the Sussex contingent finally made their excuses and left the party. Most of them had to be up early in the morning even though it was Sunday.

'Phew! Thank goodness that's over.' Teddy exclaimed as he flopped into the seat in the train carriage and undid his tie. He was now a young man of seventeen who, unlike his father David, had been able to attend Agricultural College in Plumpton. 'I see what you mean Granny, there are just too many people in London, all in a hurry and there is too much noise. How uncle Tom can live there is anyone's guess. I can't wait to get back to civilisation.'

'The houses are big I grant you but so close together. They all live on top of each other. I don't know why Tom chooses to live here: he can keep it. It was odd to see all those gaps in the houses where the bombs must have fallen. And people are living in those prefabs which look like a stiff wind would blow them away.' David added looking out the window at Battersea.

'Tom told me it is far worse in some of the other areas like the docks where whole streets were flattened. They did suffer in the Blitz…I don't see how Grace is ever going to keep that house clean with those high ceilings and all the soot from the fires… They did look happy though' Vera was ever the practical one but smiled with pride as she believed that her youngest son had found happiness at last.

'Well, I thought it was lovely and they both looked very happy. Maria looked really sweet too and so grown up in that outfit. She'll catch the eye of one of those doctors I expect.' Sue paused before adding: 'What do you think of Grace's family? Her father looked pleased as punch. But that Peter didn't look particularly happy, did he?'

'No, he didn't. I don't think Maria is very fond of Grace either. I suppose it must be difficult when your parent remarries.' Georgie was thoughtful. 'I'd like to see a bit more of the world.

Maybe I can train to do a different job like Uncle Tom and cousin Maria.' Georgie was thirteen and still at school.

'What is it you would like to do?' asked Vera.

'I don't know yet. But I'm not going to be just a farmer's wife.'

'What's wrong with that? It was fine for your mother and your granny.' David said with some exasperation.

'It's ok David. She is much more clever than I was. There are so many things that girls can do now.' Sue defended her daughter but Teddy couldn't resist another quip:

'Yeah. Marry someone with a fancy job like Grace did.'

'That's not very kind Teddy. I think she will make Tom happy and that's good enough for me.' Vera considered the subject closed and gave Teddy a stern look. He raised his eyebrows and looked out of the window where he could now see green fields as they had left Croydon and suburbia behind. He was tired and felt happy to be getting closer to home.

Imogen and Maria stayed at the wedding reception a while longer to watch the bride and groom leave in a taxi and they both cheered and waved. The newlyweds were going to catch a train from Paddington and stay in a hotel in the Cotswolds for a couple of nights as Grace didn't want to leave her son Peter for too long.

'Let me know when you would like to leave and we can get a taxi for ourselves.' Imogen said as the taxi turned out of sight.

'I'm tired from dancing already and quite happy to go now if you'd like to.' Maria turned to look at Imogen who smiled in agreement. They took their leave of Grace's father and family, picked up Maria's travel bag and waited for a taxi near the station at Angel. The driver made his way across town past St Pancras Station, London University and Oxford Street where Imogen had pointed out Selfridges. Even here in the West End, there was evidence of bomb damage but not as much as she had seen in the east of the city. When the car stopped outside a large four-story Georgian house in one of the most expensive parts of London, Maria was not entirely surprised. Her father had told her a lot about Imogen and she knew that her world was quite different to theirs. They walked up the steps and Imogen rang the bell. In a few minutes, the door was opened by an oldish man who inclined his head to the visitors.

'Good evening, Miss Imogen' he said while taking her coat. 'Would you like to take some supper this evening? Cook has some cold cuts and your favourite fruit cake.'

'That would be lovely Wilton. What would you like to drink Maria: tea, cocoa or perhaps some lemonade?'

'Cocoa would be lovely, thank you.'

'And please ask Mrs Brixham to show my young friend where she can freshen up.'

'Certainly,' the old man replied with a slight bow. A woman in a black dress came to show Maria the bathroom and the bedroom where she would be staying. Maria put her bag in the room, checked her hair in the mirror and put her night things out before she went back downstairs. She found Imogen consulting what looked like a large diary on a desk in the front room.

'Ah there you are' Imogen said picking up a silver-framed photograph from the desk. 'Here, this is my niece Marianne with her husband Nicholas and their young children Antoine and Delphine outside their house in France. "Les Trois Chemins" is the house where we will be staying in Summer. I took that photo when I was there last year.' Maria noticed that Imogen pronounced all the names with a French accent, just like their French teacher had.

'Marianne looks very much like you but her husband looks dark and strong like my uncle. It's a lovely photo. I'm really looking forward to our trip. It really is very kind of you to ask me.'

'I'm sure you will like Marianne. She is a real countrywoman – like your grandma really: she can cook, make jam, kill and prepare a chicken without thinking about it. It's a simple life you understand, not like my own. I love the sunshine there and there is so much beautiful, open countryside. France is so much bigger than England you know: it is open and spacious. And. of course, I have my sister and all her family to catch up with. I think, I hope you will enjoy it.' Imogen looked at Maria and put the photo back on the desk.

'I am sure we will. Are there any hospitals nearby? Sarah is keen to see how nursing is done in other countries.'

'I'm not sure but will ask my niece. I spoke to your friend Sarah's aunt and uncle and heard their tragic story. I understand that they are thinking of moving to America.'

'Sarah has mentioned that, but it isn't finally decided yet.' At that moment, the man called Wilton reappeared to announce that supper was ready in the dining room. Maria followed Imogen into the adjoining room where a number of plates were laid out at the end of a large table.

'No formality tonight, Wilton. We can help ourselves from here. Can we have breakfast for eight o'clock tomorrow. I have a number of things to attend to around town during the day and will not be back until late. You and cook can take yourselves off for the day.'

'I'm most obliged madam.' Wilton bowed slightly as he left. Maria tried to hide her smile as she couldn't quite believe what she was seeing. She thought people only lived like this in books.

'Perhaps you think we are rather unusual or even comical.' Imogen said as she poured cocoa from a silver pot into two cups.

'I'm so sorry, I didn't mean to offend you. It's just...' Maria was mortified.

'Actually, I like your honesty which reminds me of your father. And you are quite right: this way of life is an anachronism. Wilton has been with us since before I was born and doesn't want to change. He adored my mother even when she was arrested as a suffragette. "Never judge a book by its cover" is the most useful maxim I ever heard. You remember that, young lady.' Imogen smiled at Maria which put her at ease. 'Now tuck in and don't look so worried. Are you hungry at all? The cake is very good but I will have a little of this ham and chutney first.'

'Thank you, I will have some bread and cheese and then perhaps try the cake.' Maria found that she was in fact hungry as they had not eaten anything since the wedding lunch and she had spent a great deal of time since then dancing with a variety of partners. She helped herself but only started to eat once she had seen which cutlery Imogen used.

'I noticed that you like to dance just as I did when I was young. Do you play the piano at all?' asked Imogen.

'No, I never learned. I enjoy playing chess as well as dancing though.' Maria answered taking a sip from her cup of cocoa.

'Ah, I expect your father taught you to play chess. He tried to teach me but I just couldn't get the hang of it. And are you seeing a particular young man you like to dance with?'

'No. But I am in no hurry to find one right now. I am too busy with other things' Maria answered truthfully. Her friend Sarah had been seeing Lizzie's brother John recently and when that happened, Maria started spending more time with Lizzie. They were too busy with training to spend much time socialising.

Imogen thought that she understood Maria only too well as they had both suffered significant loss. This had made it hard for Imogen to trust and commit to another person and she thought that it might be the same for young Maria: especially now that her father had left.

'Your father looked very happy today. I think being married again will suit him. I suppose it might mean some adjustments for you. How did you find today?'

'I think you are right: my father does seem happy with Grace. I am old enough now to understand that life can't stay the same and I am pleased for him. Grace is more like a new elder sister than a stepmother. I will get used to it in time I suppose.' Maria reached out for the cake and Imogen passed the plate to her.

'I see you have a level head on those young shoulders. So, next week, I will be down in Sussex. I would like to take you and your friend Sarah to Hanningtons in Brighton so that you can look for some light summer clothes for the trip. It's so pleasant to be able to shop for clothes again, don't you think? And don't worry, I have an account there so it will be my treat. Would Saturday be the most convenient day? Or would you like to leave it for another time?'

'I'm sure that will be fine. I will check with Sarah when I see her on Monday at the hospital. She sometimes goes to the synagogue on Saturday morning but not every week.' Maria ate a bite from the cake and took in her surroundings. The room was rose coloured with a beautiful Art Deco mirror on one wall and a painting of a landscape on another. The furniture all looked old and expensive and she could just make out a walled garden through the large sash windows. Maria felt tired and stifled a yawn.

'Are you tired? Well, it is nine o'clock so feel free to retire whenever you like. I usually sit and read until ten. I keep a fairly good library of books as you know, so if you would like to borrow any, just let me know.'

'Thank you, Miss Clements, I think I will go to bed now. I have a medical book with me that I am reading because we have some exams to pass at the end of the year. But I think I am too tired to read it tonight.'

Maria went up the stairs past an array of portraits – presumably of the Clements ancestors. It was a beautiful house but it seemed odd that one person rattled around in it with only servants for company. She wondered why Imogen had never had a family of her own and then her thoughts turned to her father: how would she feel if he had another family with Grace? She decided that she really would not mind at all: just so long as he still made time to see her and Vera. She slept well that night and found it surprisingly quiet considering she was in the middle of such a big city. She awoke only once in the night to the sound of a siren somewhere in the distance. It was a change from being woken by owls or foxes.

The next morning, they had breakfast together and Imogen called a taxi which took them to Victoria station where they parted. Maria took the train home while Imogen went on to church followed by a stint with the WRVS. In truth, Imogen missed the wartime days when she had felt more useful than she had ever felt before. She found a number of causes to pour her energy into but she missed the buzz of wartime and then she would feel guilty for having such selfish thoughts.

Chapter Twelve - Summer 1950 A Trip to France

The trainee nurses all got a six week break over the summer. Maria went to stay with her father in London for a week after which she was glad to return home to Vera. Grace was pregnant and was feeling unwell a lot of the time so Maria found herself having to keep her step-brother Peter amused. Her father had asked her to do this to give Grace time to rest in bed. She had taken him to some of the museums in London but this turned out to be more interesting for Maria than for Peter. His main interests appeared to be playing with toy cars and aeroplanes and making the right sound effects for each one. Maria thought that her father had changed since his marriage and in a way that she could not quite articulate: there was a distance between them that had not been there before.

Vera welcomed her back with open arms and they enjoyed a couple of weeks together walking the dog, working in the kitchen garden and helping out on the farm generally. Vera grew potatoes, carrots, cabbages, runner beans, onions and several types of fruit in her garden behind the house. They both loved to spend time outside and Maria was almost sad when it was time to pack for the trip to France. She took mostly practical outdoor clothes but also a couple of smart dresses and a straw sunhat that Imogen had insisted on buying for her. These were quite a change from the 'make do and mend' clothes that Vera was used to providing for her. During the war, Maria and Vera had had to wear clothes made out of old curtains and anything else that came to hand. These new dresses were still 'utility' but at least they had some style about them. She also took the passport that her father had helped her to apply for and the new camera that he had bought her for her birthday.

Maria met Sarah at Lewes station on a Monday afternoon so that they could take the train up to London and spend the night at Imogen's house. The following morning, the three of them took the early 'boat' train from Victoria down to Dover and by nightfall, they were settled into a hotel in Paris. When Maria and Sarah woke, they opened the curtains to look out at the city that had been in darkness when they had arrived exhausted the previous evening. They couldn't wait to go out and investigate the wide boulevard with its little café tables sat under the shelter of matching canopies. These took up more than half of the pavement ans still there was plenty of space to walk. It looked so foreign to them: even to Sarah who had spent her early childhood in the port city of Rotterdam. They both got washed and dressed in one of their new dresses before knocking on the adjoining door to Imogen's room.

'Just a few minutes girls' they heard her say from the other side of the door. Before long, she emerged and they went downstairs to a large room where breakfast was being served. Imogen seemed to slip back into speaking French with ease where the two girls stumbled over the words. They were served strong-smelling coffee, pastries, white bread rolls, butter and a large pot of strawberry jam.

'Don't they have tea then?' Maria asked in a loud whisper.

'It is quite difficult to get tea anywhere here so it may be an idea to give coffee a try my dear.' Imogen said. Maria tried her cup and screwed up her face at the bitter taste.

'Try adding plenty of milk and sugar?' Imogen suggested.

'I love coffee' said Sarah, 'my aunt is always complaining about the coffee in England. She goes to a special shop in Brighton to get ours. '

'I suppose I can learn to like it. But what are these things?' asked Maria picking up a crescent-shaped pastry and putting it on her plate.

'That's a croissant: they are very good. And do try the jam. You may find it is almost as good as your granny's.' Imogen said with a grin. Maria tried the croissant and jam and found it so delicious that she reached out for another one as soon as she had finished the first.

'So, this morning, I thought we could visit Notre Dame and the Louvre. We can find somewhere for lunch and then just go wherever you wish after that: perhaps along the river or to the Tour Eiffel. We can take dinner at the hotel and get an early night as we will have to catch the nine o'clock train down to Montpelier. It will be a long journey so you shouldn't overtire yourselves today.' Imogen looked over at her two young charges for a response.

'I'll go with whatever you think Miss Clements as I'm just happy to be here.' Sarah said as she spread some more butter and jam on her bread and smiled over at Maria.

'Can we just wait and see how we feel later?' asked Maria.

'Of course. I think you will be impressed with Notre Dame. It is one of the most beautiful churches I have ever seen.' Imogen said to them as she summoned the waiter to bring more coffee.

'What other countries have you been to?' blurted out Sarah before adding 'If you don't mind my asking.'

'Of course not. Before the war, it was much easier to travel and we went to Switzerland, Austria and Italy as well as France and New York.'

'You've been to America! What was it like? I have family there and my aunt and uncle are looking into emigrating.' Sarah asked enthusiastically.

'That was quite a long time ago. I was still in my twenties: not yet an old maid.' Imogen smiled in a deprecating way but they could see she was controlling an undercurrent of emotions. 'The first war had been devastating for us: both my brothers and my fiancée were killed. I was grieving as we all were; and I thought my parents were trying to distract me by getting me married off to some rich American. I didn't pay much attention to New York or Boston or indeed many of the people I met. I just wanted to get back home. So, as you see, I'm sorry, I can't tell you much about America.'

'I'm so sorry, I didn't mean to pry.' Sarah said with genuine feeling.

'Don't apologise. We have all lost people we love in stupid wars. And yet life must go on.' Imogen looked at them both with a determined smile. 'Now, have you two had sufficient to eat?' Imogen looked at the two of them in turn and they nodded.

'Let's get ready for Paris then. It looks like it will be a bright day and the Cathedral is only a short walk from here. And don't worry, Sarah: many people who visit are not great believers: myself included.' Maria was quite shocked by this as she knew Imogen went to church regularly. For Vera, the church was more a social than a spiritual thing so perhaps it was the same for Imogen. She knew that Sarah went to a synagogue in Brighton with her aunt and uncle on Saturday mornings.

As they got up, a man went past smoking a cigarette and Maria was hit by a pungent smell that was both strange and yet also familiar. She threw a questioning glance at Imogen.

'Gauloises - black tobacco. Not something you often smell in England. But it is very common here in Europe.' Imogen replied and wondered if this had triggered a memory for Maria from her early years.

They walked across the bridge to the front of Notre Dame and went inside. Maria was transfixed by the beautiful Rose Window: she had never seen anything like it. Afterwards, they walked around the outside of the building where Maria took lots of pictures from various different views of its buttresses, gargoyles and spires. Maria vaguely remembered that both her parents were contemptuous of the catholic church because it had taken Franco's side in the Civil War. She herself was too much of a pragmatist to set much store by religion but was in no doubt that this was a magnificent building. She looked at Imogen curiously when she saw the older woman sitting on a bench with her eyes closed. She was wearing a beautiful blue suit with a lilac-coloured silk blouse and looked very content. She opened her eyes and smiled at Maria:

'You are deep in thought. Is there anything you want to share?' asked Imogen.

'It may be impertinent to ask..'

'I can see you have a question, go ahead my dear.' Imogen patted the space next to her on the bench and Maria sat down trying to articulate her thoughts.

'It seems to me you believe in something. If not the church, what makes you want to help so many other people?' asked Maria.

'Ah well, I am what is called a humanist. I believe that there probably isn't another place to wait for: call it heaven or the afterlife. Therefore, we should all do our best to enjoy what life brings and to make it better in any way we can. Does that answer your question?'

'Yes. I think I understand. You are quite an unusual lady aren't you?' At this, Imogen laughed and got up to walk towards Sarah.

'Yes, I suppose I am. Now, let's walk down by the river, shall we?' and without waiting for a reply, off she went followed by the two girls.

At the Louvre, they had to wait some time to see the Mona Lisa. Maria felt nothing but disappointment. She could not understand why so much fuss was made of this one picture among thousands and found that part of their visit completely forgettable. She would rather have spent more time at the Cathedral. Sarah on the other hand, along with Imogen, enjoyed the gallery and discussed the exhibits enthusiastically.

As they emerged back on to the street from the museum, the sun was high in the sky. Imogen suggested they find somewhere to sit in the shade and have a drink and perhaps something to eat. She selected a place where she had gained the attention of a waiter and the two girls followed their leaders to their seats.

Imogen ordered what turned out to be a lovely blackcurrant flavoured drink for the girls and a glass of wine and some water for herself. Imogen then had a conversation with the waiter in French that the girls only just followed. They agreed that they would eat whatever Imogen ordered as long as it wasn't a large amount and ended up with a basket of bread along with some sort of fish salad. Maria and Sarah both thanked Imogen for ordering something that they both really enjoyed. This was followed by Tarte Tatin and cream washed down with water from a bottle along with a tiny cup of coffee for Imogen.

Maria noticed that there seemed to be a lot of injured beggars on the streets; many of whom were old men. They were often waved away by the waiters or the other customers. She also could not help noticing that many of the customers seemed very well dressed compared to English people. The Parisian women looked particularly stylish and seemed to have spent a lot of time on their hair and make-up,

'Aren't the women here so very glamorous' she said as quietly as she could.

'Ah, now perhaps you see why I wanted to buy you those new clothes.'

'My aunt says that English women do not know how to dress. That's maybe a bit too strong. After all, there have been so many shortages. But it does seem more important to look nice here, doesn't it?' Sarah said. 'People in America all seem well dressed too, don't they?'

'Perhaps that is only in the movies, Sarah. Everyone looks gorgeous in those don't they?' Imogen suggested. 'Paris is known for fashionable dress. The rest of France is a bit more relaxed I find.' At this point, Imogen caught the attention of the waiter and asked for the bill. 'Now then girls, what would you like to do now?'

'I don't know. What would you suggest?' asked Maria.

'How about a slow walk though the Tuileries Gardens. From there, you can see the Arc de Triomphe and the Eiffel Tower so perhaps, you could get some good pictures with your camera Maria. But you must hang on to it as there are plenty of thieves around no matter how glamorous the people look.'

So, they followed Imogen's suggestion and walked up to the Tuileries and the Arc de Triomphe. At some point, Sarah decided that she had done enough walking so they took the Metro back to Hotel de Ville which was close to their hotel. They sat at a table in the shade where Sarah and Imogen had coffees. Maria would really have liked a cup of tea but had to make do with a hot chocolate. She was pleased that this arrived with some lovely almond-flavour biscuits. They sat and talked about what they had seen and Imogen told them about the family that they were going to visit the next day.

Maria already knew how she came to have a sister living in France so didn't listen carefully as Imogen repeated the story.

'So, Les Trois Chemins is the house where my niece Marianne now lives with her husband and children while her brother Jean-Paul and his family still live in the bigger house. Obviously, I wasn't able to visit for several years during the last war when Claude died and all the grandchildren were born. We will be staying with Marianne and her husband, Nicholas. He came from somewhere in southern Spain originally: I can't remember where exactly.' Maria pricked up her ears with interest at the mention of Spain but was disappointed when Imogen continued: 'They all run the farm and vineyard together and so you will have to be prepared to help out where you can. We will not be living in style but Maria at least is used to a similar way of life. But I hope you will enjoy it: the weather will be warm and the scenery is so beautiful.' Imogen stopped talking for a while and looked into the distance with a wistful look on her face.

Although the story sounded romantic, Sarah was not all that impressed with the idea of a working holiday. Maria on the other hand, loved the the idea of seeing new places and she particularly liked the idea of meeting someone from Spain. She also wanted to go to the Mediterranean Sea. She remembered her father telling her that, unlike the grey, rough sea around Sussex, the Mediterranean was blue, calm and very warm.

The next day, they got on the train at the Gare du Lyon and watched through the windows as the landscape changed through towns, fields of crops, forests and vineyards. They had lunch in the restaurant car and finally arrived in Montpelier in the late afternoon. Imogen had written to say when they would arrive but wasn't sure if they would need to find transport to the estate, as she called it. As it turned out, a woman waved at them from the platform as they got off the train and shouted:

'Imogen! Je suis ici!' She was a young woman in her early thirties with wavy light brown hair and blue eyes. She wore a floral dress with a brown jacket and stout brown shoes. She ran up to embrace them one by one: hugging and kissing in the French style and so, they were introduced to Marianne. She picked up Imogen's bags and waved them over to a van type of vehicle parked outside the station and all the time she was chattering away in French to Imogen. Then she suddenly stopped and thought before saying in heavily accented English.

'Can you understand in Francais or should I explain in English for you?'

'Speak in French but slowly please so that we can understand.' Maria was the first to reply and

Sarah nodded in agreement. Marianne carried on in French.

'Two of you can sit in the front with me but one of you will have to go in the back with the luggage. Sorry for the inconvenience but this is the only vehicle we have. It is better than trying to find a taxi to take you to our place. OK?'

'I go in the back' said Maria trying out her French and climbing onto the rug that somebody had kindly put there. It didn't entirely hide the animal smells that she could detect. However, she was used to being close to such smells and didn't mind. The engine made unfamiliar sounds to Maria's ears but was obviously working as it was supposed to. The van made its way out of the city of Montpelier roughly southwest towards Pezenas. It was not going to be a comfortable ride and although Maria did not complain, she was very relieved when they parked up outside a large house where Marianne opened the back up and helped her out.

The house was a fairly unremarkable two storey house from the outside with the most notable feature being a large wooden structure that ran along one side and was holding a vine of some sort. A number of people had assembled outside to greet them although the two small children were probably there to welcome their mother home. Marianne introduced them:

'This is my mother, Ermine, my husband Nicholas, our son Antoine and our daughter Delphine. Here are Maria and Sarah from England and of course Imogen.' There were hugs and kisses all round and then Marianne led them into the house while Nicholas picked up Imogen's bags and took them inside. Ermine linked arms with her sister Imogen as they climbed up the stairs,

Once inside, they could see that the house was bigger than it seemed from the outside as it was L-shaped. They were taken to a set of rooms on the short leg of the 'L' that had their own bathroom. One bedroom was for Imogen and the other was for Maria and Sarah to share. From the window they could see a huge orchard extending away from two sides with another grander house visible through the trees. Maria took a photo of the grounds from the window.

'Come down as soon as you are ready and we will have a drink before dinner.' Marianne said to them as she turned to go back down the stairs. Maria was loathe to go down without Imogen but it was clear that the older women were deep in conversation and had forgotten about everybody else. So, the two girls went down together to find Marianne. It wasn't difficult as they could hear her chatting away to her two children in the huge kitchen: the sound reverberated due to the flagstones that made up the floor. Maria could smell something cooking but could not quite identify what it was.

'Ah, there you are. Would you like some coffee while you are waiting? Or perhaps a glass of wine?' asked Marianne

'I don't know, I have never drunk any wine. Is it strong?' asked Maria who had never been allowed to drink at home and didn't particularly like coffee. What she really wanted was a cup of tea but didn't want to ask.

'A coffee would be lovely' said Sarah who was more accustomed to such worldly habits and liked people to know it. 'I am not English, I grew up in the Netherlands you know,' she added.

'Ah I see,' said Marianne as she prepared a percolator and put it on the stove. Meanwhile, Nicholas who seemed to be a man of few words was playing a game of catch with his two children. Maria was watching them intently and Marianne asked:' Would you like to join in the game?' Maria smiled and went outside to play ball. She found herself fascinated by the man who had come from Spain. She wondered if she could ask him what the country was like.

Imogen and Ermine came into the kitchen and they started to organise the tasks that were needed to get dinner ready. They prepared a small glass of Kir for everyone except the children. Ermine proposed a toast to the visit and all of them drained their glasses quickly. Maria had discovered that she liked Kir: it tasted like blackcurrant but there was another unfamiliar note. A few minutes later, they all sat down at a large table that was set up outside. Marianne passed round a basket of bread and a platter of sausage. Maria found the sausage very strange as it was not a texture or taste that she was familiar with and was nothing like an English sausage. After that they had a kind of chicken stew, potatoes that were roasted with herbs and a dish made from different coloured peppers. This was an exotic vegetable that Maria had not encountered before.

Imogen encouraged Antoine and Delphine to tell her how they were doing at school. She also asked about Ermine's son and his wife. Apparently, they would all be having dinner together another day. Ermine and Marianne cleared away the plates and bought out fresh peaches and cheese. Maria had never seen fresh peaches before as she had only had the type that came in tins and covered in sweet syrup. The meal took over two hours as eating seemed to be taken slowly and there was quite a lot of conversation. Ermine took the children to bed as soon as they had finished their dessert but she was soon back at the table.

Nicholas excused himself and reappeared with a guitar. He sat down in a seat close to the table and started to play quietly. He seemed to be making the notes up as he went along: either that or he was playing from memory. The others took little notice of the music but both Maria and Sarah looked at each other in wonder. Sarah was a great lover of music and could play the piano well. Maria had not had any opportunity to learn an instrument but was drawn to any type of music: especially if she could dance to it. Her father and Vera had taught her to dance to music they heard on the radio but she had never heard anything like Nicholas's playing: it seemed to change beat and tempo regularly and follow no set pattern. Maria felt quite emotional and wondered if the music was stirring up long forgotten memories from her childhood. She slept well that night with the music playing over and over in her head.

They spent most of the next day picking apples, pears and small Mirabelle plums from the orchard. Ermine and Imogen peeled huge quantities to cook and then preserve in stoneware jars that were stored in a large cool room under the kitchen. This storeroom also contained rows of bottles of wine and other preserves. Maria was fascinated as this reminded her of Vera and yet some of the ingredients that went into the preserves were different. Maria asked whether some of the things they grew here like peaches, peppers and garlic could be grown back home. Ermine had laughed:

'There isn't enough sun back in England to grow fruit like this.' She said holding up a peach. 'But if it can be done anywhere, it will be in the south where you live. You are welcome to take some seeds but you may need a glasshouse to get anything worth having.'

'There are some glasshouses up at the Hall. I could introduce you and to the Head Gardener if you are really interested, Maria. I know your granny is a keen gardener.' Imogen suggested and Maria smiled and nodded in reply.

Marianne raised the subject of going for a trip out to a local town and the seaside the following day. In the end, she took Maria, Sarah and her two children while Ermine and Imogen stayed behind to catch up in peace: besides, there would not be room in the van for any more people to travel comfortably. They went to visit the old town of Pezenas and afterwards went to the sea close to Agde. They all went into the sea and Maria had to admit that she didn't know how to swim. Nevertheless, she enjoyed splashing her feet in the warm sea and walking along the sandy beach in the sunshine. She was struck by the beautiful expanse of clear, blue water: it was so unlike the grey sea in Sussex. Somehow, Maria had the feeling that she would come back to this place again but perhaps she was just wishing for it. Marianne bought some fish from the quayside and they could smell their salty, fishy smell all the way home. However, they made for very good eating at dinner.

Another day, they did some grape picking and had a long, slow meal with Marianne's brother Jean-Paul, his wife Corinne and his sons at their house. Maria and Sarah struggled to understand the conversation at first as they seemed to be speaking quickly and using phrases that they were not familiar with. The house itself was bigger and older than the house where Maria was staying with Marianne and her family. It was a three-storey stone-built chateau with two large green shuttered windows on either side of an impressive looking double door with an enormous knocker. One side of the door was open and the broad-shouldered figure of Jean-Paul was standing with Ermine to greet them.

Inside, Corinne was wiping her hands on a blue apron and she was followed by two boys of similar age and height as Antoine. The boys all scampered off outside together. Maria noticed that rather them embracing, Jean-Paul and Nicholas merely exchanged a nod and a look. Ermine and Corinne returned to the kitchen while Marianne and Nicholas watched the children and Imogen exchanged pleasantries with Jean-Paul about the weather and the progress of the harvest. Maria and Sarah sat quietly taking in the sight of the children running around the grounds until Ermine emerged with a tray of long glasses and a jug of pear juice for the youngsters. She went back for wine glasses and a couple of bottles of white wine for the adults.

Corinne asked them all to sit at the table where she had placed baskets of bread and bowls of tapenade.

'Come and sit with Corinne and I, Imogen. Mother and Marianne can see to the children down there.' Jean-Paul sat at the head of the table and pulled out the chair next to him. The children sat towards the other end with Marianne and Nicholas and Ermine at the very end opposite her son, Jean-Paul. Maria threw a questioning look at Sarah and, receiving no reply, she watched Imogen spread some of the tapenade on her bread and take a bite. Seeing the hesitation of the English girls, Marianne explained that tapenade was made of olives and small fish called anchovies. Maria didn't like the sound of it but decided to give it a try.

'It's delicious, don't you think?' asked Imogen.

'It tastes very salty' replied Maria without thinking.

'Humph. We learned to eat whatever we could get when the Germans were here. They took most of the food we grew for themselves. We could only dream of eating like this. Perhaps the English didn't suffer like we did.' Jean-Paul grumbled.

'We all had shortages during the war, Jean-Paul. But thank goodness that is all over now.' Imogen replied. There was silence for a while before Jean-Paul started again.

'Who knows what will happen next with these socialists in charge. I say we should bring back General de Gaulle. I was surprised you English voted out your Mr Churchill. How are things there? Do you still have food rationing?' Jean-Paul directed this at Imogen while Corinne went into the kitchen and Ermine collected up some of the dirty plates.

'Hardly anything is rationed now so food is not such a problem: especially in rural areas where people can produce food themselves. Just like here of course. Ah look at this.' Imogen exclaimed as Corinne carried an enormous heavy pot and put it on a side table where she dished out differing portions of cassoulet and asked for them to be passed down the table. At last, everybody had a plate of the thick bean and sausage stew and Ermine bought out more wine and water to drink.

'Shall we start on the grape harvest this week Jean-Paul?' asked Marianne.

'That is for me to decide and I do not think that they are ready yet. We should continue with the tomatoes and the fruit. I already told Nicholas, he should carry on with what he is doing for another two weeks at least.' Jean-Paul smiled at Marianne as if that would counter his harshly spoken words.

It was obvious that there was a tension between Marianne and her brother Jean-Paul. Maria could sense it all through the evening and was relieved when they returned back to the other house. The children seemed oblivious to the atmosphere and played and squabbled just like any other cousins. There was no music to stop Jean-Paul from talking: he seemed to be one of those people who felt the need to speak even if he didn't have anything interesting to say. Maria did not see Jean-Paul or his family again during the trip and did not want to ask any questions of Marianne or Imogen for fear of offending them.

One evening, Ermine, Imogen and Sarah were discussing Mozart piano concertos. Maria, feeling rather left out from the conversation, went to help Marianne to tidy up the pots from dinner. She was drawn to one of the pictures she saw: it was a black and white photo of a group of people sitting at the same table where they had just eaten dinner. She could see that one of the men was holding a guitar which looked very much like the one that Nicholas had been playing. She took it off the shelf to get a closer look.

'Ah, you have the picture of my Nicholas and his comrades.' Marianne said as she finished the last of the washing-up and walked over to Maria.

'Is this an old picture? Can you tell me who they are?' asked Maria.

'Of course. That photo was taken before the occupation. That is my father and I, then Nicholas and Ermine. This one is an Englishman called Martin who Aunt Imogen and your father knew.' Marianne was pointing to a suave looking man with a moustache who was smoking a cigarette and holding up a glass of dark wine.

'Oh, that must be Martin Lascelles: my father said that he helped us to leave Spain when it became too dangerous. So, he came here?'

'Yes. He really was incredibly charming and spoke French very well. He was involved in the Resistance in some way but we stopped hearing from him during the occupation. I believe that he was killed by the Gestapo.' Marianne's voice wavered and she coughed and took a breath before continuing,

'He was a very brave man and I will always be grateful to him for bringing Nicholas here. I think I had fallen a little in love with him when he first arrived. That was before I realised that Nic was the man for me.' Marianne passed the picture back to Maria who put it back on the shelf. It was then that she noticed a chessboard with a wooden box on top of it.

'Is that a chess set? Do you play?'

'Yes, a little. Actually, it was Martin who taught me.'

'My father taught me. Perhaps we could have a game one day?'

'Yes, let's. But not now, I'm too tired. I noticed that you enjoy Nic's guitar playing: perhaps you remember hearing similar music when you were a child in Spain?'

'I love to listen to him playing but I am not sure if I can remember much from when I was a child. I seem to have forgotten it all. Your husband would have more to remember than I do. But I haven't heard him talk about it at all.'

'Nic does not talk much about anything in the past: he keeps his secrets locked away. He lives in the present and puts all his emotions into his music...' Marianne paused in thought for a while before continuing:

'It must have been very hard to lose your mother and move to another country when you were so young.' Marianne was a very direct person and Maria found herself being open and honest with her in return. The French words seemed to come to her more easily now.

'I was very young so I don't remember much about living in Barcelona but I do have a couple of pictures of my mother. I still have my dad and my granny so I think I am very lucky really. There are so many reasons to be happy. Don't you think?'

'And what do you like apart from playing chess?'

'I love to dance.' Maria replied.

'Oh yes, so do I. Let's see if we can find some music on the radio.' Marianne turned the dial looking for a station playing music. They danced around the table together giggling.

'Do you have a beau at home in England?' asked Marianne.

'No, I did have a boyfriend for a while but I am too busy learning to be a nurse. And my papa says that there is plenty of time. It's funny because he and my mother were married when they were only two years older than me.'

'Your age does not signify: just make sure you choose the right person. Don't let anyone make that decision for you: not your family and not the man. *You* must choose.' Marianne smiled at the shocked look on Maria's face.

'I can't imagine being as courageous as you' answered Maria.

'You are lovely girl. But you must take control of life or it will take control of you. Believe me, if I had listened to my brother, I would never have been this happy. Do you see?'

'Yes, I think I understand.' Maria looked at Marianne in admiration and wondered if she would ever be that self-assured. She wondered if Jean-Paul disapproved of his sister's marriage to Nicholas and that might explain the atmosphere she had observed between Marianne and her brother. She didn't dare to ask although she was curious to know more.

On another day, Nicholas found Maria sitting alone at the table reading a book. He sat down opposite her and hesitated before speaking:

'Marianne tells me that you grew up in Spain. I have seen you listening when I play the guitar. Does it remind you of when you lived in Barcelona?' he asked softly.

'I really don't remember very much about it. I remember my mother of course; her name was

Teresa. She used to sing to me in the evenings so maybe some of those tunes are the same ones. I remember playing with my cousin Luis and my aunt Pilar in the yard outside the hotel where we lived. There were old barrels and many other places to hide. Do you come from Barcelona too?' Maria was surprised by how much she did remember.

'No, I came from much further south: a place on the coast called Malaga. My family were all killed when the Nationalists took the city: there is nobody left there for me. I was imprisoned after the fighting in Madrid …and then I was lucky to escape with some other prisoners and find myself here.'

'Have you ever been back to Spain?'

'No. It is a very beautiful place: it's very hot in summer, there are beautiful, tall mountains called the Sierra Nevada, fertile land to grow grapes, tomatoes and olives. I miss it but Franco's Spain isn't safe for people like me. One day, I hope I can return and show it to my children. They are the only family I have now.' Nicholas looked at Maria with a wistful look in his eye as if he was picturing someone or somewhere special from within his memory bank. Maria understood then that many families, apart from her own, had been affected by the war. She had read about it but hearing from this man made it all more real.

'The fascists killed my mother too. I can never go back while Franco is alive.' Maria's perspective was a simple one and it surprised Nicholas. In truth, she wanted him to carry on speaking about Spain but couldn't find the right words to say in French.

'I see. Then, let's hope that he won't live for much longer.' Nicholas got up, put a hand on her shoulder and then walked away to one of outhouses. He didn't raise the subject again but occasionally looked up at her curiously when he played guitar. She smiled in reply as if they were co-conspirators in a game that nobody else understood. Maria turned her feelings over in her mind before she went to sleep. She saw it as a betrayal of Vera's love to hanker for the mother that she could barely remember. Nevertheless, she did want to know more about the country and the family that she had left behind. She would ask her father about it when she next saw him. She had noticed that he seemed to find it difficult to talk about the time they had spent with her mother. She could see now that there was a part of her that was missing and she needed to know more about her mother.

When they left for home, Maria vowed to Marianne that she would be back one day. Marianne in her turn, said that they would all be welcome to visit and Nicholas nodded in silent agreement. Imogen was very sad to leave and hugged them all repeatedly. Maria and Sarah both noticed that Imogen was tearful as she said goodbye to Marianne at the station. It was unusual to see a crack in her composure.

Over the course of the following year, Maria sometimes thought back to the beautiful house in the South of France. She never seemed to find the right moment to speak to her father and thoughts of her mother drifted to the back of her mind. Most of the time, she was too busy learning new things to give it too much space in her thoughts.

Chapter Thirteen May 1951 near Lewes

It was the fifth anniversary of Ted's passing and Tom had come down from London for the day. Grace's son had not been well so she had stayed home to look after him. Tom and David linked arms with Vera as they walked up to the churchyard with some flowers picked from the garden. Maria followed behind with Sue, Georgie and Teddy with his two sheepdogs trotting at his heels. Hats were removed and they all stood around the grave for a few minutes with heads bowed. Vera put the flowers in the heavy vase that was always left there, kissed her hand and touched the gravestone and then got up to walk away. The family shared a lunch that Sue had made at David's house after which Tom hugged everyone goodbye and went back up to London. Vera thanked them all and went back to her cottage with Maria. Once there, Vera put the kettle on and made them both a cup of tea.

'You know, I can't see the point of being sad about today. Your grandad died far too soon but I was lucky to know him for nearly fifty years and have so many happy memories.'

'I'm sure you have. I knew Grandad for only eight years but the very first time I met him, he made me smile just by playing with a dice. He was a lovely man.'

'That he was.'

'I used to love going for walks with him. Sometimes he wouldn't say a word, just listen to me chattering away. But he knew so much about the countryside and would show me where a blackbird was nesting in the hedge or where the wild garlic and columbine was flowering or when there was some frogspawn in the ponds. He taught me so much. I'll always remember him with that twinkle in his eye.' Maria was cheered by these happy thoughts and hoped that sharing them would help her granny too.

'He loved spending time with you, you know. He would have been very proud that you are going to be a nurse. I often think he is still here watching over us. But then that's daft. He didn't believe in anything like that you know. He didn't have much time for church and vicars and all that. He preferred being outside with his animals: that was his church.'

'Yes, I think you are right there.' There was a pause until Maria continued, 'So, I know you met each other in school but how did you end up getting married Granny? Did he ask you on a date? Did he get down on one knee and propose?' Vera laughed.

'We all used to go out as a crowd of friends. We would go for walks and sometimes to a dance in the village. My family weren't as well off as the Lamberts you know: that was mainly because my father couldn't stay away from the drink. Of course, that was where my brother Jim got it from but that's another story. I started to notice that Ted was looking at me in his own shy way so I asked our Jim to find out if he was interested in going to the next village dance with me.'

'Really? So, you made the first move Granny?'

'If I'd waited for him, I could have waited forever. He was quite a catch was Ted - but he didn't know it. I decided I'd have to give him a helping hand.'

'Granny! And did you two end up going to that dance together?'

'Oh yes. He called round to pick me up, gave me flowers and all. It turned out he wasn't a bad dancer either. Less than a year later, he took me for a walk up Cliffe Beacon and asked me to marry him. We didn't have an engagement ring so he used a ring he'd made from grass.' Vera laughed and looked slightly embarrassed.

'You know he used to take me up to Cliffe Beacon. I didn't realise it was your place too'

'That was his favourite spot, I think. He used to take David and your father there too. I hope you find somebody as wonderful as Ted, Maria.'

'I'm not in any hurry for that. I'm happy enough here as I am.' Maria squeezed her granny's hand. 'I'm going up to study for a while before bed. Goodnight, Granny.' Maria had been out dancing with several boys since she had broken up with Stephen Dixon but none of them had become especially important to her.

Maria, Sarah and Lizzie all completed their nursing course successfully in July 1951. Maria and Lizzie had both been offered places at the Royal Sussex to undergo further training to achieve SRN status. It was decided that Sarah would emigrate to the USA with her aunt and uncle and her qualification was going to give her a good start there. She liked John Fletcher but was too ambitious to let their relationship hold her back. All three of the girls went to the Graduation Dance held at the Metropole Hotel but Sarah had left early after telling John the news that she was leaving in three weeks.

Maria was dancing with one of the trainee doctors when she noticed Lizzie turning down a dance with Dr Maxwell, who was one of the younger hospital doctors who were at the event. At the end of that dance, Maria asked Lizzie why she hadn't joined in.

'John warned me about Dr Maxwell. He told me that he is not as nice as he appears and is a hopeless flirt.' Lizzie told Maria as they got themselves another drink. 'Why don't you dance with my brother. He needs cheering up now that he knows Sarah is definitely leaving for America. I think he was more keen on her than he let on.'

'Ok, I wonder where he is…' answered Maria looking around the room for John Fletcher but found her eyes locking instead on the attractive face of Dr Maxwell who headed in her direction. Maria panicked and ignored her friend's advice by accepting his invitation to dance. He was a good dancer and afterwards, they went outside for some cooler sea air. Lizzie saw them go and followed out of concern for her friend. She was just in time to see Dr Maxwell pushing Maria towards the wall of one the enclosed benches that were dotted along the promenade. He was pinning her against it while trying to kiss her so Lizzie ran towards them and called out:

'Maria, are you ok?' Dr Maxwell turned towards her with his hands held up as if there was nothing wrong. But Maria looked upset as she turned towards Lizzie and then covered her face with her hands in shame. At that moment John arrived panting as he had run up from beach level when he had heard his sister shouting. He looked from Maria to his sister and saw the look of disgust that Lizzie shot at Dr Maxwell.

'Is everything ok here Maria?' asked John seeing his sister's friend had shrunk into the shadows in fear. Lizzie put her arms round her friend to reassure her. 'Do you get some kind of kick out of frightening young women. Shame on you.' John said.

'Nothing happened here Fletcher' sneered Dr Maxwell as he walked back across the road to the Hotel. John turned to Maria.

'Are you ok? Maybe you should report this' John said gently as his sister was stroking Maria's hair.

'No. I don't want any fuss, I'm fine - really. Please don't tell anyone else about this.'

'As long as you are sure... I can walk you back to the train station if you like. Or you could stay with Lizzie as we live just round the corner.'

'My granny is expecting me home tonight.'

'Would you like us to see you to the train. It isn't far and I would feel better to see you get on it safely.' Lizzie was gentle but firm in her tone.

'Thank you, that's kind of you. I just need to pick up my coat from the cloakroom.' It was a warm summer evening as John and Lizzie walked Maria up to the train station.

The incident knocked Maria's confidence for a time. Not long afterwards, Dr Maxwell moved to another hospital. When the news was announced, Lizzie couldn't help saying to her friend.

'Well, we won't be sad to see the back of him.' Maria could only agree as she registered a sense of relief that she would not have to hide from him anymore.

Maria found herself spending more time with Lizzie as Sarah became preoccupied with the move to New York. She had agreed to stay with her father for a while that Summer. He was taking Grace, Peter and their new baby, Keith, down to Eastbourne on a caravan holiday for two weeks in August. Maria had agreed to go along for the first week as she was on duty for the following week. Vera would be staying with them for a few days too as she loved to help out with her new grandson. Vera had encouraged Maria to come along as she thought the change might cheer her granddaughter up. She hadn't been herself of late.

Tom had told George Fletcher that he would be down in Eastbourne and they organised a joint family outing from Beachy Head to Cuckmere Haven. The clifftop walk was much too far for the children so they stayed on the beach with Grace and Vera. Tom, Maria, Lizzie, George and John Fletcher drove up to Beachy Head and they set out on the walk.

It was a beautiful sunny day but there was a steady breeze coming off the sea. The walk had a lot of ups and downs and took much longer and was more tiring than they had expected. They stopped in a café at Cuckmere Haven to have tea and sandwiches before making the return journey. George and Tom enjoyed putting the world to rights just like they used to years before. George was a Quaker and member of the Peace Pledge Union but Tom thought that the allies were right to go to war with Fascist Germany so they had many a lively debate on political issues. By the time they got back, Lizzie had cooked up a plan for Maria to go back to Brighton with them and stay overnight with her. Having dropped back to where her father and George Fletcher were walking, Maria asked:

'Dad, Lizzie says they have a bike I could have to help me get to hospital and back, the bus from the station is so unreliable. Lizzie and John say they can help me fix it up. Can I stay there tonight so that we can sort it out tomorrow. If that is alright with Dr Fletcher of course.' She added looking at her father's companion.

'This feels a bit like an ambush. I am happy with the arrangement if your father is. It's so nice for Lizzie to have a good friend like you.'

'I didn't know you wanted a bicycle, my dear but I can see it would be useful. It's fine with me so long as George can cope with you.' George nodded in silent agreement.

'Thank you.' Maria shouted as she skipped back to Lizzie to tell her.

Maria knew where her friend Lizzie lived but had never stayed over before. It was a huge house with several storeys on Regency Square but there were three bells with name plates outside the enormous front door, as well as another separate flat in the basement. Maria followed Lizzie up the stairs to the second floor where George let them in with one of the keys he was jangling. They went into the living room which was very light and airy due to fact that the glass doors onto the balcony were open to welcome in the evening sun. A lady sitting on the balcony got up slowly with the aid of a stick and turned to welcome them.

'Hello, my dears, have you all enjoyed your walk?' Mrs Fletcher was a petite, dark lady wearing a dress with a bright paisley pattern in shades of blue and pink. Her dress was in contrast to the plain clothing that the rest of the family seemed to favour. 'Ah, is this your friend Lizzie?'

'Yes mother, this is Maria who is training with me. She is going to stay over so that we can fix up that old bike for her.' Lizzie answered.

'Ah yes. Your father is Tom Lambert the photographer, isn't he? I've met your father you know. You don't look anything like him so you must take after your mother. Sit down by me and tell me about yourself. I don't get out to meet many people now what with these blasted lungs.' She said patting her chest as she sat on the sofa and pointed to the chair beside her. Maria sat down as instructed while George and Lizzie left the room as if on a pre-arranged mission. John sat down at the piano on the other side of the room and started to play a quiet tune.

'Play something a bit less dreary would you John?' John gave his mother an exasperated look and then started to play something a bit livelier. Mrs Fletcher continued. 'So, Maria, tell me about yourself and how is your father? We haven't seen him for a while.'

'My father is fine. He lives in London now with his wife Grace and their new baby. He seems very happy.'

'Will you move up there with him?' As she spoke, Maria noticed that she wore several unusual rings on her fingers one of which had a large turquoise stone. She also wore several bracelets that jangled together when she moved her hands.

'Oh no. I live with Granny Vera just outside Lewes. I wouldn't want to live in such a crowded, busy city. I love it at the Royal: Lizzie and I want to become really good nurses together.' Maria answered earnestly and she could not help noticing that Mrs Fletcher was wheezing when taking a breath. Lizzie had explained that her mother had breathing difficulties but some days were worse than others. It meant that Lizzie and the rest of the family had to take turns to do the things around the house that their mother used to do.

'What do you do for some fun then. All young people need something more than work in their lives.' She said this looking briefly but meaningfully in her son John's direction.

'Well, I like to help Granny at home. I also enjoy playing chess, dancing and the movies.'

'Ah, you like dancing. I used to love to dance, and I was a dance teacher when I was younger you know. My mother taught me but after she died, I used to dance with the ayah.' Maria was puzzled:

'What's an ayah?'

'Oh yes, perhaps you don't know. My father was a civil servant in India so I grew up there and "ayah" is their word for a Nanny. My father was often out so I spent a lot of my time with the ayah. She was a wonderful woman who wore beautiful saris and sang strange songs to me. India was so colourful and warm. Then I was sent home to England where everything is as grey as the sky.. and I have been cold ever since. Do you feel the cold?' Maria was puzzled:

'Well, no, I just put warmer clothes on.' At this, John stopped playing momentarily and smiled while Mrs Fletcher looked slightly put out and said:

'Well, that told me I suppose.' Maria was clearly embarrassed but Mrs Fletcher winked at her.

'Oh no, don't you worry young lady. I like someone with a bit of spark who speaks their mind. You are your father's daughter after all, he and my George used to have some lively discussions. And it puts me in mind of when I was young.'

At this, Lizzie appeared to say that dinner was ready. John went over to help his mother out of the chair and into the dining room.

After dinner, they played a few rounds of whist and then went to bed. Before they turned the light out in Lizzie's room to go to sleep, Maria confided in her friend:

'I had no idea your mother had had such an exotic life. To be born in India! Is that where she got her illness?'

'Oh, I've heard all those stories a hundred times before. She did suffer from fevers in India but her breathing problems started when she got TB when I was nine or ten. My aunt had to come to look after us for a while. Mother is better now but she won't ever be as strong as she was. That's why I often have to come home on time to make sure she is ok.'

'She seems lovely and has such unusual jewellery.'

'Ah yes, mum loves bright colours. She keeps saying that England is too grey and too cold. Anyone would think that she hadn't been living here for most of her life.'

'Do you know how your mum and dad met?'

'Oh yes, my father used to play the piano at dance classes to earn extra money when he was training to be a doctor. My mother was one of the dance teachers so that's how they met.'

'Ah, so she is a good dancer then?'

'Oh yes, and she taught me. My father tried to get me to learn piano but I was nowhere near as good as John so I gave up. '

'I suppose it was music that drew John and Sarah together?'

'Yes. He's pretty much refused to do anything but work since Sarah left. I've tried asking him to come to the movies or out dancing but he just says he isn't interested. Mother is losing patience with him. Ah well, what can we do?'

'I'm going to miss Sarah too. We had been friends since we were eleven.' There was a pause and Maria could see that Lizzie was mulling something over.

'You know Gerry Markham keeps asking me to go out with him. What do you think of him?' asked Lizzie.

'He's the anaesthetist isn't he. He seems nice enough. Do you think you will go out with him?'

'Probably. I'm not sure yet. But how come you aren't going out with anyone. You have plenty of admirers you know.' Lizzie goaded her friend and she coloured.

'I've been out with a few boys but don't want to get serious with anybody yet. Granny says that I will know when the right one comes along.' Maria had stopped taking an interest in young men recently.

'I suppose you will have to get back to your Granny before lunch tomorrow. Are you going to take the bike with you if we get it going?'

'Maybe, let's see first. It's ages since I even rode a bike. My cousin Teddy and I used to share one but that was years ago.'

'You'll be fine. I'm going to turn the light out now. Goodnight Maria.'

'Goodnight Lizzie.'

In the morning, after breakfast, Dr and Mrs Fletcher and their son went the short distance to the Friends Meeting House for a Quaker service while Lizzie and Maria cleaned and serviced the bicycle. Lizzie was clearly familiar with bicycle maintenance and they soon had it working well enough to go for a ride down the seafront to Hove and back.

Maria was curious and when they stopped on the seafront at Hove, she couldn't help asking Lizzie what being a Quaker meant.

'Quakers are Christians who follow the Testimonies which are Simplicity, Truth, Equality, Peace and Sustainability. Most people associate us with conscientious objectors and campaigning against slavery. We hold simple services and place a lot of importance on charitable work. My father encourages us to join him when he helps at the Brighton soup kitchen that is run for the homeless and hungry.'

'Shouldn't you have gone to the service with the others then?'

'I often go with them but not always. Usually, my father or John will be there to play piano accompaniment if hymns are sung. Do you go to church with your granny?'

'Yes. But really it is just to keep her company. I am not sure whether either of us believe in all of it. I agree with treating others the way that you would like to be treated. But I am not sure if there are such things as Heaven and Hell. Do you believe in that?'

'You are a deep one, aren't you? To be honest, I don't give it much thought at all. I quite like helping in the soup kitchen and some of the old men who go there have interesting stories to tell: especially about their wartime experiences. Perhaps you would like to come along one time?'

'Oh, I don't know what Granny would say about that. Speaking of whom, I should really be getting back. Thank you so much for your help with the bike.'

'Let's ride back now. I'll come up to the station with you to make sure everything is ok.'

'Thanks. That's really kind of you. Please thank your mum and dad for having me.'

'Of course.' They went back to collect Maria's things and then Lizzie accompanied her to the station.

A few weeks after this, Lizzie started going out with Gerry Markham and she tried to get Maria into a couple of foursome outings. However, Maria didn't like either of the young men who had come along. Lizzie's family were not keen on her going out alone with Gerry so in desperation, she suggested that John come along with Maria. John was resistant to the idea, but their mother persuaded him to go along with it for his sister's sake. Maria felt more comfortable partnering with Lizzie's brother. Ever since the incident with Dr Maxwell, she had felt nervous around young men but John was someone she could feel safe with. They went to a dance at the Corn Exchange and Maria took the opportunity to wear one of the lovely dresses that Imogen had bought for her the previous summer. The dress was in brightly coloured rayon and flowed well as she moved around while dancing. She didn't get many opportunities to dress up so took advantage when she could.

'Don't look so worried John. We may only be here to chaperone Lizzie but I intend to enjoy myself.' Maria said when they met Gerry outside the venue. In fact, John was surprised at how well Maria had looked when she emerged from his sister's room. He hadn't paid much attention to her before but had found himself looking at her differently.

'Yes, well, I have to look out for my little sister, don't I? How are you doing with the bike? I know it isn't easy getting up that hill to the hospital whichever way you go' He asked avoiding eye contact.

'I've tried most ways and they are all hard going. I think maybe I should leave it at Lewes station and just use it for that part of the journey.'

'Chicken! Lizzie and I both make it up Marine Parade.'

'Talking of chickens, I don't think I have seen you dance before, are you any good?'

'I couldn't say. But no doubt you will give me an honest opinion.' John and Maria followed Lizzie and Gerry onto the dance floor for a jive. John looked rather serious all the way through the dance as he was concentrating on not making a mistake and treading on her toes.

'So, was that up to your standards?' John asked nervously.

'Not bad. You could try relaxing a bit more. Shall we go for another?'

'Fine with me.' The band started up. 'Ah, an old-fashioned waltz. Miss Lambert, may I have this dance?'

'You may.' John bowed his head pretending to be formal and led her onto the dance floor where he seemed to hit his stride and even smiled as he spun her around the floor. At the end of it, the four of them went for a drink and then Gerry took Maria's hand to dance one of the new Latin American dances with her.

'Well, brother, I have to say you two danced very well together. If I am not mistaken, you might even be in danger of enjoying yourself.'

'It isn't as bad as I thought it would be.' He looked over towards Maria and realised that he did enjoy her company. She was different to most other girls somehow.

'How are things going for you? Do you really like Gerry?'

'Too early to say. He is good company and a really good dancer as you can see. Thanks for coming along though. I thought you were going to dig your heels in and refuse.'

'It's fine. I didn't want to spoil your fun.' Lizzie noticed that John's eyes were following Maria and Gerry.

They all enjoyed the evening and John even suggested that they should do it again soon. Maria was staying over with Lizzie again. When they got back to the flat in Regency Square, Lizzie embarrassed her brother and Maria by announcing that they made a really nice couple.

Chapter Fifteen – August 1951 Brighton

Over the next few months, John, Maria, Lizzie and Gerry went out dancing, to the movies, for walks along the beach and to a music concert. They gradually moved from being friends to being two couples. For Maria, this was sealed when John asked to visit her home to meet Vera. She had only bought two boyfriends back to the farmhouse before but Vera felt that Maria was more enthusiastic about John than she had been about the previous two. At the news, Vera had gone into overdrive cleaning and baking to be ready for the appointed Saturday afternoon. They had had to wait for some time as John did not get many weekends when he was not on duty at the hospital. Maria liked that he was as dedicated to his work and family as she was. He was more grown-up than the other young men she had spent time with and she felt both safe and happy in his company.

Maria went on her bike to meet him at Lewes station. She was struck by how blue his eyes were in the sunshine and noted that he had made the time and effort to look smart and have a shave. He had an attractive face when he smiled but when in repose, he always looked like he was frowning at some private thoughts. He let her lead the way as they cycled up the hill out of Lewes and along the road to Blackthorn Farm. Vera welcomed them at the back door of the brick and flint cottage as they were leaning their bikes against the garden wall. John shrugged his backpack off and took out a gift for Vera. It was a small box of chocolates which she thanked him for as she led them into the kitchen and made the obligatory pot of tea.

'Shall we have some lunch and then you could take Trixie out for me?' Vera was always in charge in her domain in spite of being a small grey-haired old lady. John was not particularly tall for a man but he towered over Vera as he sat down next to her. Maria sat opposite him and smiled encouragement. Vera offered tea accompanied by bread, ham, cheese, salad and pickles. They all helped themselves to a plateful.

'So, John, I know that you are George Fletcher's son and that you work in the hospital with Maria. Tell me a bit more about yourself: how do you like to spend your time?'

John took a long breath while he thought about his answer:

'I'm a junior doctor and I have at least two years to go until I am fully qualified. That means I don't have much time for anything else but, when I do have time, I like to spend it with my family and playing piano. Recently, your granddaughter made me realise that I quite like dancing too. She is a much better dancer than I am though.' John looked over at Maria and she smiled back.

'Maria's grandad wasn't much of a dancer but he tried his best and got better for my sake bless him. I can't imagine what it's like living surrounded by so many people in Brighton. Is it really noisy?'

'Sometimes, but it isn't the people that make it noisy where we live so much as the seagulls. We are right next to the sea and you just get used to their squawking. Come to think of it, it is really quiet here, isn't it?' John directed this at Maria.

'I hardly slept when I stayed over with Lizzie. The seagulls seemed to make a racket just after we went to bed.' Maria said laughing.

'I suppose you two girls were talking too much to get much sleep, were you?' Vera asked with a chuckle and then turning back to John, she continued to exchange pleasantries to try to get to know him better while they ate.

'Now, you must try some cake. There's fruit cake or jam sponge. Which is your favourite?' asked Vera. John looked to Maria for guidance.

'Both are good but the jam is made from our own fruit so perhaps you should try that.' Maria advised.

'That's decided then.' John replied as Vera went to a cupboard and came back with a blue and white china platter with a huge cake brimming with buttercream and jam and dusted with icing sugar. She cut three large slices and handed them round while Maria topped up the teapot.

'That is a really delicious light cake. How come you are both so slim. I think I would soon put on weight if I lived here.' John said. Vera was secretly pleased by the compliment. Maria could see that he had passed her test and they decided to go for a walk to work off some of the cake. As they were leaving by the back gate, Teddy and David were walking back to the barn. They made quite a pair: both wearing boots and flat caps and carrying shotguns. David also had a brace of rabbits on a string over his shoulder and there were a couple of black and white sheepdogs trotting along close behind Teddy.

'Hello there, so, you are the young man Maria is walking out with? I'm her uncle David' said Maria's uncle holding out an enormous hand that was tanned and calloused from working outside. John shook his hand in spite of seeing evidence of dried blood on it.

'Another fine hand like my brother Tom's' David said with a smirk.

'Afternoon. I'm Teddy.' There was another vigorous handshake. 'Where are you going to take the doctor to?' asked Maria's cousin. He was a slightly taller but less weather-beaten version of his father.

'I thought maybe up Cliffe Beacon to get the view, then down to the river and back up through the Long Field.' Maria replied.

'That might be too far for a townie,' laughed Teddy who noticed the sensible stout boots that John was wearing.

'I'll manage fine, don't you worry,' answered John looking Teddy straight in the eye.

'OK. We'll let you get on your way then.' David pronounced as if their inspection was over. When they got out of earshot, Maria apologised:

'Sorry about that. They seem to think they have to protect me.'

'That's fine. They are a bit intimidating I suppose. Actually, it is good to know you have family close by looking out for you. I hope I pass whatever test they have all set for me.'

'It's not like that.'

'I think it is like that, Maria. By the way, my parents have told me that they like you.' They both laughed and walked on before starting to climb the hill. After a while, they both stopped to catch their breath and John cleared his throat:

'I need to tell you something… I am going to be really wrapped up in my training for the next couple of years. That means I may not be able to spend as much time with you as I would like. It's different for Gerry, he's qualified already. I know you really enjoy going out…'

'Stop there. I remember how important qualifying was to me so I think I can understand how important it is for you. I am fine with that. In fact, I am thinking of continuing my training: I could specialise in midwifery or surgical nursing.' Maria wanted John to see that she took her work seriously but she wanted to have some fun too. She lacked confidence in herself and had a nagging feeling that she wasn't quite good enough for a doctor. 'Now, let's see if we can catch up with Trixie. Vera will never forgive us if we lose her.' They walked quickly up the hill and found the little terrier sniffing around and wagging her tail at the top. They also took in the great view down towards the sea on one side and right across the valley of patchwork fields to the Downs on the other side.

'Is this one of your favourite places?' asked John.

'Yes, it is. That's why I brought you here. I used to come up here with my Grandad when I was younger: we would often just sit here looking at the views without speaking. This place has a way of making any worries seem less important.' Maria rested on a flat rock leaning against a chalky outcrop near the edge of the cliff. They were several miles from the sea but could just about see it through the haze on the horizon.

'My place to think is down by the beach: especially in winter when the weather is bad, the sea is rough and there aren't so many visitors.' John was normally reserved about himself but for some reason, he couldn't help being open to sharing his private thoughts with Maria.

'You know, my favourite beach was the one I saw when I went to France with Imogen Clements. It was so sunny and so blue and the sand went on for miles. I would really love to go back there one day.'

'Ah yes, Sarah told me about that. But she seemed to prefer Paris to the house in the country where you stayed.'

'Yes. I think she did. I'm sorry it didn't work out for you and Sarah.' Maria thought that she might be compared unfavourably to Sarah. Trixie ran up to Maria with a stick she had found so Maria threw it down the hill.

'Really? I'm not sorry about it anymore. It wasn't meant to be.' The little dog soon returned with the stick and she threw it again. But this time, John took her hand and they ran down the hill after the dog.

Maria took them down to the riverbank where she and Vera always picked berries in September. The bees were busy on this year's flowers. She pointed out a kestrel hovering in the next field and they sat down together on the grass watching the river. Then she lay back looking up at the clouds. John picked a blade of grass and tickled her cheek with it. She swatted the grass and then, on an impulse, reached over to kiss him on the cheek. He kissed her on the mouth in return and they stayed close for a while holding on to each other. She was surprised by the unfamiliar feelings that were taking hold of her and didn't want him to see. So, she got up, dusted down her clothes and started to make her way up the bank towards home.

'Come on. Race you up to the chestnut tree.' John ran after her quickly so that he reached the big old tree first. The dog thought it was a great game and carried on running up the field. John reached down to pick up a decent sized stick and threw it away from the dog who soon retrieved it. He threw the stick again and they carried on until they were back at the cottage flushed with the exercise.

Vera opened the door when she heard the dog barking to be let in and asked them if they would like another cup of tea.

'Yes, please. And then I will need to go and catch a train home.' John said looking at Vera.

'I could come with you to the station.' Maria offered as she got two extra cups out for tea.

'There's no need for you to come out, I can find my own way back. I'll see you next week: I am working next weekend but I have next Wednesday off. Perhaps I can meet you for lunch or after you finish?' John asked as he took the cup that Maria handed to him.

'Maybe after work as we often don't get much time for lunch. I am supposed to finish at 5:30' answered Maria.

'There is plenty more cake. Would you like another piece? Or a biscuit?' asked Vera.

'No thank you. I can't say I'm not tempted but I'm really not hungry.'

After John left on his bicycle, Vera looked at Maria and said:

'What a polite young man and nice looking too. As I would have expected from the son of George Fletcher. You two seem quite a couple now. Have you told your father?'

'No. There isn't anything to tell. We are only just getting to know each other. It isn't anything serious...'

'Yet. I think I know that look he gives you. But don't give your heart away too quickly, Maria. Make sure you are right for each other first.' Vera loved to give out advice.

'What's got into you granny? Don't worry about me so much. I'll be fine.'

'It's my job to worry. You may find that out for yourself one day.' Vera said sipping her tea and smiling to herself. Looking back, Maria realised that that was the day she fell in love with John.

Chapter Sixteen March 1952 Brighton

Lizzie and John's mother died in February and Maria and her father went to the funeral. The service was a simple one at the Friends Meeting House in Brighton. Maria could see that the whole family were devastated and it was hard to see it as she knew them so well now. The following Saturday, she had arranged to meet John by the West Pier. The day was cold and windy and his mood was as grey as the sea.

'I'm sorry but I can't take you anywhere this weekend. I just don't feel up to it.' Maria noticed that he had not greeted her with the usual kiss or taken her hand as they walked along the promenade towards the other pier.

'I understand really. You are allowed to feel sad about your mother, you know. Just because you are a man, it doesn't mean you are made of stone. And if you can't bring your troubles to me, who exactly are you going to take them to? Your whole family are grieving for your mother. In our jobs, we see people die so often: but it is such a different thing when it is someone close to you isn't it? I know that from when grandad passed. It isn't something you can get over in five minutes or put in a box and forget about.'

John was throwing pebbles into the sea but then spoke quietly without looking at her: 'Maybe, but I've been thinking that we should stop seeing each other for a while.' Maria was so shocked that she stopped walking and looked out to the waves. He carried on as if he had had a speech ready: 'I need to concentrate on my training and I don't want you to wait around for me to feel like taking you dancing again. I'm sorry but I think this is for the best. Shall I walk you back to the station?'

'John, I don't think you are thinking straight. You need to give yourself time to get back on an even keel.'

'Please don't make this any harder than it is. I'm not good for you right now. I can't do this any more. I can just about get through a shift at work.' He looked tired and distraught and Maria accepted that he needed time to deal with his grief.

'Ok, if you are sure. I'll leave you to yourself for a while. Drop me a line when and if you would like to talk. I'd rather walk back to the station on my own now.'

'Are you sure?'

'Yes, now go home and try to rest.' Maria hadn't wanted him to see how upset she was and took the train back to Lewes. She went for a walk before going back home to her Granny. She told her that their work patterns were keeping them apart but Vera could see that Maria wasn't happy and invented some chores to keep her busy.

Just over a week later, John sent a note to Maria via Lizzie asking her to meet him in a teashop on Edward Street. He set a time that was after she had finished a day shift and he was on his way to a night shift. It stayed open late as there were many customers who worked at the hospital. He looked tired and his hair was rather messy but she still found him attractive. He turned and smiled nervously as he heard her footsteps and they kissed each other on the cheek in greeting before going in.

They ordered a pot of tea for two and some toasted teacakes before sitting down at a table by the window. This offered some privacy when the place was relatively empty, as it was when they arrived.

'Is Lizzie not with you today?' John asked to Maria's puzzlement.

'It's Wednesday so she's off. I thought you would have seen her at home?' she asked.

'Oh yes. Sorry, I'm not really with it today. I never have enjoyed working nights as you know and since mother passed, I don't sleep as well as I used to. How was your day?'

'I'm fine. It was a pretty typical day, nothing out of the ordinary. How are you? You look full of cares.' Maria's tone of voice was soft and full of concern.

'Well, I need to apologise for what I said the other day. I am so sorry. I shouldn't have said those things to you. It wasn't kind after all the help you have given to me.'

'It's fine really.'

'Thanks for understanding, Maria. You've been through so much and yet none of it seems to knock you off balance. I wish I had some of your strength. I'm sorry…'

'Don't apologise, there really is no need. I don't have the answers, but Granny always told me to hold on to the happy memories that you have.'

'I keep going home and expecting to find her there. And then she isn't there and the place feels so empty. I feel so empty and I'm not good company.'

'I know how that feels. Silence can be deafening as they say. But you just need to hold on to the things that count: you have your music. Perhaps you should sit and play as if your mother is still there. It might be a comfort as it seems to be to my friend Nicholas. He lost his entire family; but I could see that he found some solace in playing his music.' Maria paused to look at John who was staring at his hands and she continued. 'Have you had anything to eat today?'

'No, I just got up here in time to meet you. I start my shift at seven so we only have half an hour or forty minutes.'

'So have the teacakes and perhaps order something else. You need to eat especially if you aren't sleeping properly. You know Vera will have enough food at home to keep me going for a week.' Maria smiled and John laughed.

'Always the practical one, aren't you?' John said. 'Sometimes, I wonder how you put up with Lizzie and I. We are all so grateful to you for helping us with the funeral and so on.'

'I was happy to. Your mother was a wonderful person and was always kind to me. You will get through this, John. It may not feel like it sometimes, but you will.' Maria had been touched that John's mother had left her some jewellery in her will. It was a pair of silver bangles that she had admired.

'You are probably right. You usually are.'

'Is that a fact?'

'Oh crikey. I shouldn't have said that out loud should I.' They both laughed and John realised again how much he enjoyed being in Maria's company. The spark between them was still there.

'Maria, you are so beautiful, and clever and kind. I can't imagine my life without you, I really can't.'

'I'm so happy that you said that. I wasn't sure if you felt the same way as I do.' John took her hand and kissed it.

'My mother left me a turquoise ring. Would you wear it for me?'

'Of course, I'd be happy to wear it.' Maria felt so happy that she wanted to dance.

John couldn't quite believe what had just happened. He hoped he wouldn't let her down by failing the exams that were coming up. The waitress came over to check that everything was ok. He was suddenly hungry and ordered some eggs on toast. They held hands under the table until the food arrived.

'I suppose I will need to go and catch my train soon or Granny will worry,' Maria said although she didn't really want to go.

'I'm off from Saturday through to Monday night this week. Would you like to go to the movies or something?' John asked her.

'Perhaps you should be sleeping?' Maria joked. 'Let's go dancing. We haven't been for ages. Or we could just go for a walk on Sunday if the weather is good?'

'Sounds good to me' John said in between yawns. 'Sorry, I really need a good night's sleep.'

Maria was thoughtful for a while before asking: 'Have you thought that maybe you should follow your father and go into general practice rather than staying on at the hospital. It would mean you don't have to work night shifts so often, wouldn't it?'

'Yes, I have thought about it, but I need to qualify first. I always thought I didn't want to follow in my father's footsteps but perhaps that shouldn't matter. Working nights doesn't seem to work well for me. I have some doubt about whether I will pass the exams that are coming up this summer. I sometimes wonder if I have what it takes to become a doctor at all.' John turned a tired looking face towards Maria.

'Don't doubt yourself, you will be a wonderful doctor, I know.' She put her hand on his and tried to re-assure him.

'How about you? Do you think you will stay on the surgical ward? Dr Fraser seems to think you could be a theatre nurse. Or can you see yourself cycling around the countryside as a district nurse looking after old people's bunions?'

'Well, you make that sound very appealing. Lizzie is talking about training as a midwife you know.'

'Yes, she mentioned it. She also said that Gerry has applied for a job at St Thomas's in London. I wonder if she will follow him if he gets it. I wouldn't want to work in London, would you?'

'Definitely not. I'm too much of a country girl. Every time I visit my dad and Grace, I can't wait to get back to the green fields once the train passes beyond Croydon.'

'I know what you mean. Brighton is a big enough place for me.'

'Would you want to join your father's practice?'

'Oh no, I don't think so. I'd rather find my own way.' Maria knew what he meant. John's father was larger than life and he didn't want to stay in his shadow for ever.

John did fail an exam that Summer, but he retook it and passed in the autumn. After that, they started to talk about when they would get married.

Chapter Seventeen - August 1953

Tom came down from London with his family to give Maria away at her simple wedding in Lewes Register Office. He and John's father had bought them a Morris Minor as a wedding present. They had both learned to drive and planned to take it down to the South of France for their honeymoon. Imogen had given them a cheque that covered the deposit for a flat in Kemptown that they wanted to buy. They spent their wedding night in the Old Ship Hotel in Brighton and in the morning, Maria drove them down to Dover where they crossed to Calais and then John drove to the Bois de Boulogne where they were going to camp for two nights.

Maria wanted to show him Notre Dame but she had forgotten how expensive everything was in Paris. Last time she had visited, Imogen had paid most of the bills without flinching at the cost. John just laughed it off when they paid almost as much for two drinks in a café as they would have got paid for a whole day. They made the drinks last a long time as they watched Paris go by from their pavement table.

It took them another couple of days to get down to the campsite by the Mediterranean Sea. They had booked to stay for a few more nights before making the return journey. Imogen thought they should have stayed with Marianne but Maria didn't want to impose and thought that she and John could just visit them for a day. Imogen assumed that as newlyweds, Maria and John wanted to spend time alone so did not press them on the subject. Maria had written to Marianne to tell her that they would like to visit as they were passing nearby.

On the appointed day, John drove while Maria navigated their way to Les Trois Chemins using a combination of a map and her memory. As they drove up the short drive and parked up outside the house, Maria was surprised to see a newish fence with young trees planted next to it running close to the house and down through the orchard. She was sure it hadn't been there before and wondered why it was there. Perhaps they had sold some of the land? Maria waited for John to join her before knocking on the door. A pretty girl of around ten answered the door and looked at them curiously:

'Allo?'

'Good-day, is your mother or your father in? My name is Maria… are you Delphine?' Maria spoke in broken French as she had been in the country for only a few days and found the right words with difficulty.

'Maria! Come in, come in' said Marianne emerging from the back of the house smoothing her hair back into place as she walked towards them.

'Marianne!' They exchanged kisses on both cheeks.

'This is my husband John,' Maria gestured towards John and Marianne kissed him on both cheeks before turning to Maria:

'It is lovely to see you both. Please, come in and tell me all your news. Nicholas and Antoine are out somewhere, but they will return soon. Would you like some coffee or some wine?'

'Could we have kir?' asked Maria excitedly. John looked puzzled.

'Ah yes, what a lovely idea. Delphine, please go and tell your father that Maria and John are here.'

'Ok.' The girl, who was around ten years old, shouted in response and then ran off with her ponytail swinging behind her. Meanwhile, Marianne prepared three glasses of kir, handed them round and took them outside to the table in the courtyard. John's eyes took in the expanse of the vines growing on three sides of the courtyard entwined in their wooden supports. On the fourth side, they saw rows of fruit trees that ended with a fence. Meanwhile, Marianne had bought out a plate of little cheese pastries.

'Your good health and a happy future. Tell me, how did you two meet?' Marianne asked. She could see Maria looking at the fence but didn't want to talk about it yet: she wanted to hear her news first.

'John is a doctor and we trained at the same hospital. We both still work there. John is the brother of one of my good friends.'

'Love at first sight?' Marianne was bold as ever and Maria did not hesitate to reply.

'No, it wasn't. I don't think I believe in that. Do you Marianne?' Marianne looked at John who seemed to be frowning.

'I agree, that only happens in the movies.' said Marianne. 'And what do you think John. Do you understand what we are saying?'

'Yes, I think I understand. I knew Maria for nearly three years before I was certain that I wanted her to be my wife.'

'I see and did your families agree with your choice?'

'Yes,' they both said together and then they giggled.

'That's lucky. My family did not approve of Nicholas. But I didn't listen to them and I was right. Jean-Paul told me that Nicholas would run back to Spain as soon as things got difficult. But then it turns out that Jean-Paul is a fool. Look at that fence he put across the orchard. It's madness.'

'What happened Marianne?'

'Ah no. This is a happy day. You don't want to hear our troubles on your honeymoon.'

'It's fine. Tell me what happened. And how is Ermine?' Maria put her hand on Marianne's hand.

'It's a long story so maybe later. Ermine is fine, she is with Jean-Paul. Stay for dinner tonight. You two can have Imogen's room and go back tomorrow, yes? Please say yes'

'Let's see. I think I see Delphine coming back. Nicholas and Antoine are behind. Antoine is so grown up now.' Maria saw that they all looked well. Of course, the children were older and taller but Marianne and Nic had both filled out a bit from her last visit. She looked over at John to try to read what he was thinking.

'I must make some coffee for Nicholas. Would you like some?' Marianne asked as she stood up to go to the kitchen.

'No, thank you Marianne. I still do not like coffee.' Marianne smiled and looked towards John for a response.

'Yes, please' said John loudly but then he lowered his voice:

'If you want to stay, that is fine. I did put some things in a bag in the car just in case this happened.' John said quietly and Maria smiled as she got to her feet to tell Marianne the good news and to meet the rest of the family. She wondered what John had packed in the bag.

'Hello Nicholas. It's so good to see you again.' She held out her arms in anticipation of the embrace.

'It's good to see you too.' He looked over to John who introduced himself and they embraced just like the women had.

'This girl is special. I hope you know that?' Nicholas said to John.

'I know she is special and I am a very happy man.' John replied after some thought about what words to use. Nicholas clapped him on the shoulder.

'Good. Good. Now, time for some coffee' Nicholas went into the kitchen to get his coffee. He spoke to Marianne briefly and came back to the door holding up a small cup of black coffee for himself and a question for John: 'Would you like your coffee like this?'

'That looks good, thank you,' answered John as he got up to get his cup. The two children came out each holding a glass with a cold drink. Marianne followed with another two glasses of Kir for herself and Maria.

'Antoine is learning English at school. He asked to have a conversation in English with you later, is that ok?' Marianne asked John.

'Of course. I'd be happy to.' John sipped his coffee and found it to be as good and as strong as any he had tried. 'Let me know when you are ready,' John said to Antoine.

'Now? I can show you round so that the others don't hear us. Is that ok?'

'Of course.' John said in English as he finished the coffee. 'You go first' he continued gesturing to the gangly boy.

'OK. We can go this way,' Antoine said leading them out towards the orchard.

'Delphine, can you run down to the boulangerie and get some bread for tonight?' asked Marianne.

'Sorry are we making work for you?' said Maria.

'Oh no, one of us usually goes to get it around this time,' Marianne answered.

'I'll go with her. We can call in on Madame Toussaint on the way back. I will find out when she wants me to help her. We won't be long.' Nicholas leant over to kiss Marianne and left with Delphine.

'How about that game of chess?' asked Maria.

'Ah yes, I remember, what a good idea. As long as it doesn't take too long and I forget about dinner…' Marianne went to pick up the board and the box of chess pieces. They went outside to set up on the large table. Maria took two pawns to juggle behind her back and Marianne choses the white one. She made her move and looked at her opponent:

'You look very content Maria. Is married life good or is it too early to say.'

'I am very content but I must know – why is there this thing' Maria said pointing to the fence 'in the middle of the field?'

'It's a long story. Do you really want to know?'

'Yes, of course I do.'

'OK. Where shall I start?' Marianne collected her thoughts for a few moments before continuing.

'I was twenty in May 1939 when Martin turned up at Imogen's house – this house – with three other men who had escaped from one of Franco's jails in Spain.'

'Three!?'

'Yes: Nicholas and Antonio were from Spain and Diego was English. Soon after, Martin took Diego to catch a train back to England.'

'Diego is not an English name.'

'Agreed. But that is what they called him. I called them The Three Musketeers with Martin as D'Artagnan!' Marianne laughed at her naivety back then.

'Martin was assigned to Marseille but he came back several times while the situation with Germany was getting more tense, They spent hours talking about whether it would be safer for them in Spain or France. My father and brother were not particularly keen on them staying but this was always Imogen's house not theirs. Martin had got French papers for both the men but while Nicholas stayed, the older one they called Antoine moved south saying that he missed his family and wanted to go back to Spain for them. He was taking a big risk as back then, ex-Republicans were being caught all the time and kept prisoner in France or sent back to Spain. Nicholas stayed here and became really useful around the place. He knew about growing grapes and he was very practical: he could make things with wood and shoot rabbits. He spoke very little at first but Ermine and I helped him to learn French.' Marianne smiled and took another sip of her drink. Maria was transfixed by the story but wondered where it was going.

'Nico and I started to fall for each other but all my family objected to it. Jean-Paul was married with a son of his own so I don't know what business it was of his. Imogen had left this house to me. She did that because she knew that my father had left everything to Jean-Paul. And it was lucky that she did once war was declared. But somehow Jean-Paul was angry with that too.'

They carried on making moves while Marianne spoke but she obviously wasn't concentrating and Maria soon got the upper hand by taking Marianne's queen.

'Shall we stop playing until you've finished?' asked Maria.

'I think I resign this one. We can start another game if we have time later. Shall I carry on?'

'With the story? Yes, if you don't mind.'

'Ok, so in 1940, France was invaded and the Vichy regime started in this part of France. That summer, we were all mourning as my father died of a heart attack. Jean-Paul took it very badly and tried to blame his death on me. Of course, it is far more likely that he had a weak heart and was broken by the sight of Paris being in the hands of the Germans.

The whole of the original Bernard estate was left to Jean-Paul and I was a bit surprised but after all, he was the son and I was the daughter and I had moved into this house with Nico. It didn't seem to be a problem as there had always been plenty to go round.'

'Things got more difficult as the occupation went on and we ran short of all sorts of things. The Germans took so much of what we grew here and left us with very little to eat at times. Jean-Paul would pick silly fights over small things. He obviously didn't like it when Martin visited and so Martin came less and less. By then, he was working with the Resistance, the Maquis as some people called it. He could easily pass for French and we let him use one of the barns to store things. It was a risk and we wondered if we could trust Jean-Paul and his wife Corrine. Obviously, my mother, Ermine, was now a naturalised Frenchwoman but there were still people alive who remembered she had originally come from England so we all felt vulnerable and not sure who we could trust.'

Marianne took another sip as it she was trying to avoid getting to a particular point in the story.

'Martin stopped coming entirely and we heard a rumour that he had been taken prisoner by the Gestapo in the winter of '42 and '43. Finally,

Imogen told us in a letter that he was reported as missing in action. He taught me to play chess you know. Anyway, that isn't the end of the story. After the war, things were never the same between Jean-Paul and me and I heard rumours about Corrine: some said that she had betrayed Martin to the Germans but I was never sure. There were also rumours about Joelle's mother. Joelle used to work for us but in 1941 he was taken to a so-called work camp in Germany and was never seen again. This happened to a lot of young Frenchmen during the Occupation. But his mother was lost without him. Everybody was under suspicion at that time. The children still played together but Jean-Paul would always find reasons to have words with Nicholas: who had done the most work, who deserved what share. Anyway, finally it all came out after you and Imogen visited last time.'

'Oh?'

'Jean-Paul got into another argument with us and he told me that the reason I had not been left anything in **his** father's will was because Claude Bernard was not my father.'

'What?'

'Yes. Claude Bernard knew that he was not my father and he told this to Jean-Paul before he died but not to me. Apparently, Jean-Paul started asking all the older people in the village about his mother. He thought that she had been having an affair but he eventually found out the truth from someone and told me in front of Ermine and Nicholas.'

"You are not even my half-sister. You are Imogen's bastard daughter. Isn't that true mother?"

At this point Marianne broke down and Maria took her friend's hand in hers while Marianne insisted on continuing:

'I thought he must be lying and shouted at him but the look on Ermine's face said it all. She tried to comfort me but Jean-Paul carried on:

"Come on mother, we don't have to stay here and pretend to care about these people any longer." And of course, Ermine had to stand by her own son, so off she went.' Marianne looked at Maria who was in shock at the news but had instantly gone over to put her arms around her friend. After a few minutes, they parted.

'So don't you see Ermine anymore?' asked Maria.

'We don't see much of any of them now and even then, they usually pretend they haven't seen us. Last year, that fence went up. We checked with a local notary and the correct line has been taken. So now we only have the land that Imogen – my real mother - bought with this house. '

'Oh, my god, this is terrible, are you ok? What does Imogen say about all this?'

'Oh yes. She came over to see us not long after the row. She and Ermine tried to resolve it but Jean-Paul and Corrine are clear. They are doing this for their children and they do not want anything to do with us. It is very sad but there it is. Of course, Imogen was sorry about the big secret she had kept for all those years and she explained that things were different when I was born. Her fiancé, my real father, had died in the first war but it would have been impossible for her and for me if she had kept me.

The sisters thought they had found a perfect solution but Jean-Paul had to go and ruin it all. Imogen – my mother- has been so good since. She wants to come more often, to put a telephone in, to do this for us and that for us. There is no need: we are happy. Nicholas is able to find work elsewhere quite easily but he talks more and more about going back to Spain for a visit. I think he really misses it and wants his children to see it even though it may not be safe for him. You see, we are both in a country where perhaps we do not belong. I was so sure of myself but my whole identity was a lie. Now I must try out a new version of myself and make it fit! What a mess eh? Sorry if I am speaking too fast. Did you understand it all?'

'Yes, I think so. But what a lot to take in. You know, Imogen has been very kind and generous to me and my father. I always thought she had no family of her own. But all along she did. She really is a wonderful woman you know.' Maria felt a bit guilty about having accepted so much from Imogen.

'She is well off and has plenty to spare so don't worry about that. She has a generous heart too.'

'She is always happy to talk about you. I think she is very' Maria had to look the word up in her pocket dictionary 'proud of you.' She said and Marianne looked embarrassed.

'I am quite proud of her. She did what she thought was best for me. And she adores Nicholas and our children...Speaking of which, where has Antoine gone with your husband? They have been gone a long time, haven't they?'

'I hope John hasn't started on politics. He may be telling your son about pacifism or the National Health Service.'

'Oh yes, I have heard about your NHS. Now, I think it is time we forgot about my unhappy story and prepare the dinner.' Marianne wanted to be busy so that she did not dwell on her troubles.

'Something smells good already,' said Maria.

'That's just some rabbit in red wine. Do you think you will like it?'

'Sounds lovely,' Maria was used to having rabbit stew at Vera's. It was a staple when food was short during the war. But naturally, Vera's version never had wine in it.

'Let's see what we have ready to eat in the garden...' they walked out to one side of the orchard where there were some vegetables growing. Marianne cut some broccoli stems, a few courgettes, some purple onions and some enormous tomatoes. These were all placed in a large basket while they looked for some herbs. Meanwhile, they could see that Antoine and John were making their way slowly back through the orchard.

'Your husband is a handsome, isn't he?' Maria blushed in response as she could only agree with her friend.

'I suppose you are going to tell him my secret. But I must ask you: please do not tell anyone else. I do not think that my mother – Imogen – has told anyone in England. So please ...' Maria interrupted her friend.

'Of course. He is a doctor and I am a nurse. We understand about keeping a confidence. I promise we will not tell anybody else. I must ask, what is this?' Maria was pointing to a huge plant with enormous spiky purple flowers on it. It looked like some kind of giant thistle.

'Ah, that is an artichoke. You do not have these in England?' Marianne asked.

'We grow very different vegetables. Perhaps because of the weather. My granny did grow some tomatoes from the seeds I took home last time. They were very good.' They could see that John and Antoine were close now.

'Ah, here you are back again. How is Antoine's English? He says he wants to visit Imogen in London one day. Perhaps we all will.' Marianne looked at her son with pride.

'He speaks English very well. Imogen will be very impressed. You would be welcome to come to visit us although our apartment is very small. This is a beautiful place.' John said struggling with the words.

'Thank you so much. Now, Antoine show our guests where Imogen's rooms are please.'

Maria and John settled themselves in and then went back down to help with dinner preparations. Meanwhile Antoine and Delphine played ball with a dog who looked like a black wolf. Antoine explained that it was a Belgian Sheepdog who had turned up at their house as a stray one day and never left. They had named it Surcouf after a famous French pirate.

They had a wonderful evening eating and drinking followed by some guitar playing from Nic. Maria told them that John could also play the guitar and Antoine bought down a second instrument for him. He started a couple of classical pieces and they found that they both knew one of them and played on together.

'You play well for an Englishman' joked Nicholas.

'The piano is my favourite instrument. You are a fantastic player. You could be a professional.' John really was incredibly impressed.

'Ah no, my friend. You should go to Spain. There is a player like me in every bar in every town. Even Franco can't have stopped that.' Nic was dismissive of his talent but he clearly loved to play.

'Have you been back yet?' asked Maria during a break in the music.

'No. But I hear that many political prisoners who survived have been released and most likely, I would not be locked up if I returned. Anyway, officially, I am a Frenchman now. I am planning to go over the border this winter to see for myself. Are you still waiting for Franco to die before you go?'

'Yes, that's right. You remembered. But, I would be interested in your impressions.' Maria was actually less interested in looking for her mother's family now that she was making a home with John in Brighton. She had left Spain when she was a child but she understood that it was different for Nic. He had spent his first twenty years or so there and she could see that it was important for Nic to make the journey back and see what had happened to his old home. She had been so shocked by Marianne's story and was thinking about how hard it must have been for Imogen to give up her daughter. She wondered if her father knew about it and decided that he probably didn't and she wouldn't tell him. She would tell John about it though.

The following morning, John and Maria decided to leave and said their goodbyes promising to return soon. They spent the next couple of days alone at the campsite next to the Mediterranean Sea and Maria learnt to swim in the warm sea. They returned to England with some precious memories.

Chapter Eighteen Summer 1962 South of France

In the Summer of 1962, John and Maria took their two children on a trip down to the South of France in their VW Combi. It was much more luxurious than the trip that they had done for their honeymoon in the Morris Minor. They planned to visit Paris, Dijon, Aix-en-Provence, Arles and of course Pezenas to visit their friends Marianne, Nic and family.

They now lived in Lewes as John had taken over a GP practice there soon after their first child, Robert had been born. Maria had given up work and a couple of years later, they had had a second child. When their daughter was born, they had decided to call her Teresa Sonia after the mothers that they had both lost.

It had been a busy year what with work and the children. John had followed his father, George, in his belief in pacifism and found the speeches of Fenner Brockway and Bertrand Russell inspiring. He had asked Maria what she thought about joining the CND Easter march from Aldermaston to London again.

'Do you get any criticism from your patients about your pacifist beliefs? I would have thought some would disapprove of their doctor having such opinions?' asked Maria.

'There have been some comments but when I tell them I am a Quaker they seem surprised but also, reassured somehow.'

'You know that I like to see to the little'uns, Maria, if you want to go too. But it seems odd to me you gadding about at demonstrations like that.' Vera was spending some time with them and liked to offer an opinion. She didn't wholly approve of Maria going back to work but was often on hand to help when needed. Their lives were not all serious though as Maria still loved to dance and John loved to join the fun and games with the children.

Both Rob and Teresa were excited to be going to France. Up to then, they had been to places like Hastings, the Isle of Wight and Cornwall for their Summer holiday so the South of France sounded like an exotic location. Rob was now seven and Teresa was four and turning the van into a bedroom each night was such fun that they had practised it several times before leaving. It all had to be very well organised and John and Maria enjoyed planning the route, making lists of the things they needed to take and organising the bags and boxes in the van. They had both taken two weeks off work to make the trip.

They drove to Newhaven to take the slightly longer crossing to Dieppe and were lucky that the crossing was fairly calm. John drove the first leg from Dieppe to the Bois de Boulogne in Paris and they had arrived just before it got dark. In the morning, Maria took Teresa to the shop at the campsite and bought bread and croissants while John and Rob got the table ready and made tea.

'Mmm, these are lovely,' pronounced Teresa.

'They are too. Why don't we get them at home?' asked Rob.

'I don't know. I've never found anywhere that makes them and I gather they are not easy to make at home.' Maria had indeed searched around Lewes and Brighton and even asked her father if he had seen croissants for sale in London but it was all to no avail. They packed a small rucksack to take on the metro into Paris,

'Is there anything fun where we are going? Can I take my ball and skipping rope please?' asked Teresa. John sighed as he knew he would end up carrying them in the bag but he found it hard to refuse his daughter's requests and she knew it.

Teresa had dark brown eyes which reminded him of Maria and of his own mother.

Both children loved the metro and Rob enjoyed counting out the stations on the way to the Cite station. Maria was rather disappointed that they did not seem to be in awe of the building as she was. She had to tell Teresa to calm down and stop running up the aisle. When shown the Rose windows, Teresa just said: 'Yes, pretty, can we go now?' Maria smiled at John and they went outside to sit on a bench while the children played catch for a while. Rob had learned to be quite patient with his little sister.

They went on the metro again to the Tour Eiffel where John and Rob decided to climb up while Maria watched Teresa skip around the grounds and chase pigeons. Later on, they found an Algerian restaurant on the Left Bank where they ate couscous for the first time and went back to the campsite feeling tired. Back in the van, Rob picked up the bread that had been left from breakfast and discovered that it made a good bat for hitting a ball.

It took them four days to get from Paris to Pezenas as they took detours along the way: stopping at Montelimar, Aix-en-Provence and Arles so they reached 'Les Trois Chemins' one rainy afternoon and were welcomed warmly by Marianne and her family. During the evening meal, Delphine got out a book of photos that she had made of their trip to London to stay with Imogen the previous year.

'Grand-mere has such a beautiful house and the location was superb' Delphine said as she shared the pictures.

'This page has some pictures of that day we all took a picnic to Hyde Park,' Maria said as she passed the album along to John.

'Mother and I had a fantastic time. We loved the shops and the bars and meeting so many of Grand-mere's friends,' Delphine said

'I don't think our father likes big cities though,' Antoine continued as he took a turn at rocking the baby.

'Hrmph' groaned Nic as he poured more wine.

'I was sorry to have missed being with you on that trip but we hope to go another time.' Antoine said looking over at his wife, Florence.

Nic and John discussed music and both had records to share with each other: John had bought a record of a guitarist he had been to see in London called John Williams. Marianne and Maria discussed their children while they looked at what was growing in the kitchen garden.

They sat around the table outdoors surrounded by vines as they did on most nights. On some evenings, they needed to take turns to calm the baby or take Rob and Teresa to bed and on others some of them would play cards or ball games while the others discussed political subjects like the cold war and social reform. They drank wine and often Nic would play guitar.

Nic told Maria that he missed Spain more as he had got older. He asked if she was still against going back there.

'Maybe I will one day,' had been her non-committal reply. In truth, she had asked her father to tell her more about her mother the last time she had seen him. He had opened up about how they had met and about the day she had died. She was intrigued to see Barcelona but it seemed a long way to go to search for a ghost.

During the long sun filled days, they went to the beach or up into the mountains. The children learned to play boules and speak a little French. They all enjoyed their stay and the two couples kept in touch over the following years. As the years passed, Imogen and Marianne spent more and more time together either in London or the South of France.

Chapter Nineteen 1966 Lewes

It was just after 7pm, Maria was putting the children to bed and John was doing the washing up when the phone rang. John dried his hands quickly and answered it.

'Good evening, Lewes 32678 Dr Lambert here, how can I help?' This was his usual way of answering the phone but the reply in a mixture of French and English was not what he expected to hear.

'Allo, it's Marianne here, I am so sorry to bother you, John. I have some problems here, is it possible for me to speak with Maria?'

'Ah ok, please wait a moment' he replied in English and then in something close to French. He went upstairs and whispered loudly to Maria that he would finish putting the children to bed as she needed to speak to Marianne on the phone.

'She sounds unusually panicky' he said as Maria raced down the stairs.

'Hello Marianne. What's happened?'

'I am so sorry to call you.'

'Really, it's fine.'

'Ok. I have just got off the phone to mother. I had to tell her that her sister passed away yesterday. I heard it from the baker, can you believe not from my cousin Jean-Paul.'

'I'm so sorry Marianne. This will be very hard for you and for Imogen.'

'Yes, but my mother says that she wants to come over for the funeral. Of course, I am worried that she is too old to make the journey on her own and offered to collect her from London. But she tells me I am being ridiculous and she will make arrangements to come alone as soon as she can. Have you seen her recently? I am worried about her health as she is sixty-seven and perhaps is not as strong as she thinks she is. Jean-Paul will not make this easy for us. Should I tell her that she cannot come. What do you think? Am I being crazy?'

'No. I understand. Let me think a minute… I think the solution is for me to accompany Imogen to your house. For me, it is only two journeys but for you, it would be four journeys. I need to help Imogen just as she has helped me and my family.'

'No, this is too much.'

'On the contrary. I must do this. When is the funeral? Do you know?'

'Not yet but probably next week. One of our friends in the village will let us know.'

'Ok, let me know the date as soon as you can. Leave it with me Marianne. I will call Imogen and let her know that I am coming. Whether she likes it or not.'

'Thank you so much. Are you sure?'

'Yes. I am sure. Is everything else, ok?'

'Yes. How about you? The children?'

'Everything is fine.'

'I'll call you with the date then. Goodbye Maria. You are a true friend.'

'Goodbye Marianne.'

Maria sat down to think about who could help with picking up the children from school: there were neighbours, Granny Vera, Auntie Sue, John's father. It wouldn't be so hard to cover for a short absence during term time. John came down the stairs having finished the bed time routine.

'Teresa is asking for her bedtime kiss,' he said on his way back to the washing up which might now be cold. Maria went to kiss their children goodnight and came back downstairs to give John the news. He took it in his stride but remarked:

'I understand. But Imogen has always struck me as stubbornly independent. Do you think she will go along with your plan?'

'She will if I tell her, I want to do it to help Marianne. If she gets a whiff of us doing it because she is getting old, I agree it would not work.'

'I see you have it all covered as usual. Do you know exactly when you will be going yet?'

'No, Marianne is going to let me know the funeral date as soon as she can.'

'OK. Of course, I'll help however I can, but you know that my hours can be a problem. Dad may be able to help us: he enjoys spending grandad time with the children. I hope Lizzie hasn't already asked for help with Stuart. And no doubt Granny Vera will be up to the challenge. She might even bring a cake if I'm lucky.' John teased Maria and she laughed. Granny Vera's cakes were a legend in their family.

John's sister Lizzie had moved back into Regency Square with her son Stuart following her split with Gerry and had stayed on at her father's request. He didn't want to live in their big empty flat alone and was happy to both help Lizzie with Stuart and to have her company. Lizzie went back to full-time nursing once Stuart was at school and her father took the opportunity to step down as head of the GP practice and only worked mornings so that he could pick up his grandson from school. This arrangement seemed to suit them all and Stuart saw his father every other weekend and for some of the school holidays. Lizzie had been hit hard by Gerry's affair and vowed that she would never marry again.

The arrangements were made to travel by train and Maria went over to France with Imogen the following Monday. The funeral was to take place on the Wednesday and they would return on Friday. They made the whole journey in one day as trains now ran faster down to Narbonne and the two women had enjoyed catching up: Maria told her that Teresa was now an energetic eight-year-old and Rob was starting at the local Grammar school in the autumn. Imogen enjoyed talking about all the changes that were happening in London and about the charities that she still worked with. They avoided talking about Ermine and the funeral. When they arrived at about nine in the evening, Marianne collected them in a comfortable Renault saloon. The following morning, Maria was surprised to wake up so much later than usual: she must have been tired. She got dressed and went downstairs to find Marianne and Imogen sharing coffee at the table in the dining room.

'Ah, Good Morning, Maria. Did you sleep well?' asked Imogen.

'Oh yes, thank you. I didn't realise it was so late. Is everyone out?'

'Yes. Nic and Antoine are working and Florence has just left to take the children to school.

I'm surprised they didn't wake you. What would you like for breakfast? I kept you a croissant and there is some bread left. Or would you like ham and eggs? I also have some tea here if you would like some?' Marianne asked.

'Oh lovely. I'll make some tea and have some bread and jam please.' Marianne showed Maria the brown teapot and tea caddy full of loose tea that they had bought back with them last time they had visited Imogen in London. This made Maria laugh and she put some water on to boil while Marianne retrieved the croissant and bread that had been hidden in a basket under a cloth.

'I had no idea that Antoine's children were old enough to go to school' exclaimed Maria as she took her tea to the table.

'Chantal is in school but little Michel only went along for the ride in his pushchair. They will be back soon unless they stop off in town. Florence often takes him to see her mother or one of her friends.' Marianne spoke while Maria was spreading butter and jam on her croissant. She had never lost her love of these and still struggled to find them in England. Imogen was looking out of the window at the cloudy sky.

'What is the plan for tomorrow, do you know Marianne?' asked Imogen.

'My friend Vianne came over to see us yesterday. The notary had trusted her to bring a letter from Ermine for me and a gift that she left for you Maman,' Marianne reached over to a cupboard and took out a small package and an envelope. She handed the package to Imogen and tapped the envelope on her hand.

'She wrote me such a lovely letter.' Marianne waved the letter at Imogen before continuing. 'I won't read it out, but she apologised for any hurt that Jean-Paul had caused over the years. She told me that she always had loved me like a daughter but had to support her son as she thought I was always stronger in spirit than him. She asked me to watch over Jean-Paul's sons as she was worried for them. I am not sure what she meant by that as I hardly see either of them. Anyway, you are welcome to read the letter if you wish.' At this Imogen shook her head and smiled reassuringly at Marianne.

'Vianne told me that the funeral is to be in church. She converted years ago but I thought that was just to fit in. It seems that Ermine had turned to the priest for guidance more and more. The service is at 11 in the morning and then pretty much the whole town, apart from us, are invited back to drinks at Rene's café across from the church. Apparently, we would not be welcome and Rene asked us not to cause a scene by trying to attend. As if we would want to!!' Imogen went over to Marianne to give her a hug.

'I'm so sorry Marianne. This is going to be difficult for all of you.' Maria spoke with sympathy. 'I'm glad Ermine wrote you that letter though. It will be something to remember her by.'

'Yes. I am grateful for that. Are you going to open the package?'

'Oh yes, let's see. I think I know what it will be.' Imogen opened the package and found a box of photographs and a gold locket. Some of the photos looked very old and Imogen started to go through them identifying who they were. She explained that the locket had belonged to their mother and this would now be left to Marianne.

The women spent the day together: walking outside, amusing the children and preparing food for the family. Imogen suggested that they might want to extend the house to give more space to Antoine's growing family. Maria and Marianne spent some time in the garden exchanging information about what they each grew in their plots and how the children were doing. Nic and Antoine came back for a quick lunch and again at the end of their day. In the evening, Delphine arrived from Marseille where she was currently working and Nic played the guitar.

In the morning, breakfast was a sombre affair and after they got ready in their black mourning clothes. The rain held off in the morning as most of them walked the two kilometers to the village. Antoine drove Imogen down in the car to save her legs and besides, the car would be needed to ferry them all back after the service. Imogen automatically went towards the front pews, but Marianne urged her back take some free seats in the middle, where they would blend in with the rest of the congregation. Marianne did not want a confrontation with Jean-Paul and could see Corinne already sitting in the front pew.

Shortly after the priest emerged, the coffin was brought in with Jean-Paul, his two grown sons and three other men acting as pall bearers. They placed the coffin on a dais at the front and then Jean-Paul turned a look of red-faced anger towards Marianne and Imogen as he strode towards the front pew directing his sons to take the seats next to him. Jean-Claude was the eldest and shot a look of annoyance and curiosity at Marianne. The younger son, Andre was looking down as if deep in thought. The priest started talking in Latin and seemed to go on for a very long time. Maria did not understand what was going on and couldn't help feeling restless. Nic whispered something to Marianne and went outside to get some air.

272

Outside in the graveyard, Nic walked past the freshly dug grave and out into the street where he leaned against a wall, opened a box of Gitanes and lit one. He saw that Rene and his son were laying tables outside the café. Then he saw another man walking with a slight limp towards him having stubbed out his own cigarette under his shoe.

'You're not one for this religious circus either then? I didn't think this was Ermine's style either, did you?' Corrinne's elder brother, who was the local clock and watch repairer addressed Nic in a quiet voice.

'No, I'm not much of a churchgoer. But we were out of touch with Ermine towards the end.' Nic replied.

'Yes, that was all a bad business... I wish my sister were not so caught up in it. Jean-Paul hasn't been the same since his father went. At least I managed to get Andre away from that house. He's a good lad you know,' Nic nodded slowly in reply as he wasn't sure what to say. Most people avoided talking to him about Jean-Paul and he was inclined to err on the side of silence on the subject.

'Ah well, I'd better put in an appearance. Hopefully that priest will have nearly finished by now.' The older man winked and shuffled off into the church.

The mourners emerged slowly sometime later and the coffin was laid in the ground while the priest concluded the service. Imogen stepped forward to put a single white lily into the grave and Jean-Paul shot her another glare before leading his family out towards the gate. Maria thought that he looked more than a little ridiculous and had to stifle a laugh. Some of those around the grave looked at each other in collective discomfort. Andre looked over to Marianne with embarrassment before following the rest of his family.

Imogen asked Antoine to take her back to the house and leaned on him as she walked towards the car. Marianne lingered a while longer and turned to Nic when she was ready to leave. They walked home arm in arm without speaking until the spell was broken by Michel announcing that he needed a 'peepee'.

'Oh, bless him. You know, Ermine wouldn't want us to be sad. She was seventy after all and had a long and happy life.' Marianne said to nobody in particular.

Later that evening, they were disturbed by an unexpected knock on the door. Nic went to answer it and was surprised to see Andre standing outside.

'Good evening. Sorry to disturb you. I just wanted to share my condolences with your family. If I may?' Andre said.

'Of course, come in.' Nic replied opening the door wide in welcome. Andre followed him into the living room which was filled with family members who were all surprised to see him there. Marianne got up to greet him and offered him a glass of wine or a coffee.

'I'll take a coffee, thank you Madam. I just wanted to share my condolences with you. And to apologise for my father. He hasn't been himself recently. But I am sorry for your loss.' Andre was clearly struggling to find the right words. Marianne recognised that it must have taken a lot of courage for him to call on them.

'Thank you, Andre. It is very kind of you to come. You are very welcome here.' She put hand on his shoulder and invited him to sit down. Antoine jumped up and offered his seat while he went to get another from the next room.

'I hear that you are working with Monsieur Garnier now.' Imogen said hoping to give the nervous looking Andre a safe conversation starter. Monsieur Garnier was Corinne's brother. He and Jean-Paul had never got on well.

'Oh yes. I enjoy working with him. I find it fascinating to take something apart and make it work. I suppose I might eventually need three sets of spectacles like he has though.' Andre looked up and smiled at Imogen. Marianne bought in a tray with coffee and some fruit tarts and Andre took just a black coffee.

'Do you remember when you used to come over here to play as a child?' Imogen asked.

'Yes, I remember that uncle Nic played guitar really well and Aunt Marianne had a beautiful garden and there was a lovely old clock in one of the rooms. Wasn't there?' It seemed like he wasn't sure of his memories.

'Ah yes. I found that in Paris years ago. And it was old when I bought it. Perhaps Marianne could take it into your uncle's shop for a service. It used to chime but doesn't anymore.' Imogen replied.

'I would be happy to look at it for you. Thank you for the coffee and for seeing me in these difficult circumstances.' Andre put his empty coffee cup back on the tray and took his leave.

'I'll be sure to look in on you soon, Andre. Thanks for coming.' Antoine offered his hand and they shook hands in parting. Marianne kissed him on both cheeks and thanked him as she saw him to the door.

'Well, that was certainly a surprise.' Marianne said as she returned to the room and sat down.

Later that year, Marianne called Maria to tell her that Jean-Paul had died from a heart attack at the age of only fifty-one. Jean-Claude carried on working the land alone as Andre chose to remain in town working with his uncle. Antoine had visited shortly after to offer his condolences to Corrine and her eldest son. He said he was happy to help in any way they wanted. Jean-Claude had thanked him but said that they did not need any help.

Chapter Twenty Boxing Day 1969 Lewes

On Boxing Day afternoon, the Fletcher and Lambert families all went for a walk to Cliffe Beacon with Vera, who was now 75 and Dr George Fletcher who was 68. They were accompanied by Teddy with two of his four children Suzie and Will and a dog as well as Lizzie, her son Stuart and her partner Barry. Lizzie had introduced them to Barry fairly recently. He was a musician and had had a chart hit a few years earlier. He was slightly older than Lizzie with unkempt brown curly hair, green eyes and a soft Irish accent. He had created a small recording studio in the cellar of his house in Brighton and seemed to do quite well out of royalties from his songs.

Maria had more time now that the children were older but still worked as a nurse part-time. Teresa was in secondary school and was a tall, leggy athlete and dancer who was often out with friends. Rob was a spotty teenager with a talent for science and music: he spent a lot of time in his room studying. All the family except Teddy and his children went back to John and Maria's house for tea. Maria read a long letter that they had received from Marianne's son Antoine a few days earlier,

"Dear John, Maria and family,

I am writing this letter at my mother's request. Please let me know if there are mistakes. Also, I write because we have much news to tell you. Some is good news and some is bad news.

Firstly, my mother and my father and my sister are in good health. My wife, Florence and I are going to have another baby next year. Our daughter Chantal is nine now and has started to learn English in school. She has started teaching English numbers to her brother. I heard them practicing the other day when they were eating some grapes.

Next, there is news from the old house. Perhaps you know that my cousin Jean-Claude was always a big drinker and was not so good at looking after his affairs after the death of his father. Also, his mother was ill and his brother Andre was making a life in Pezenas away from the farm so he was more or less alone. In September, Jean-Claude was in the middle of his grape harvest. He had taken on some temporary workers from Spain to help with it. One evening, he rode his bicycle into the village and got very drunk on Pastis with some other men in the village. While riding back to his house late that night, we think that he was knocked off his bicycle and did not make it home. When the workers went to look for 'le Patron' in the morning, they found that he had not slept in his bed. Two of them walked along the road to the village and found his body by the side of the road."

At this point Maria stopped reading briefly at the gasps of some of the listeners. She dropped the letter on the table and took a sip from her tea. John continued to read out loud.

"The news of what had happened spread very quickly. When Andre went back to the farm later that day, he found that his mother had suffered another stroke and had to be taken to hospital. She died a week later, and we went to both of the funerals. It was a very sad time for Andre and we went to visit him to pay my respects and take him some food that my mother had made. He told us that he had no interest in going back to the farm as it was full of bad memories for him. He asked if I wanted it and of course I said that he should not make any hasty decisions. He is well set up in his own business now and he continued to tell us that his family had no interest in farming and we all considered what to do. We had no use for that huge house but could put the land to good use for him. We came to an arrangement to buy some of the land and manage most of the rest on his behalf.

He put the house up for sale and, last I heard, an English couple were in the process of buying it. Who knows what old Jean-Paul would have thought about that? My mother asked me to knock down the fence that Jean-Paul had put up and it gave me great pleasure to make a hole in it with the tractor. My father also helped with this while my mother stood by and cheered.

I think that Andre and his family will remain friends with us in the future. At one point, I asked him if he knew whether his parents had betrayed your father's friend Martin but he said he did not know anything about it. He also pointed out that if they did, it might have been for the best reason: to protect the family. My parents say that you never knew who you could trust during the Occupation or how hardship can change even the best of people.

I hope this finds you all in good health. It would be lovely to see you all in 1970. We are expecting Granny Imogen to visit us for Christmas. My mother and sister will be going back to London with her to stay for a few days so perhaps you will see some of us sooner than you think.

With love from all of us"

John held up the letter to show that there were several signatures at the bottom of the page. 'So, what do you think of that?'

'Very sad for the boy Andre to be left all alone like that isn't it?' Vera said.

'He isn't a boy anymore, he must be nearly thirty and he has children of his own. What an unlucky family! But how lovely that the farm is re-united. And we get to see Marianne and Delphine.' Maria answered.

'Did you know they were coming? Are they coming here, or will we go to Aunt Imogen's to see them in London?' asked Teresa excitedly.

'Imogen invited us up to lunch next Sunday but kept all this to herself. She does love secrets and surprises.' Maria exchanged a look with John.

'They sound like a crazy family to me. Maybe I should write a song about them.' Barry said raising another glass of Irish coffee. He had been making and drinking them since they got back from the walk and this was the third or fourth one. Dr Fletcher would be driving them back to Brighton and that, along with it being Boxing Day, was enough of an excuse for Barry. John found him to be good company as they had an interest in music in common. He was pleased that his sister Lizzie and her son had found some happiness at last.

Chapter 21 - September 1970 near Lewes

Maria drove her mini over to Blackthorn Farm one rainy Sunday morning expecting to check the garden for any fruit and vegetables that needed picking. Then she would take Vera back home with her to have lunch with the family. She and Sue had started to take turns to do Sunday lunch as Vera was now seventy-six years old and no longer had the energy to be the feeder of the family. She parked on the gravel by the side of the cottage and as she walked round to the back door, she could see that the bindweed had started to take over the flower border at the back of the house. The cottage seemed very quiet and when she put the kettle on, she noticed that it was cold.

'Granny!' she called but there was no response. She checked the front room but there was nobody there so she went upstairs and was surprised to see that Vera was still in bed. The surprise turned to disbelief when she saw that there was no life in her beloved granny's tiny body. She touched the wrinkled face for confirmation and found it to be cold. She sat down on the bed collecting her thoughts, trying to adjust to the whirlpool of emotions that were churning up her insides. She didn't move for some time and then the sound of some crows squawking on the roof brought her back into the room.

She went downstairs and called John: he would know who the on-call doctor was for that day and would deal with that for her while she went to tell David and Sue. Sue and Carol were in the kitchen discussing dinner preparations when Maria knocked at their back door. They could tell that something was amiss from Maria's shocked pale face.

'She's gone,' were all the words that Maria could muster as she flopped into one of the kitchen chairs and let the tears come. Sue went on autopilot to make them all some tea. She added sugar for everyone even though she was the only one that normally took sugar. She had heard somewhere that it was the right thing to do and good for shock. The she gave Maria a hug.

'I should call my dad,' Maria said once her sobs had subsided.

'No,' said Sue taking charge of the situation by putting her hand on Maria's shoulder. 'Drink that tea first and then we can organise things.'

'I'll send Suzie and William out to get the others. Or should we wait for them to come back? And don't we need to call a doctor in?' Carol asked in some confusion.

'I already called John and he will contact the doctor.' Maria said as she blew on the hot tea.

'I don't think we should call David and the boys in yet. There isn't anything they can do and they'll be here soon enough anyway won't they.' Sue said.

'I expect so,' Carol said absently. They sat in silence for a while and heard the telephone ringing in the cottage next door. Maria rose to go to answer it but it had rung off by the time she got there. When she returned to Sue's kitchen, she could hear her talking on their telephone. Carol mouthed the word 'John' at her.

'Yes, she'll be back in two shakes of a lamb's tail...here she is.' Sue was saying. Maria was a little short of breath as she answered.

'Yes. It's me.' Maria said trying to catch her breath.

'Ok, love. I am so, so sorry about Granny. I managed to contact Dr Brown who is the doctor on call this weekend. He should be with you within the hour. I also called the Co-op and they will send somebody over to discuss the arrangements once Dr Brown gives the word. I'm going to organise a lift over there as I don't think you should be driving back today. How are you doing?' Maria found the quiet authority of her husband's voice calming.

'I can't really think right now,' she answered truthfully.

'Okay. You sit tight there and I'll see you soon. Is there anything you need?'

'I don't think so. Thanks love, see you later.'

'Bye for now.' Maria put the receiver back down and told Sue and Carol that a Dr Brown would be over shortly. She decided to call her father and while she was doing that, Teddy and his eldest boy, Ben returned to the kitchen. For the next few days, the house became full of the chaos of sharing the sad news with friends and family and organising what needed to be done. Sue and Maria took on most of the work that was required to organise the funeral. Maria took some comfort from the ease of her Granny's passing: she had always said she wanted to die quietly in her sleep and she had got her wish.

The funeral was a simple affair but they were all taken aback by the number of people in the village who had wanted to come. Vera had touched so many lives with her quiet kind heartedness. The wake was held in the village hall and they had put on a good spread. George Fletcher played some old-fashioned dance tunes and a good time was had by all. Vera had requested that they have a simple service and enjoyed themselves rather than being sad and so that is what they did. Tom came down from London with his family, David's daughter, Georgina and her family made the trip from Vancouver. Imogen, now quite frail, came from the South of France accompanied by Marianne and they stayed on for a while in London.

Vera did not own much herself as the farmhouse and land had passed to David but she did leave a small sum to each of her great grandchildren and there were two additional unexpected requests in her will. One was for a bench to be placed at the top of Cliffe Beacon with an inscription for herself and Ted on it. The other was for Maria to continue to take care of the kitchen garden and so David had a legal document drawn up to show that she owned the two-acre plot. Maria thought about Vera whenever she went there to tend the fruit and vegetables and often made the trip up Cliffe Beacon to visit the bench. It also meant that she kept in regular contact with David, Sue, Teddy and the rest.

The loss hit Maria hard and she seemed lost for a time: she tried out several new hobbies such as singing in a choir and taking an active role in the Fireworks Society. She even tried to learn Spanish and went to a fortune-teller by the pier in Brighton. She never told John about the fortune-teller as he would have teased her about the lost dark-eyed relative that the gypsy said she must cross the water to find.

Less than two years later, Imogen lost her fight against cancer and passed away with Marianne by her bedside. The loss of Vera and Imogen left a huge vacancy in Tom and Maria's lives and they seemed to grow closer as a result. This may have been due in part to Maria having to spend more time in London. She had been appointed to the Board of the Clements Charitable Trust and chose to take an active role. She often consulted her father, as well as Marianne, about the decisions that the Trust made.

Maria and her sister-in-law Lizzie walked down to the war memorial to meet the coach that was bringing Teresa and some of her school friends back from Gatwick airport. Teresa's father John had rung the airport so they knew that the flight from Malaga had landed on time. It had been a wet April morning in Lewes but now the sun was trying to push its way through the clouds. They had still bought an umbrella just in case. The coach was due to arrive at 3:30 but finally appeared at nearly four o'clock.

'Stew was a good idea as it will only get better being left in the oven.' Lizzie said as they were waiting. She was wearing a warm coat and hat and stamped her feet to try to keep warm.

'I like a roast but it is all in the timing isn't it' Maria agreed with her companion as they waited for the children to gather up their things and appear.

Teresa seemed to be one of the last to get off the coach as she spent ages chatting to her friends and hugging goodbyes. It was almost as it she hadn't spent most of the last two weeks in their company and wouldn't be seeing them at school on Monday. Finally, she wheeled her case over to her mother and aunt.

'Hiya mum, hi Auntie Lizzie. Why is it so cold in England! Where is dad?' Teresa asked glowing with a healthy tan and sparkling dark eyes. She looked very much like her mother but already towered over her by several inches.

'He's waiting at home, reading the papers as he is expecting a call about a patient tonight. I take it the weather was good then?' asked Maria as they started to walk back to the house that was close to the GP practice where Teresa's father worked.

'Did you have a good time?' asked Lizzie.

'Yes, it was fantastic: so much sun and lovely sandy beaches. There were huge mountains, a desert where they make cowboy movies and old castles that are totally different to ours. I can't wait to show you the pictures when they are developed. I took loads of them.'

'How was the family? I hope you were polite and tried all the food.' Her mother hoped that Teresa had behaved herself while she was away. After all, it was an exchange trip so the Spanish girl would be coming to stay with them in Summer.

'Sofia and the Gonzalez family were really nice though they do have different routines to us. Like, they eat dinner really, really late. My stomach was rumbling so loud the first evening, I was sure that they must have heard it' Teresa laughed.

'Actually, I liked nearly all of the food. Except Octopus – yuk - don't ever ask me to eat octopus again. It was so disgusting: you could see all its suckers – ugh' she shivered to reinforce her revulsion. 'I'm glad to be back home though.' She smiled over at her mother as they reached the road where they had lived for most of her childhood. They often shared Sunday lunch with their grandad George, Aunt Lizzie, her son Stuart and partner Barry. They usually alternated lunch between John and Maria's house in Lewes and George's flat in Brighton.

After dinner, they played music while Teresa showed them the gifts she had bought back: a bright blue dish with a sunflower emblazoned on it, some turron, some vegetable seeds and an Indalo man fridge magnet. She had also bought some recipes home that she had noted down in the Gonzalez kitchen in Spain. She was very keen on Domestic Science at school as well as sports and languages and she enjoyed helping her mother with the cooking. When Teresa went up to bed, her mother followed to say goodnight.

'How come we have never been to Spain? Loads of people go there on holiday now. And you were born there. I don't understand why don't you want to go back and see it?'

'I've told you before. My mother was killed during the Civil War in Spain and I vowed I would never go back until Franco had gone. Unfortunately, he is still in charge after all these years and so it looks like I will never go back. Besides, my home is here now.'

'You really should go. I just know that you would love it. Grandad obviously did. How come he went there anyway?'

'I'm sure I've told you. He worked for a newspaper: he went to take pictures and report on what was happening in France and Spain in the 1930's. It was a time of great change in Europe. He met my mother there and they married in Barcelona: her name was Teresa too. We named you Teresa Sonia for both your grandmothers. When my mother died in a bombing, my father took me back to England for safety. I don't think he wanted to stay once she had died. He went to report on the war in other countries and was often away from home. It was mostly Granny Vera who bought me up.'

'But you may have other grandparents or family in Spain who we don't even know about.' Teresa did not want to drop the subject.

'We did have an address for an aunt and your grandad wrote but we didn't keep in touch. It was all so difficult in wartime and people didn't have phones back then. So, I wouldn't know where to start looking. Anyway, that's all in the past now and long forgotten. Goodnight, Teresa. I'm really glad you had a good time. I wonder, did you know that Malaga is where my friend Marianne's husband Nic is originally from? He had to escape from Spain too.'

'Really? I knew he was Spanish but didn't know he was from Malaga. I'll have to tell him all about it next time we meet. Can you find that address so that I can write to your aunt?' Teresa asked.

'I'll see what I can do,' replied Maria. Teresa knew that this was her mother's way of fobbing her off. Maria thought that the address must be somewhere in her father's muddled papers in the attic. For some reason she could not put her finger on, she was not enthusiastic to rake over those memories. She hadn't thought about all that for a long time and neither her father nor her granny had encouraged it.

On Saturday morning when her mother was out gardening and her father was doing a brief morning surgery, Teresa lowered the loft ladder, made her way up and pulled the light switch. The attic had been boarded out in the middle to allow them to store boxes and old cases. They were covered in old dust sheets and dust rained down when she pulled one off. There was a large case

293

with a recent label on it 'Tom Lambert – 1940s photos'. Teresa pushed the metal buttons and the wooden case sprang open to reveal hundreds of boxes and canisters of film. She knew that her grandad had been a photographer and closed the case back up. There was a smaller black leather case with an old label saying 'Tom Lambert, The Observer, 01-330-1582'. Teresa opened the case to find a jumble of old newspapers, cardboard files, old keys, calling cards, black and white photos and letters. She heard a noise downstairs so she closed the case and went back downstairs. It was only her older brother coming back from playing football.

'What are you up to?' Rob laughed as he tossed his filthy kit by the washing machine. His light brown hair was still wet and he smelled of shampoo. 'You look really guilty. Have you been raiding dad's whisky or something?'

'I'm not that stupid,' Teresa answered evasively and noticed that her brother's spots seemed to be clearing up.

'What's that in your hair?' Rob's hand reached down to his sister's head but Teresa turned away to the hallway mirror. Seeing the dust in her dark hair, she brushed it away.

'Ok. Keep your secrets,' Rob whispered in her ear before rushing up the stairs two at a time, he continued in his deep tone. 'I've got homework to do so you're on your own until Mum or Dad get back.' With that his bedroom door closed and she could hear music drifting out.

'Do the Strand' Teresa sang to herself. At least Roxy Music had a dance beat and made a change from his usual choices. She was getting really bored with Pink Floyd's Dark Side of the Moon: she quite liked it but Rob had played it over and over again. Teresa decided not to go back to the attic alone. She would wait for her mother to get back from her vegetable garden. It was a small plot that she had been given at the Lambert's farm. She went upstairs to finish her homework so that her mother would not have any reason to dismiss her request.

An hour or so later, Teresa had finished her English essay and was doodling on a pad when she heard a car door slam. She glanced out of her sash window and saw that her mother's light blue Ford Escort was back on the drive. She gave it five minutes and then left the table that she used as a desk and skipped down the stairs.

'Hi mum. I've done my homework. Can we look for that address today?' Teresa asked as her mother poured water from the kettle onto a teabag in a small red teapot. Maria turned her dark eyes to the kitchen clock and looked thoughtful.

'Your father will be back shortly. Let's just have a bit of soup for lunch and then we can have a look in the attic afterwards.'

'Oh great, thanks mum. Can I help with lunch?'

'Is Rob in?' Teresa nodded. 'Can you ask him if he is coming down to eat?'

'Ok' and Teresa trotted off upstairs, anxious to make herself useful. Maria poured the home-made soup into a pan to warm and then put some oil in a large frying pan to make croutons from some stale bread. Teresa returned to say that Rob would be down in five minutes.

'Can you get the table set please?' said Maria as the front door slammed. Teresa set spoons and knives on the kitchen table with some plates. The bowls were already warming in the oven. John Fletcher greeted his wife and then his daughter with a kiss and a hug and then his daughter. His dark hair was thinning slightly at the front but his large blue eyes and easy smile meant that he was still an attractive man even in his forties.

After lunch, John announced his intention to read the paper and listen to a concert on the radio for a while. Rob went back up to his bedroom with a plate of home-made flapjack. After helping her mother with the washing up, Teresa looked at her expectantly.

'Ok, ok, let's go then,' Maria said as she made her way up the stairs past the familiar pictures of the children on holiday in some of their favourite places in France. There was a picture of Vera outside the farmhouse with the little terrier who kept her company in later life. Maria liked to think she had inherited the artistic eye of her father and loved to take pictures. They could hear Rob playing the guitar when they passed his room. He was taking lessons at school and was a pretty good player. Both children had learned piano from an early age having been encouraged by John and his father, George but Rob clearly had more talent for it. Teresa preferred more active and sociable pursuits such as gymnastics and dancing to playing music. Maria grabbed the lever and pulled down the loft ladder. They made their way up and turned on the light.

'Goodness, it's dusty up here. I'm not sure where to start. There are some old cases of your grandad's over here.' Maria pointed to the black case that Teresa had opened earlier. It had metal handles and locks which opened suddenly with a thunk.

'How come this stuff is here and not at his house?' asked Teresa.

'He left it up in Granny's attic at the farm. Your dad and I bought it here after the funeral as David wanted it cleared to make more space. I think my dad's house already has too much junk in it as it is. Look at this!' she said holding up a shiny old black and white picture of a group of people grouped around a horse and cart in a field.

'Who on earth are all these people?' asked Teresa as she turned the photo over and saw 'Harvesting Sadler's Field 1938' on the back.

Maria pointed to the people in the photo in turn: Grandma, Teddy, Georgie, Sue, David, my cousin Billy who died in the war, me, my great uncle Jim next to the horse. My dad would have been taking the picture of course.'

'Wow, Auntie Sue looks so young doesn't she? And look at Georgie! But what on earth are you wearing mum?'

'Probably something Vera made. That was the year we came to England and I didn't have many clothes.'

'Where is this? It doesn't look like England' as she passed over a black and white photo of a dark-haired woman holding a small child on her lap.

'This must be me and my mother in Barcelona. There is something familiar about that mosaic fountain... so unusual isn't it?' She turned the picture over and saw her father's writing 'Teresa and Maria Parc Guell 1936'. She remembered that she used to have a similar picture in her childhood bedroom.

'Cool. So that is my Spanish grandma. Looking young and stunning. Don't you agree?'

'Well, she was young. I don't know about stunning as they say that you and I both look like her. That was taken in Barcelona. But that isn't what you're looking for is it,' Maria said putting the photo to one side.

They found some old newspapers, more pictures, an old passport, some keys and then some letters addressed to Tom Lambert.

'This letter is from someone called Martin Lascelles. Do you know who that is?' Teresa asked.

'Ah that was a friend of my dad's who died in the war. I seem to remember it was a rather sad story but I'm not sure now.' Maria was looking thoughtful as she tried to remember the story she had been told about Martin. Meanwhile, Teresa pulled out an old brown envelope with 'Leaving documents – keep safe' written on it. She poured out the contents and found a load of papers: some in English and some in Spanish. They looked official and uninteresting so she put them back. Then she found a manilla folder which had several letters, train tickets and receipts but they were all in English. Underneath there were some small books that looked like diaries and a wooden box with a pile of black and white photos, an old book of matches. A piece of paper headed 'La Llanterna' with a printed address in Barcelona followed by a hand-written address fell out of one of the notebooks:

Antonio y Pilar Reyes

La Casa Blanca

Avinguda de la Diputacio

Salou

Tarragona

'This is it. Pilar's address!' exclaimed Teresa. 'Was Antonio her husband?'

'Yes, he was my mother's brother. He fought for the Republicans and was taken prisoner. I don't know what happened to either of them for sure but I understood that they had died too. Apparently, I used to play with their son when we lived in Barcelona but I can't even remember his name.'

Wrapped in the paper was a black and white photo of two men and two women who looked unmistakably Spanish standing in front of a bar. On the back was written: Senor Garcia, Pilar, Antonio, Teresa 1936.

Maria had seen plenty of photos of her mother but was struck again by how young she was when she had died. It was always a shock to be reminded;

'At least one and possibly all of the people in that photo died in Franco's war. That's why I cannot go back while he is still in charge.' Maria almost spat out the words as if it would stop the emotions rising up.

'But mum, it was all so long ago and your Aunt Pilar may still be alive. And your cousins. Can't I at least write to them?' Teresa was quite insistent and wasn't going to let the subject drop.

'Ok. You can write. Can we put all this back now as you have what you were looking for.' She quickly put the photo of herself and her mother at the park in her pocket.

'Thanks mum. I know you don't always like to look back on what's passed.'

'Plenty of other people lost more than we did. I had my dad and Granny and now I have my own family.' Maria smiled at her daughter who was like her in so many ways.

'Yes, I know, even so...' and they climbed down the ladder and secured it back in place. 'I for one would like to know about our Spanish family. I am proud to be a bit different. I'm going to look this place up in the Atlas.' Maria grimaced at the implication that she was ashamed of her family. During the war, she had always wanted to fit in in England: she didn't want to be called a foreigner. But she also recalled that she herself had looked up Barcelona on a map when she was younger. She had put that curiosity aside having had so many other priorities in her life.

When she got down, Maria suddenly said to her daughter:

'Luis. My cousin's name was Luis. Funny how things come to you when you stop thinking about them.'

'That's great mum. I will mention his name in the letter I write.'

Teresa carefully wrote a letter in Spanish which she asked her Spanish assistant Juan to check before posting it. She did not receive any reply. Juan said that there had been a lot of tourist hotels built in that area so the house may no longer exist let alone have the same people living there. Teresa forgot about the letter after a while.

However, a couple of weeks later when she was alone in the house, Maria's curiosity got the better of her and she went back up into the loft to look at her father's things looking for anything relating to her mother. She skimmed through some diaries but they were all work related rather than personal. Then she opened the letter from her father's friend Martin Lascelles which was written on headed notepaper and dated March 1939.

'Dear Tom,

As you can see, I am sending this with the diplomatic post so that it cannot be intercepted here by the Spanish authorities. I have been able to locate your brother-in-law and he is not in a good place. Jimmy is in the same prison camp and I intend to get both of them out.

I informed Pilar of the situation and she agreed that it would be too dangerous for him to stay in Spain due to widespread reprisals taking place against former Republicans. The plan is to get both of them out to another country – probably France. We have been able to get in touch with one of the guards who seems to be willing to help in return for payment. I do worry about Pilar though as Franco's reprisals have not left women and children untouched. People are disappearing without trace so I fear we need to move quickly. I advised her to leave the city and lay low for a while.

As the British government remains neutral on Spain, all this has to be done unofficially and discreetly. By the way, your friend Imogen has given me some useful information so you may need to thank her again. I will send an update and hope to see you soon.

All the best from your friend as ever.

Martin'

Maria was surprised to read the letter and looked for another but could not find one. Not only was it possible that her uncle Antonio had escaped from imprisonment but it seemed like her father and his friend Martin had helped him. She thought it was more than possible that he was the Antonio who escaped with Nicholas and stayed in Marianne's house. They had mentioned that there was another man with them. She folded the letter up and put it back in the envelope and held onto it. When she was back downstairs, she telephoned her father. After the usual pleasantries, she asked him:

'You know, I have been thinking. Did you ever find out what happened to my mother's family after the Civil War?'

'Crumbs. I haven't thought about that in ages. You know I had a friend in the diplomatic service in Spain?' Tom began.

'Yes. Martin. He helped to get us out, didn't he?'

'Yes, he did. And afterwards, he helped your mother's brother, Antonio, to escape from a prison camp. He was in there with a British member of the International Brigade that Martin knew. He arranged for both of them to escape to France and stay at Imogen's place for a while. It was all quite risky and hush hush, you know. I don't know much about what happened after that. As you know, the war changed everything.'

'And you never kept in touch with my aunt Pilar or Antonio?'

'No, there was no way to do it once the war started. Martin was moved to other work. I wouldn't have known where to start as it was difficult and risky to play detective in Franco's Spain. By which I mean it might have been risky for them as those who fought on, or even sympathised with the Republican side were punished and the regime was suspicious of any foreign interference.'

'I see. And do you know what happened to Martin?' asked Maria. She was curious to know how much her father knew and was willing to share.

'He died in action in France around 1943. He was working with the French Resistance in some way so I didn't hear from him. His father contacted me to let me know about his memorial service. He was a pretty extraordinary man was Martin.'

'Did Imogen and Marianne know anything about all this?' Maria continued as she wondered whether to tell her father what she and John knew about what happened in France.

'Oh yes, Imogen came to the memorial service for him. Those two seemed to enjoy each other's company. Martin used Imogen's place as a safe house during the Vichy regime. It was the house that you stayed in that summer when you were training. But you have been back there since haven't you? You've kept in touch with Imogen's niece who lives there - Marianne isn't it?'

'Yes, she told me that Nic escaped with two other men but she didn't connect them to us.'

'I only remember Martin saying he rescued two men. He never mentioned Nicholas,' her father replied.

'I see. I remember they were suspicious that someone had betrayed Martin but didn't know anything for sure.' Maria frowned as she tried to remember.

'Well, I suppose occupied countries are always very keen on stories of the Resistance: all so much more romantic than the collaboration that must have gone on with the Germans.' Maria thought that her father was getting too cynical in his old age.

'Nobody can tell how brave they would be in such circumstances though can they? Imogen was very close to Marianne and her children and Marianne is always very welcoming when we visited them since. Surely, Marianne couldn't have known that I was related to Antonio though. She would have told me, wouldn't she?'

'I don't think she knew anything about that. Martin had to keep a lot of secrets in his line of work. If you didn't need to know, he wouldn't tell you. I suppose it was the only way to survive.' Tom found himself feeling guilty about not telling Maria what part he had played in that story.

'Martin said that Antonio was unhappy in is France. I always assumed that he had either gone back to his family or, more likely, got killed in the attempt. I never knew for sure and forgot all about it I'm afraid.' He changed the subject back to Imogen.

'Imogen left Marianne a large amount of money in her will as well as setting up the Trust. You know, I often wondered if Imogen had a secret lover hidden away somewhere.'

'Dad, what a thing to come up with: must you always think like a journalist? She was a lovely lady who helped a lot of people including us. If she had any secrets, she should be allowed to keep them. Why rake them up now?' Maria would continue to keep Imogen's secrets as she had promised.

'I suppose you are right. But she was a very attractive woman back in the day and had a lot of suitors as they were called then. Martin was always flirting with her but then he always got on well with women. You are right, as usual, she was a wonderful person and quite a character. I owe her so much: as do many others. I still miss the old girl.'

'I don't understand why you never told me about my uncle Antonio. Have you ever thought about going back to Spain, dad?' Maria asked after a moment of reflection.

For Tom, that life with Teresa in Spain had happened to some other young man he had left behind and yet here was Maria: a constant reminder. How could he explain it without hurting her? He wasn't sure if his good intentions would bear up to her scrutiny.

'I've thought about it many times. I will never forget your mother you know. I don't know what happened to Antonio and if Martin knew, that secret probably died with him. Most of those exiled republicans did not survive the war you know. Many of them were hunted down by Franco and Hitler's forces. I doubt if there is anyone left who would have known your mother. I didn't want you to go chasing after relatives when there was more than likely nothing to find except another sad story.'

'For me, it never seemed fair to ask Gracie to revisit that part of my past. I often wondered if you might want to go one day: the land of your birth and all that. But I thought you said you wouldn't go while Franco is still in charge. Of course, they welcome tourists from all over Europe these days. Have you changed your mind about going?'

'Not for now, but perhaps I will go one day. Franco can't last forever, can he?' Maria wondered why her father had never given her the information about her uncle. If only Imogen was still here to ask but she could ask Marianne and Nico if they knew anything. She was definitely going to tell John what she had found out and see what he thought.

After dinner that evening when Rob was upstairs and Teresa had gone down the road to see a friend, Maria took the letter and photo out from the drawer where she had hidden it and went to find John. He was sitting in his favourite chair by the window listening to some piano music on the radio and looked up as she came through the door.

'This looks like something serious. Is everything ok?' He turned the radio down a touch, sat down next to her and took her hand in his. She saw that his forehead was furrowed with a frown and reached up to smooth it away.

'Yes, don't worry. I just wanted your opinion on something. I've been looking at my father's things in the attic as Teresa wanted that address for my aunt and uncle in Spain.'

'Yes, I know. So, what did you find that has you looking so worried?'

'Well, first I found this' she said handing over the photo. John put on the gold-rimmed reading glasses that were laying on the table close by.

'But that is lovely. I can see that it is you and your mother. Such a good photo' John was puzzled.

'Yes, it is a lovely photo. It's this letter from my dad's friend. Read it.'

John read the letter slowly and raised his eyebrows before he put it down and thought for a while.

'Why on earth did my father not tell me that my uncle escaped to France and may still be alive?' asked Maria looking hurt.

'Did you find anything else? And have you asked your father?'

'No, I rang him earlier to ask him what he knew. He said that Martin took Uncle Antonio and another man to Marianne's house to hide out for a while but he left soon after and nobody knew what had happened to him. Marianne and Nic did not know that he was related to me apparently. Dad assumes that he was captured and killed. He didn't seem very interested or keen to talk about it. But why wouldn't he have told me about this?'

'I can see that this has upset you but think about it. Your father was almost certainly trying to protect you. You already had the tragedy of losing your mother. He didn't want you to look for this man and only draw a blank or find another sad story. It is quite likely that he did disappear, either because he was caught or he needed to stay under the radar. Those Republicans were hunted down by both Franco's men and by the Germans. Many died in German prison camps and even France wasn't safe for them. I've read a bit about it as I'm sure you have. Your father was just trying to protect you. I'm sure of that.'

'Maybe you are right. It does seem strange. I want to tell Nic that the Antonio who escaped with him and stayed in their house was my uncle.

Perhaps he knows more about what happened to him. What do you think?'

'I suppose it is worth asking. But only if you are prepared to either find out that he didn't get a happy ending or that they know nothing. Perhaps this is the right time to think about going for a holiday in Spain? I know you always said that you wouldn't but the country is much more open now and the regime must be on its last legs just as Franco is. Beach holidays aren't really my thing but there is a lot more to see there: Barcelona, Granada, Seville. And I can see that both you are Teresa are curious about your past. What do you think?'

'I am not ready for that yet. I think I will speak to Nic and Marianne. If I can get back into speaking in French. I might get Teresa to help. Also, you never know, she may get an answer to that letter.'

'Ok. Why don't you see if you can get that lovely picture enlarged? I don't suppose you have the original?'

'No, but I think there is a place in Brighton that can do it. If not, I'll ask my dad.'

'Yes, he would like that and it would let him know you aren't mad with him.' John winked at Maria and she smiled and kissed his cheek before taking the photo and the letter back upstairs. He went back to listening to the radio and doing the newspaper crossword while she went outside into the garden. The garden and her allotment were her places to escape and think.

The next day, she decided to call France in the evening when there was a chance of finding somebody at home.

'Hello, this is Maria from England.'

'Hello Maria, this is Antoine. Do you want to speak to my mother?'

'Yes, please or your father'

'Wait a minute. I will find her.' Maria waited and then heard a woman's voice:

'Hello Maria. Is everything ok?'

'Oh yes. I'm fine. How are you?'

'Yes, everything is good here too. How can I help? Are you coming to France again this year?'

'No, it isn't that. Marianne, I just discovered a couple of things about my mother's brother, Antonio. It seems that he was taken to your house in 1939 by Martin. He probably escaped with Nic and he may even still be alive.' Maria said trying to keep her enthusiasm under control.

'Oh, my God, this is hard to believe. I don't know what to say... Antonio was your uncle. Nic

313

isn't here right now but can I tell him?' Maria could tell that Marianne was stunned.

'Of course. Can you ask him to tell me everything he remembers about Antonio please. Perhaps in a letter so that we understand all the details. My daughter Teresa wants to know all about her Spanish family now that she has been to Spain. She went to Malaga you know. Is that ok?'

'Yes. I will ask him and I am sure he will be happy to tell you anything he knows. And he may want to ask her about her trip. He has persuaded me to go to Spain with him in June. He has been back himself and seems to miss it more now that we are getting old.'

'You two are not old.'

'Oh well. I am a grandmother you know. Can you believe it: Chantal is thirteen and Michel is eleven. How are Robert and Teresa?'

'Rob is applying to go to university and Teresa is doing well at school. But I mustn't keep you.'

'Oh yes. This phone call will be expensive. But it is lovely to hear from you. Write to tell me all your news and I will ask Nic to write to you.'

'Thank you so much Marianne. It's good to hear your voice. I will ask Teresa to help me to write.'

'Ah yes. What a good idea. Perhaps Chantal can write the letter in English for you. It would be lovely to see you all. Send my love to everyone.'

'That is so kind. Goodbye Marianne.'

Maria was pleased with the call: she could still speak French but she wasn't sure about writing a letter. They had seen Marianne and Nic several times over the last few years both in France and England. Maria looked forward to hearing what Nic could remember. She told Teresa about what she had found out and about the call. Teresa had been fascinated and they wrote a letter together. Teresa told them about her trip to Spain and they also explained what they knew about Antonio, how they had found out and what they were all doing.

In late May, Maria came back from work to find a thick airmail letter from France. Teresa ran down the stairs to let her mother know it was there. Maria went to put the shopping away in the kitchen before taking the letter into the front room. Teresa was shadowing her every move and they sat down together on the sofa to read it. Straight away, they were surprised to find that it was written in English.

Dear Maria,

Chantal and Antoine are writing this letter for me so that it will be easier for you to understand. I am happy to tell you everything I (Nicolas) know about Antonio.

Antonio and Diego (Jimmy) arrived to share the prison cell that already contained three men and myself in early 1939. They had been moved from another prison near Leon. I don't need to tell you what the prison was like: it was as bad as you can imagine. I soon became friends with Antonio and for some reason I will never understand, he told me that they were arranging an escape and that I should come too. True to his word, when the time came, the three of us escaped, with help from one of the guards. We were taken in a car to a boat which eventually took us to Marseille. It was as well that both Antonio and I can handle a boat because we were able to help when the Captain fell asleep from too much drink at one point. We were thin but at least looked like crew when we arrived in the port. We had been given French papers and were then driven by Martin to the house that I now live in. Jimmy had British papers and soon left to get a train back home.

Antonio had heated conversations with Martin because he did not want to be exiled from Spain without his wife and son. He must have thought that they were escaping at the same time. He talked about going back often. Eventually, he told me that Martin had obtained French papers for both his wife and son and he was leaving to find them. He heard about the reprisals against Republican families in Spain and he thought that they would all need to come back to France. He said that if they did come back to France, he would come to see me. He could see that it was my intention to stay as I had nobody back in Spain and I was already making a life here. I gave him all the money that I could spare and he took a set of tools so that he could pose as a Frenchman looking for casual work. Martin had told him to avoid the obvious route via Perpigan and Banyuls as this was heavily patrolled on both sides. Somehow, I had the impression that he had a plan worked out and he would succeed.

After that night, I never saw Antonio again. As you know, the war changed everything. Unfortunately, I have no idea what happened to him or his family. I asked Martin if he ever heard from him and he said that Antonio and his family were safe but would not give any details. Antonio is a common name in Spain so I never connected this man with you. I did wonder when you mentioned that your aunt was called Pilar but then that is a common name too. I have written to the address that you have as I am sure you have. From what I know,

Salou is a large tourist resort now and has probably changed completely. I can tell you that I have been back to my own hometown of Malaga and only recognised it from the few old buildings that remain. The coastline around it is crowded with huge hotels full of German and English tourists and many locals have become rich from tourism. I know that Teresa enjoyed her visit in April but that is not the Spain I remember.

As you already know, I have been back a number of times and I can tell you that although the country is now safe for ex-republicans, most people do not want to talk about events that happened nearly forty years ago. I have looked for several of my old friends and comrades but could never find any of them. Franco and his regime had done a thorough job of 'cleaning up' after the war and the catholic church helped them. One day, I went into a church near the old prison camp, the one where Antonio and I were held, and I found a priest. This man said that many of the prisoners had been sent by train to a death camp in Germany 'and good riddance to them' he had said. I know that I could easily have been on that train. Unfortunately, this is still how some people feel about things. Very few republicans, including the wives and children had escaped Franco's terror campaign and neighbours were encouraged to betray neighbours. I would say to you: go back to see the beauty of our homeland but stay away from the beach resorts. And don't expect people to want to talk about the Civil War. I think that if he is still alive, you are just as likely to find Antonio in France as in Spain. He may still be using the name Antoine to match his papers but I am sorry to say that I don't recall the second name.

I owe my life to Martin, Antonio and all those people who helped us to escape. If you have any luck finding him, please let me know. I would love to see him again and thank him.

Marianne says thank you for the letter. We would be happy to see Teresa here over the summer. If she wants to visit in the last two weeks of August, Delphine will be able to collect her in Paris and take her back to the return train. She will be staying with us too. We hope to see you all soon.

Sending love and good health

The Clement-Blanchet Family

Maria was a little disappointed with the letter as she secretly hoped to find out more clues about what happened to her uncle Antonio and where he might be. She could see how obsessed her daughter was becoming with the subject and she was getting sucked in too.

The Spanish girl Sofia visited in June and told Teresa that the address in Salou no longer existed. Teresa asked if she could find the name Antonio Reyes in the phone book but Sofia warned that this is such a common name that there are likely to be hundreds of entries. After Sofia left, Teresa started nagging for them to go to Spain on holiday and her parents agreed to think about it. They already had a holiday booked in the Lake District that year and they would need to take time off work to go to visit universities with Rob. Teresa was taking both French and Spanish O'levels the following year so John and Maria had agreed that a trip to France would be helpful for her. The offer of a lift from Delphine had made the arrangements much easier.

Maria took a trip up to London on one of her days off to meet her father for lunch. She took the picture she had found of herself and her mother in Barcelona. She intended to ask if he could get it enlarged. Tom had retired from full time work but still took occasional assignments from magazines. They met in The Albert Pub on Victoria Street which was one of Tom's favourites and was close to the train station for Maria. He was already there with a pint of beer when she arrived. His hair was greying now but he still looked relatively slim and healthy for his age. After they exchanged greetings, he ordered an orange and lemonade for Maria. They took a chess set and menus over to a free table and sat down.

'Lovely to see you my dear. You are looking well.' Tom said as he started to set out the pieces.

'Thanks. You're looking well yourself. How are the family?' Maria asked.

'They are all good. Grace is excited about being a granny again. Everyone seems to be doing well. I think I'll go for the sausage and mash. How about you? Don't tell me you'll just have a sandwich: this is my treat and we have plenty of time.'

'Ok. I'll try the chicken pie, please.' Maria finished setting out the game while her father ordered the food at the bar. Then she reached into her bag for the envelope containing the photo. As Tom sat back down, she passed it over.

'I have a favour to ask you.' But before she could ask, her father looked at the photo and exclaimed.

'What a lovely photo, I remember that day. That's Parc Guell in Barcelona you know. Your mother loved that place: it's so unique: very quirky and artistic. I'm sure you would love it too and I'd forgotten I had this photo. Where did you find it?' he asked.

'In the attic with some of your other things. Do you think you might have the original or is there some way to enlarge it without the original?' she asked.

'Yes, of course. I can look for the original but I don't need it these days to get good quality enlargements. How big would you like it?'

'I'll leave it to you. Whatever looks good. You will know best.'

'It would be my pleasure. I suppose you found it when you found that letter from Martin. You know, our last chat got me thinking. There is a lot of interest in wartime stories these days. Did you watch 'A Family at War' or 'Manhunt'?' Maria nodded. 'I put it to a features editor I know and he suggested I should put something together about Martin: see if there is enough there to make a small piece. They have another colleague looking into some other SOE stories that are coming to light as more government papers get released with time. It seems that there is some interesting stuff about codebreaking that one of the others in the team is investigating so we may have some linked pieces on forgotten war heroes.'

'That sounds interesting.'

'Yes, I thought so. I rang Martin's sister to ask if she would help and I'm going down to their place in Gloucestershire to chat to her about it. She remembered him talking about a friend in the French Resistance called Antoine. He lived in France but was actually Spanish. He had a wife and also a son called Louis. This Antoine may be your Antonio. And I have a contact in the Foreign Office who has given some more gen on what Martin was up to in France.' Tom hoped that this information might help Maria to see that even though he had kept her in the dark about her uncle, he was on her side.

'Marianne might be able to help you there. She told me that he spent time on and off at her place during the war. You know Martin rescued her husband from the same Spanish prison as my uncle Antonio and another British man called Jimmy.'

'Oh. I hadn't realised she had married one of Martin's people. It seems that he made a habit of rescuing people then. I wonder if I could speak to Marianne and her husband?'

'You know they don't speak much English. But then Teresa is going to stay with them for a couple of weeks this summer. Would that be too late?'

'Oh no, these things take time to research properly. It isn't news so there is no deadline as such.'

'I can tell you what they told me and perhaps Teresa can see if there is anything else you might want to know?'

'That would be really helpful. I have plenty of photos of Martin and I think we all know he was something of a hero but I need specifics. I am currently trying to find what happened to Jimmy McAuley. He was the International Brigader that Martin rescued.'

'I think Marianne and Nicholas would like to know if you find anything out about him.'

'Ok. Now are we starting this game or having lunch first?' Tom took two pawns and juggled them behind his back.

'We can start if you like but I can't concentrate on a game and eat,' Maria said tapping on her father's left hand. 'I'm black then so you go first.'

They played the game for another ten minutes and were fairly evenly matched, having both lost a pawn, when the food arrived. They exchanged family news over lunch and Tom started a conversation about how awful the Heath government were performing but Maria had little interest in that. She narrowly won the chess game and Tom said that he would call her if he had any news. He took the photo with him and caught a bus back home. He had not said anything but the recent IRA bombings had put him off using the tube. Maria went into the Army and Navy store to buy a few things before catching the train back to Lewes.

Chapter 23 August 1973 France

The family had not been back from their holiday in the Lakes long when Teresa had to pack again for France. Maria took her as far as the Gare du Nord in Paris where they had lunch while they waited for Maria's afternoon train back to Dover. Before it came, Delphine arrived from work and they had a coffee together before going their separate ways. Delphine promised to take good care of Teresa and to see her back on the train in two weeks' time.

Delphine was an attractive, elegant lady of around thirty and Teresa was quite in awe of the older woman. Her dark hair was held up on her head with an unusual wooden clip and her make-up was expertly applied. Teresa listened as Delphine chatted away about her work at the Sorbonne while they took the metro to her flat near the Bastille. The flat was essentially one room with a separate bathroom but the area was divided into sleeping, living and cooking areas by judicious use of shelving and a screen. The wall in the living room was dominated by a huge reproduction of Matisse's famous image of a blue woman. Through the window, you could just about see the River Seine in between a gap in two buildings. Delphine threw a couple of additional items into a bag:

'Ok, let's go. We won't get there until late tonight – perhaps 10pm. I will stop for something to eat around half-way but let me know if you need to stop.'

They loaded their luggage into the back of the light blue Renault 4 and Delphine had soon manoeuvred out of the tiny parking space and then out of Paris towards the autoroute. They listened to a French radio station which played a combination of English and American music along with some French tunes that Teresa had never heard before. They arrived at the house just before 11pm where Marianne had waited up for them. Teresa was exhausted and fell into bed gratefully.

Delphine was absent for a lot of the time during the fortnight: out visiting old friends rather than joining in with harvesting tasks along with the rest of the family. Teresa, on the other hand, spent a great deal of time picking fruit in the orchard and helping to preserve it to last through the winter. One day she was fascinated to see how they dried plum tomatoes spread out on clothes in the sun to make into a puree. She loved to help Marianne with cooking and noted down some of the recipes. One of the career options she was thinking about was training to be a chef.

Every evening, Nic, Marianne, Antoine and Florence would discuss what needed to be done the following day. Teresa was impressed by the way they ran things: there were differences of opinion but these were worked through without animosity and without any one of them imposing their view. She felt like the whole experience was really helping with her French conversation skills.

One morning towards the end of her stay, Marianne glanced at Nic and made an announcement at the breakfast table:

'So, Nic and I were thinking that we have all worked so hard and completed so many of our tasks that we should take a break for a couple of days.'

'That sounds great mum, Florence and I have an outstanding invitation to join her family down by the beach with the children. Is that ok with you?' Antoine asked while he was preparing a bowl of fresh peaches to eat.

'That sounds like a great idea, son. You'll enjoy that.' Nic said as he drank his coffee.

'Nic and I would like to take Teresa on an adventure down to Barcelona to look for her relatives. If you would like to that is?' asked Marianne.

'Would I like to? I'd love to. If you are sure it is ok with you?'

'I want to find my old comrade too. So, it is fine with us.' Nic said.

'I found the phone number for a campsite near the address you had in Salou and Nic will call them today. You should call your parents to check that they are happy for you to go, don't you think?' Marianne looked at Teresa and could see that she was really excited about their idea.

'I hope I get to meet the mysterious Antonio at last' she exclaimed. 'How long will it take to get there?'

'I think maybe five hours down the coastal route. It's a good road.' Nic went off to make the call while Marianne and Teresa discussed what they needed to take with them for the two-day trip and loaded up the car. The three of them left early the following morning and were soon on the main road south following the coastline. Teresa thought that the mountains and the sea were beautiful. They had stopped for lunch after crossing the border to Spain where there had been a short delay arranging tourist visas. They did not reach the campsite in Salou until the heat of the August afternoon was turning the car into an oven. Teresa was glad that she had bought her sunglasses and sunhat. The shop on the campsite was closed but they were relieved to find that the bar was open and selling cold drinks.

They asked the staff for help in finding the address that they had for Antonio and Pilar and were given directions to the road. By this time, it was typical siesta time and pretty hot to walk be walking around. They could not find the house and were reluctant to call at a house randomly. They saw an older lady coming from one house with a little yapping dog and Nic asked her in Spanish if she knew the address. She shook her head and suggested that they ask in the bar along the street when it re-opened later. They walked down and found out that it opened in a couple of hours so they went down to the beach where Marianne and Teresa went into the shallows for a bat and ball game while Nic took a rest.

After a shower and change, they went back to the street where Antonio had once lived and headed into a bar that sold food. Nic ordered some drinks and started chatting with the bar staff. One of them told him that the owner of the bar at the other end of the street had lived in the area for a long time so they decided to try there. Marianne said that they should eat there as she and Teresa were both hungry. Again, Nic started to talk to the staff and asked in anyone knew of Antonio, Pilar and Luis. The man who seemed to be in charge said that he knew of a Luis Reyes who was around forty and spoke several languages.

'Ah yes, He may well have spent some time in France as a child.'

'Probably the same one then. He runs a business renting out holiday apartments and so on. It won't be open now but I can give you the details.'

'That would be really helpful, thanks. And could we also have a table for three?'

'Yes, of course. What part of Spain are you from? I can't place the accent.'

'I am originally from Malaga but now I live in France with my lovely wife.' Nic indicated Marianne to the man.

'Enchante Madame. That explains it. I'll get you the menus.'

After eating a good meal, they went back to the campsite to sleep. In the morning, they went to the café on the campsite for breakfast. As they were finishing, Nic noticed something behind the bar and ordered a drink called Horchata de Chufa and offered it to Teresa to try.

'Mmm – unusual -what is it?'

'Nut milk. I've never seen it in France or England. Marianne – try it'

'Yes. I quite like it. When would you drink it?'

'My sister and I used to get it sometimes on the way to school.' He finished off the drink 'Let's go.' Marianne knew that he had lost his sister and his parents when Malaga was bombarded by the Nationalists. He only found out about his family months afterwards as he was already fighting near Madrid when Malaga fell. Nic rarely spoke about his early life so this was a rare insight.

They took a walk to the office where they had been told Luis worked. Nic rang the bell in reception but the woman who came out to speak to them said that Luis would not be there that day as he was out with clients. She invited them to leave a message. Nic wrote out a note to explain things and gave his address and phone number. He turned to Teresa as they left the building.

'I'm sorry Teresa. I know you were hoping we could make contact today. You must be so disappointed, just as I am.'

'Yes, it is sad that we haven't been able to see Luis. But we have made real progress. So, thank you for making the trip. You are very kind.'

'It's no problem at all. De Nada as we say in Spanish. Now before we go back home, would you like to take a detour via Barcelona? We won't have time to stop long but you could see the famous Sagrada Familia from the outside if you like. It will be busy at this time of year.'

'Isn't that a lot of trouble for you?' Teresa asked.

'Well, it is sort of on our way.'

'Nic you are crazy sometimes. I hope we don't get lost.' Marianne was a bit worried but loved to see her husband enjoying himself. They spent ages driving around Barcelona but saw the strange, unfinished gothic building eventually along with a view down Las Ramblas: the long wide street that was something like Oxford Street in London. Teresa was intrigued by the beauty of the city. The buildings had not been spoiled by incongruous mixtures of old and new like most of the cities she knew in Britain, like London.

'I had no idea this place was so interesting and it is not as badly bombed as I expected. It isn't as beautiful as Seville in my opinion but next time, maybe we can stay here for a while?' Nic asked Marianne.

'If you like' she answered. They got home very late and very tired that night. The following day, Teresa left for Paris with Delphine.

On the way, Teresa told her how grateful she was for the lift and also for the help that her father had given her to find her Spanish family.

'I'd never thought about this before but there is a Professor of History at the Sorbonne who is researching into the Spanish Civil War. I should make contact with her and tell her about my father. I think someone in her family is from Spain too.'

About a week after Teresa got back, Maria picked up the phone one evening to hear Marianne's voice.

'Allo Maria, it's Marianne here. I have some good news for you.'

'Hello Marianne. It's lovely to hear from you. Have you found Antonio and Pilar?'

'Yes, we have. Do you have a pen as I can give you the address..'

'Wait a moment' Maria found a pen and their address book. 'Yes, go ahead'

Marianne read out an address in Cambrils, which was close to Salou, and continued:

'Nic went down to see them yesterday. He rang me today to say that Antonio and his family would love to see you all. They are not in great health so Nic said you should try to go as soon as you can. He and Antonio have been catching up and talking over old times.'

'That's really great. I will talk to John and see what we can do. But tell me, why didn't Antonio make contact before? He knew where you lived didn't he?'

'Ah well, he told Nic that he came to the house when the Germans had left in '44. There was nobody home so he went to Jean-Paul's house and asked for Martin or Nic. Jean-Paul told him that they were both dead and gone. He told Antonio to get off his land. Can you believe it?'

'Unfortunately, I can believe it. How sad that we could have been in touch thirty years ago. All that time lost!'

'Yes. I know. But now we know where they are and that they are all fine. Nic took a camera with him and said that he would take photos. It sounds like they are having a great time together. They are planning to go down to the place in Valencia where they took a boat to France all those years ago.'

'That's wonderful. Please say thank you to Nic from me. I think you must go with him next time.'

'Yes. I think I will. And tell me when you plan to go won't you? Take care my dear.'

'Love to all Marianne. Goodnight'

'Goodnight.'

Maria spoke to John about it and he agreed that they should book something for the following year. Franco was still alive but he was said to be ailing and no longer able to run the country. There was talk that Prince Juan Carlos may take over once Franco died. The country was starting to thrive and the last thing people wanted was another Civil War. Maria told Teresa that they had found Antonio and the rest of his family. They had an address and started to write a long letter together.

On a cold Sunday morning, Maria made up the open fire in the living room while she waited for the newspaper delivery. Her father had told her that his piece about Martin would be in the supplement along with some other short pieces about forgotten heroes of World War Two. He also told her that he had found out that the Jimmy who had escaped with Antonio and Nic had died in 1942 when serving with the army in Egypt. He had made it out of Dunkirk alive but had met his end in the desert. She had passed this information on to Marianne and Nic.

She heard the thud of it landing on the mat and went over to deconstruct their Sunday paper which now arrived in several parts: the news part which John would read when he came back from his Friend's meeting; the business part, which nobody read and served for fire lighting; the review part which she sometimes flicked through to see the tv and film reviews and then the colour supplement which was the bit she wanted to see. She took it into the front room, put it all on to the table and then took just the magazine part to a comfortable chair.

The contents page directed her to page 23 and there she was somehow surprised to see a black and white picture of Martin looking smart and worldly in a suit and tie. There was a trilby hat next to a glass of red wine on the table in front of him and the ubiquitous cigarette in his hand. The headline read 'Martin Lascelles 1907-1943 SOE agent'. It mentioned his upbringing in Switzerland and England, the fact that he could speak French, German, Spanish and Italian as well as English and that he was a very good chess player. He had entered the diplomatic service after taking a degree in languages at Oxford and the Sorbonne. He had been able to obtain false papers for a number of people escaping from Spain in the late thirties.

When France was invaded, he returned as part of an SOE group to help organise resistance work to undermine the occupation. It was thought that he had helped at least twenty Jews and several resistance fighters to escape from Vichy France to England. He was captured and executed by the Gestapo in 1943. It seems he had not revealed his secrets either to his captors or to the sister he left behind. He had never married.

There were similar articles about other people who Maria had not heard of such as a group of women codebreakers working in a country house in Buckinghamshire, a spitfire pilot, a fireman who worked in the Blitz and a young French woman who also worked for the SOE. Maria wondered what had motivated Martin: would he have risked his life if he had had a family of his own? She didn't think she would have been able to summon up such courage. She showed the piece to Teresa when she finally appeared looking for breakfast.

A couple of weeks after, they received a blue airmail letter from Spain. In it, Luis wrote in English to invite them all to visit them in Cambrils any time that they wanted. Antonio and Pilar were not in the best of health but really wanted to see their niece Maria and her family. He had drawn a family tree diagram showing Antonio and Pilar with their children and grandchildren and also an older brother, Xavier and his family. It seemed that Antonio and Pilar had a daughter called Martine during the war and also that Luis himself had three children who were similar in age to Rob and Teresa. Xavier had a number of children and grandchildren. Luis had included Teresa, Tom, Maria and her family on the tree which meant that they had received the letter that she had written with Teresa. He warned them that although he and his parents spoke good French, they could not speak much English.

He explained that the Reyes family had sold the house and land they owned to a developer who had built a block of holiday apartments on it. They bought a bar/restaurant and accommodation for Luis's family near the beach in Cambrils and a house with some land for Uncle Xavier and his family further inland and they also still had a small boat in the harbour. Luis said that he would leave the story about how his parents escaped to France and then returned to Spain for them to tell. He did reveal that he returned earlier and married a local girl but his sister still lived in France.

Maria shared the reply with the rest of the family and Teresa pleaded for them to visit. Maria's resistance had been wearing thin as she too was curious to meet her relatives. They decided that they would book to visit Cambrils in the first two weeks of the summer holidays.

In April, Tom came down to share Sunday lunch with them as he had some news. John's father George, sister Liz and her partner Barry were also coming as it was Maria's birthday. Although only fifteen. Teresa had overruled her mother and cooked lunch that day. Maria and John had cycled up to her allotment on the farm in the morning and had climbed up Cliffe Beacon together. The family made good use of their allotment and had built a shed for tools and a greenhouse to bring on young plants. This was Maria's haven and she went there at least once a week to tend it and to call in on Sue, Teddy and the family. They did not make much fuss of birthdays but this year, John had given her a beautiful book full of colour photos of Gaudi's architecture in Barcelona. It included several pictures of the Parc that the architect had designed and one of them was of the fountain that had featured in the picture of Maria with her mother. Maria thought it was a wonderfully thoughtful gift.

During lunch, Tom revealed that he had received a letter from a Frenchwoman who had seen the article he had written about Martin reprinted in a French magazine. She told him that she had worked for the French government and had met Martin in Marseille before the war broke out and started a friendship that had turned into an affair. She had supplied Martin with blank citizenship papers which, she assumed, he had used to help people escape. Her name was Anne-Marie Lavigne and she had given birth to his daughter in the summer of 1943 after he had disappeared. She was glad to finally know who he was and how he had died.

'That is such a lovely story isn't it' Maria said. 'But what happened to the daughter? And can I tell Nic and Antonio about them as I'm sure they would like to thank her.'

'Her daughter, Isabelle, is now 30 and she was particularly interested in the piece. She is a lawyer and is still living near Marseille. I have put her in contact with Martin's family. I have her permission to pass on her address to anyone who knew Martin well.' Maria was conscious that nobody else around the table knew Martin so she changed the subject to ask John's father how he was enjoying retirement. She would need to let Nic and Marianne know about Martin's daughter though.

Chapter 25 - July 1974 Return to Spain

This would be the first time that the whole family went on an aeroplane. All their previous holidays had been either in the UK, Ireland or France and they had gone on the ferry when they needed to. Teresa had been on the plane for her exchange trip to Spain and Rob had been on skiing trip with the school the previous year. Both of them had said how easy the plane was and how driving all that way just would not be fun. So, John and Maria had been persuaded to book to go to Barcelona by plane.

After landing at the airport, they took a train to Cambrils and got a taxi to the apartment that they had booked for their stay. Luis had told them to call him from the airport but they didn't want to impose too much and had insisted on getting themselves to the accommodation. They had accepted an invitation to dinner that night at Luis's house and phoned him to let him know that they had arrived safely. Once he arrived, they exchanged greetings and went down to his car. Maria asked him if he remembered playing with her in the yard behind his maternal grandfather's bar in Barcelona.

'Oh yes, unfortunately, the bar is no longer there as the port area has been redeveloped. Can you still speak Catalan, Maria?'

'No. I learned French at school and speak it with some friends but there was nobody to speak Catalan with me so I have forgotten it. I had to learn English quickly and soon started to think in English. Do you speak many languages?' she asked.

'Once we moved to France in 1939, I had to learn that and spoke French for the next ten years. I was Louis to my schoolfriends. At home, we would always speak Catalan at weekends if there was nobody else there. I also learned some German during the war. I moved back to Spain when I was eighteen to work for my uncle and I had to learn Spanish – which I found very easy. Since the tourists started to arrive, I learned English and German more thoroughly.'

'My god, that's five languages. I can get by in French and Spanish and I thought that was pretty good.' Teresa laughed but was amazed by Luis's impressive skills.

'My father will probably get very emotional when he sees you. I have seen pictures of your mother and you both look so much like her.' Luis smiled at the women in the rear-view mirror as he said this.

'That's ok. I think I will get emotional too. I have happy memories of your mother. Unfortunately, I do not remember your father so much. But my daughter has been very determined to find him. With some help from our friend Nic.'

'Yes. Nico came to see my father for a few days. I think it did them both good to meet after so many years and they had a great time talking over old times. Are you related to him in some way?'

'No. His mother-in-law Imogen Clements was English and a great friend of my father. She owned the house where your father stayed after their escape.'

'Ah, I see…We are nearly there now. It's the white house at the end there.' Luis pointed to a large white two storey house with a purple Bougainvillea growing up the wall and he drove the car onto the driveway. They followed him through a gate and round to a courtyard at the back.

Maria had a tearful re-union with both Pilar and Antonio who were both now in their sixties. They were then introduced to the rest of family who made up an enormous number. As well as Luis's wife and children, there were the children and grandchildren of Antonio's elder brother Xavier. This was a part of Maria's family that she hadn't known about. They had been less interested in politics and had remained in Spain throughout the Franco regime. The house was full to bursting and the eating and drinking lasted until after dark. An enormous round pan of delicious seafood paella had been prepared on an outdoor stove and this had been washed down with plenty of local red wine. As they walked back to their apartment after midnight, Maria couldn't help noticing that in spite of the time, it was still warm out on the streets and they were not the only ones still out and about. Some bars were still open and the cicadas were providing an unending soundtrack to the starry night. She put her arm through her daughter's arm and smiled at her.

'Surely mum, you have to admit it now. This place is fantastic, isn't it?'

'Well, I am glad that we came,' her mother conceded. Teresa was happy even if the victory was muted.

Maria had arranged to return with Teresa to visit Pilar and Antonio on the following Tuesday when John and Rob were going to play football with some of the other family members. Maria wanted to hear more about her mother and how her aunt and uncle had managed to make a life in France and later return back to Spain. When the football party left, Maria and Teresa sat down in the garden with Antonio, Pilar, Luis's wife Sofia and their daughter Gabriela. After providing drinks for them all, Sofia busied herself in the garden: picking tomatoes, trimming plants and collecting herbs. She seemed to be one of those people who cannot sit still for very long and perhaps she had already heard the stories of her mother and father-in-law. Gabriela explained that she didn't like football and enjoyed spending time with her grandparents. Maria took in the white walls of the courtyard which were covered in climbing plants. She was glad that they were sitting in the shade of a veranda. They spoke mainly in French as this seemed to be the language that they could all understand.

'Antonio, please can you tell me about when my mother was young. I know so little about her. I have these photos from Barcelona but nothing older than that.' She handed the photos that she had of herself and her mother in the park in Barcelona, another of her parents on their wedding day and the other of a group of people including her mother standing outside a bar in Barcelona.

'It's lovely to see these. Here, Pilar, it's a picture of you and your father outside the bar.'

'That is so nice to see. Thank you.' Pilar handed back the picture but Maria stopped her.

'These are all copies that my father made for you. You can keep them.'

'Really? That is very kind. Please thank your father for me. Is he still taking pictures?' Pilar asked.

'Yes, he is but he isn't working so hard these days. I would like to know more about my mother. Is that going to be very difficult for you? I know that some memories can be hard to talk about and I don't want to cause you pain unnecessarily'

'Don't worry, Maria.' Antonio said. 'I want to tell you about your mother. It is a sad story but I think you need to know.' Maria and Teresa both nodded in agreement. Antonio cleared his throat as he wondered where to begin.

'Ah yes, dear Teresita. She was the only daughter and the youngest so of course she was very spoilt. She did well at school, was a bit too talkative perhaps. She loved music and dancing and was so full of enthusiasm for life. And, by the way, you look very much like her Maria. In fact, both of you remind me of my sister.' Antonio looked at them both and smiled before continuing. 'She could twist our father round her little finger which is perhaps why she was able to stay with us in Barcelona after our wedding.' Antonio looked at his wife of more than forty years at this point and smiled.

'My little sister and I were fired up by the optimism, the atmosphere and freedom we found in the city at the beginning of the Second Republic. In 1932, Pilar gave birth to our son Luis, your mother married your father and I had plenty of work as a carpenter at a furniture warehouse. I'll be honest with you, I was not happy when your mother and father fell in love. I did not think they should marry but Teresa did not listen to advice on this subject. She was very determined and so they got married in Salou and you were born the following year. Your father had to travel around and he sometimes took you both along with him.' He stopped momentarily to drink the coffee that Sofia had brought on a tray. Perhaps this pause allowed him to reign in the emotions that the memory had stirred up.

'When the war began, I signed up to fight in complete ignorance of where it would lead us. I thought it would be over quickly. You probably don't want to know about the fighting: we were better supplied with belief in the cause than in actual guns. As you were only three when I left, I doubt if you even remember me but perhaps you remember spending time with Pilar and Luis around her father's bar. You were only five when your mother was killed by a bomb down by the docks and your father did the right thing when he took you back to England for safety. I was already a prisoner of Franco by then but it wasn't long before Pilar and Martin organised my escape. I think you already know about that story from Nic?'

'Yes, I do. Please can you tell me where my mother died? I would like to visit if I can now that I am here at last.' Maria took a colourful map of Barcelona out of her bag. They had been given it along with a train timetable in the tourist office the previous day. Pilar held out her hand for the map and Maria passed it to her along with a pen. She studied the map for a short while.

'Here, down near the port.' Pilar pointed to the right-hand side of the map. 'My father's bar was here. That part of the city has all changed now. I think you were taking a nap and Luis was playing in the bar while I served the handful of customers. Your father was away with his camera as there was some trouble reported between the anarchists and the communists over at the Plaza de Espana. There had been many bombing raids but we needed bread and took turns to queue up for it. It was Teresa's turn on that day and I often think that it could so easily have been me instead of her. A neighbour came to tell us what happened: there were several people missing when they cleared the front of the baker's shop. It must have been around here. I'll never forget your father's face when I told him the news. He really adored your mother you know' Pilar pointed and then drew a cross on the map and looked up at Maria with eyes full of sorrow. Maria nodded her head and touched Pilar's hand in acknowledgement.

'Was the bar nearby?' Teresa asked.

'Not far, it was around here.' She pointed a brown bony finger close to the 'x' she had already

350

marked. 'We all lived and worked with my father in that bar. It was popular and we also let out rooms. It was partly destroyed by another bomb a month or so later. When Barcelona fell, the police came for my father. I was out with Luis, probably looking for food. He wasn't even interested in politics but they came for him because he let Republicans meet in his bar and stay in the rooms. They shot him just like they shot so many others: because they could.' Pilar turned towards Antonio and there was a silent look exchanged.

'I'm so sorry about your father, Aunt Pilar. But thank you so much for telling us about what happened. We are going to Barcelona on the train tomorrow to see Parc Guell and some other places but we also hope to find this spot.' She folded up the map and put it back in her bag. 'But please Pilar, can I ask for more: how did you manage to get out of Spain? I have read that life was difficult for Republicans after the Fascists had won. Would it be too hard for you to tell me?' Maria was fascinated to know.

'No, no, I will tell you. But this is both a happy and a sad story. I met up with your father's friend Martin as Barcelona was being taken over. He told me that he would try to get Antonio out and that it might be safer for me and Luis out of the city where family could help me. I had already heard stories about how the fascists treated the families of

351

Republicans but I wasn't sure they could be true, even after they shot my father. I did not believe that they would kill women and children. But Martin convinced me that Luis and I could be in danger so I left the city and went to find Antonio's father and older brother. I knew that Xavier disagreed with what Antonio fought for but he and his family took us in. His wife, Maria was a strong catholic, her brother was a priest and she found our presence difficult. She had heard that the Republicans had killed priests and she believed that Franco was restoring the power of the church. Perhaps it was because they were known supporters of the church that we were safe to begin with.'

'However, after Antonio escaped, the Fascists came looking for him at his father's house. When they were not able to find him, they took his father away and they executed him. He was fifty years old so how could he have been a threat to anyone? Xavier and Maria didn't blame me to my face, but they must have been angry as well as desperately sad. I was feeling guilty that I had been spared and that was simply because they didn't know I was there. Other Republican widows were killed and their children taken away for adoption by people that the church approved of.' Teresa was looking wide-eyed at Pilar.

'But why didn't countries like Britain or France oppose what was going on. We fought Hitler so why didn't we fight Franco?' she asked but Antonio and Pilar just shrugged.

'It's a very good question, Teresa, and I never found an answer to it. But the story does have a happier ending doesn't it. Can you go on?' Antonio looked towards Pilar again. Meanwhile, Gabriela had left to join her mother inside the house.

'Yes, to continue…It was late in the Summer of 1939 when I came out of the baker's and a man came up behind me, put a note in my hand and walked away before I could see his face. The note told me to pack a bag for myself and Luis and look for a French lorry parked in the next street at 8pm. We would be leaving for France that night with a load of Spanish cork bound for France. Somehow I knew that the man was Antonio and that the plan was real so I packed my bag and we left Spain that night. We did not come back for over twenty years and that is why we all speak French. We had to learn it quickly in order to fit in and survive as even in France we were not entirely safe.'

'How did you manage to pass for French though? I speak it quite well but still everyone knows that I am English.' asked Teresa and Antonio replied.

'Martin had supplied us with a good set of papers. And there are Catalan and Occitan speakers

353

in Roussillon even now you know. We lived near Toulouse, but we said that we came from Perpignan. And most French people accepted that explanation. The authorities were on the look-out for ex-Republicans: but we had French papers, I had a job driving lorries for a reputable company based in Carcassonne and they were looking for single men not families. We stayed with a local man and his family and they helped us learn French. Renee had been a war hero from 1914-18 and was the local mayor, so he had some standing in the community. He was a socialist which was why he sympathised with our situation. All of these things helped us to remain safe.

'War was declared in September and then people had other things to think about. Luis went to the local school in the New Year. Paris fell to the Germans that Summer and we found ourselves in Vichy France for the next three years. Our daughter, Martine was born in 1941. Food became more and more scarce as the war went on with rations that were barely enough to stay alive. The Germans took so much of what was produced for themselves. Antoine, as I was now called, became part of the resistance: the Maquis. However, the news from Spain told us that we would probably have been worse off there. I could have been executed or starved to death in a camp, Luis may have been taken away and adopted by a nice Catholic family and god alone knows what they would have done to Pilar. We were better off in France living freely as Antoine, Pauline and Louis. And we had a new baby to distract us.'

Antonio looked happy but tired as he broke off from their story and he smiled when he saw Isabella bringing in a huge platter of tomato toast for them to share and some more coffee. Maria asked for a glass of water and could not be persuaded to take anything else. What she really craved was a cup of tea and she laughed inwardly at how English she had become: she had packed PG Tips teabags in her suitcase. They all shared the toast and Teresa asked Gabriela how it was made. Maria took out the article that her father had written about Martin and handed it to Antonio. She translated the words into French for him. Meanwhile a skinny tortoiseshell cat was stretching out on the sunny part of the terrace and the sparrows who had been pecking at some crumbs nearby had scattered noisily.

'My father wrote this about Martin. It tells how he helped people in Spain and then again in France during the war. Did you ever see him again while you were in France?' asked Maria.

'Oh yes. We met up a couple of times. I made some deliveries for him. He worked with a group near Beziers and had another contact within our group too. I let him know how to get in touch with me if he needed something and he did the same. He was careful but there were always risks so I was sad but not surprised to hear that the Germans had taken him.'

'Antonio is being modest, you know' Pilar interrupted her husband. 'He did far more in the war than he will say. He won the Croix de Guerre as well as the Medaille de Resistance you know. They don't give those out for making a few deliveries. Antonio was one of the only ones in his group who had shot a gun at people rather than rabbits and he knew how to handle explosives. They blew up a load of German supplies and were even busier in 1944 once the retreat had started. He was often away for weeks at a time. Who knows what he got up to in between making his 'deliveries'. But he always came back thank goodness.' Antonio just grunted in reply. Pilar spoke quite loudly like someone who was slightly deaf and every so often they could hear the squeaks and whines from her hearing aid. Antonio changed the subject.

'Did your father find out what happened to Diego, Jimmy, the one who escaped with us. I can't call him an Englishman. I did that once and he got so angry: "My god, I am not English, I am from Scotland." He would say' Antonio laughed at this, and they all joined in as if to release some of the tension.

356

'My father found out that unfortunately, Jimmy signed up for the army, escaped from Dunkirk and served in North Africa. He died in May 1942 I think.' Maria replied.

'What a shame. He was very keen to get back home to Scotland after we reached France.' Antonio offered the last of the toasts around and when nobody took it, he ate it himself. Teresa addressed another question to Antonio as Pilar had taken the empty plate into the house.

'How was it that you stayed so long in France? Didn't you want to come back here or was it still not safe for you even after the war?' Teresa asked.

'When the war was over, Martine was still at home with Pilar. Luis had a talent for languages having learned French and some German and English. We spoke Catalan at home on Sundays when nobody was there so that the children knew where they came from. Luis learned about engines from me and how to grow food from his mother: he was a very practical boy and always kept himself busy. We had a bit of land with the house at Lavaur that we moved into. We knew that the food shortages were as bad in Spain as in France. On top of that, Spain was still too dangerous as Franco's policy of "limpieza social" carried on into the 1950's. Even then, it would have been difficult for

357

me to work as you needed a certificate of good behaviour from the parish priest or Franco's party. So, all in all, we were better off in France: and we had each other. Wherever Pilar is; that is my home.' Antonio took Pilar's gnarled hand and kissed it.

'Antonio is my home and I am his. And so, to continue..' Pilar looked to her husband in encouragement.

'I was able to keep in touch with my brother as I sometimes took loads to and from Spain. Then, when he was about twenty, Luis asked to work with Xavier for a while. He met Isabella and decided to stay here.' Antonio looked at Pilar who carried on.

'We were so happy when they got married and set up home here with family. But then Martine was still young and in school, Antonio was happy with his work and I had made a life for myself as Pauline in France. Martine grew into a real French woman and she is settled there with her own family now. We still go back to visit our friends and family from time to time. They make aeroplanes in Toulouse now you know - that is what Martine's husband does. When Antonio decided to retire in 1964, we started making plans to move back here. I missed the sun and the sea and my grandchildren. Now I find myself thinking in Catalan again. Do you remember anything about Barcelona Maria?' Antonio got up and went into the house.

'I seem to remember playing a game around some enormous barrels in a courtyard with you and Luis and my mother. I remember some of the tunes that my mother sung to me: especially when Nic plays the guitar. I think some of those tunes he plays are familiar.'

'Ah yes, those barrels were just old wine barrels in the courtyard at my father's place. They probably seemed enormous to you as you were so small yourself. I like to hear Nic play too: he is a fine player. You know that my grandson Rodrigo also plays guitar. He might play later when they get back from football. They should be back soon as the sun is getting hot now. How do you feel about coming home after so long?'

Maria was thoughtful for a while before answering: 'It is wonderful to be here. England is my home but I feel like there was always something missing and now, I am finding it here. Thank you so much, Aunt Pilar…and Uncle Antonio.'

'I feel that too. We are English but we are also Catalan. I would love to spend more time here,' Teresa said earnestly. They are smiled and raised their glasses.

Antonio had come back with a cardboard box while Teresa was speaking and proceeded to empty it onto the table. It was full of old black and white photos, and he picked some out to show them.

'Here are some pictures of your mother when she was young. Xavier brought them over for you to see the other day.' He said handing them over to Maria. They chatted about the photos until all the others came back from football. They stayed for lunch and then went back to their apartment at siesta time.

The following morning, the four of them took an early breakfast before walking up to the train station to catch a train into Barcelona. They had a really full day as tourists with John taking lots of pictures with the new Nikon SLR camera he had bought following advice from his father-in-law. They had multiple pictures taken on the wavy bench in Parc Guell. There was a picture of Maria and Teresa by the lizard fountain at the park which was a close copy of the one that Maria had with her own mother except that this one would be in full colour. There were several others in Parc Guell along with a set at Sagrada Familia and Casa Mila. And then, as a change from all that gothic Gaudi architecture, there were some of the old town, near Las Ramblas. Finally, they had gone down to the harbour and watched as Maria threw some bright red flowers into the water in memory of her mother.

At nearly 3pm, they managed to get a table in one of the fish restaurants by the harbour. After all the walking around the city, they were tired and hungry. The food was delicious but not cheap and they were all grateful that Teresa could help them to translate the menu. Afterwards, they sat watching the boats come in and out of the harbour before making their way back to the Railway Station. On the way, Teresa managed to persuade her father to buy her a rather expensive bag from a stall that had not closed for siesta time. She said it would be great for carrying her books to school. Rob snorted and asked just how many bags girls needed to have for schoolbooks these days. He couldn't complain too much as their parents would be making a hefty contribution to his time at University over the following years.

It had been an exhausting day and they opted for a snack and an early night when they got back to the apartment. Teresa had seen pictures of Barcelona, some in the Gaudi book that her father had given her mother for her last birthday, but nothing had prepared her for how magical she had found it. She was absolutely loving being in the city.

The next day was a quiet one spent by the beach and the pool that was in the grounds of the apartment block. Maria was enjoying herself so much that she couldn't believe that she had been resistant to making the trip for so many years. The subsequent day, Marianne and Nic were coming down and Rob and Teresa had arranged to go to a local water park with Luis's children and a couple of their friends. The holiday continued for another week and at the end of it, they all had to admit that it was one of the best holidays they had ever had. The parting when they left on their last day was an emotional one and they vowed to return.

Shortly after they got back, Maria's father came down to visit her and they sat in the garden in Lewes drinking tea.

'We had a wonderful time. I met so many of my mother's family: Antonio was such an interesting man and told me so much that I hadn't understood. But one thing has been bothering me. Why did you and Imogen keep the story of how Martin rescued him a secret?'

Tom sighed before answering. 'I suppose that was wrong with the benefit of hindsight. I assumed that he had died: the odds were not in his favour. I was trying to protect you from finding another unhappy story about your Spanish family. I asked Imogen to keep it from you too. We started a lie and then couldn't really take it back. It was done with the best intentions but I'm sorry now that I know they survived.' He looked at his daughter hoping for forgiveness.

'I see. You were trying to protect me but once I was an adult, didn't I have a right to know and make my own choice about it?'

'There never seemed to be a right time to tell you. Other things got in the way and it didn't seem important. Look, I really am sorry. So how is Antonio and Pilar and all the rest of the family?'

Maria told him all about the family and their holiday and got out the photo album that they had made. He asked for copies of some of the pictures.

'Luis's son, Antonio's grandson, Jose has asked to visit us next Easter. He wants to make a career in tourism and to improve his English. He and the children seemed to get on well and we all looking forward to seeing him here. Teresa in particular is very keen to keep up her connection to Barcelona. She seems keen to make a career in the food industry or using her language skills. I thought I might try evening classes in Spanish again too.'

'I'm glad you are going to keep up the connection. Let me know when Luis's son is coming and we will either come down or he could stay with us in London if he wants to do the tourist things there.'

'Ok. I will. Shall I drive you over to Uncle David's now?' Maria had finally made her peace with her father.

Chapter 26 - Barcelona 1978

Maria wore a new red dress with a pattern of blue flower buds on it and had found some matching red shoes. She had made an effort with her appearance: trying to tame her long dark wavy hair with a crocodile clip and wearing more make-up than usual. She and her husband John were full of pride as they approached the now familiar building in the one of the backstreets of the city. Even their medical student son, Rob had been persuaded to wear a suit for the special opening day of 'La Llanterna' bar and restaurant. The three went through the door and inside where they were welcomed by the new proprietors: Teresa and Jose. They were both dressed in black and white except for Jose's red tie and red belt. They were business partners but nothing more than that. When they had worked together in both Barcelona and Brighton, they had found that their skills complemented each other. She was in charge of the kitchen: ordering and preparing the food and keeping the accounts whereas he looked after front of house: wine, drinks and serving customers.

There was a large bar along one side of the room with mirrors behind it and staff ready to serve glasses of Cava and trays of canapes as guests arrived. The walls were dominated by a number of huge old black and white photographs and the biggest was one of four young people standing outside a bar: they were Antonio, Pilar, Maria's mother Teresa and Pilar's father. There was another photograph of a crowd gathered in Barcelona with a banner that read 'No Pasaran'. Tom had helped them to source and enlarge the photographs and they were pleased with the impact that they had on the space. The rest of the décor and furnishings were quite plain and simple. It had already become a favourite spot for students but this was a special opening where there would be some press and a couple of speeches from experts and veterans from the Civil War. Now that Franco was gone and Spain had an elected government, some people were asking questions about what happened in the Civil War. Jose had invited two historians, one was the Professor from the Sorbonne that Delphine knew and the other was from Barcelona University, and there was an International Brigade veteran: all three were going to speak briefly.

There were many other people gathered already: Luis and Sofia were looking equally proud and greeted Teresa's family enthusiastically. Maria saw Antonio, Pilar and Nic sitting in a corner and went over to greet them too. Marianne introduced them all to Martin's daughter Isabelle who was a lawyer in Marseille. They had already made contact with each other.

The Professor from the Sorbonne spoke briefly about the Spaniards who had been exiled in

France as a result of the Civil War. Professor x from Barcelona University gave a brief summary of the War and the number of people on both sides who had died. He also mentioned the controversial subject of the children who had been taken from Republicans and given to Christian families to raise. The American International Brigade veteran told the story of why he had joined the fight and how sad he had been when they had been defeated. After this, Antonio went up to the makeshift stage and asked if he could speak. Teresa and Jose looked at each other, smiled and agreed.

'Good afternoon, ladies and gentlemen. My name is Antonio de Reyes and most of you know that I served in the army of the Republic and had to live in exile in France for many years. This bar belongs to my grandson Jose and my great niece Teresa, and it celebrates a particular time in the history of this wonderful city. It was a time of great hope and of comradeship. Sadly, there were many people who suffered on both sides of the conflict. But I for one am proud of what we tried to achieve. Don't be sad about the past: learn from it. At last, we have progress, we have democracy, we have greater freedom and tolerance. I have hope again for the future of our country.'

At this, there was a round of applause from the audience. Antonio smiled but after a few minutes, he raised his hand and asked for quiet:

'So please, let's celebrate our children and our future. But I have one final request: please join me in raising a glass for all those who cannot be here. I am thinking in particular of my sister Teresa but also of a man, not a fellow Spaniard, but an Englishman called Martin Lascelles. Without him, many of us would not be here today. And so, to those we have lost. To Martin!'

'To Martin' everyone echoed. Martin's daughter Isabelle was so moved that she had to wipe some tears away. When Antonio went back to his seat, Nic clapped him on the back and spoke to him:

'Well said, my friend. You know, you never did tell me why you asked me to escape with you.'

'I didn't want to be left with those two Brits: Martin and Jimmy. I needed an ally.' He clinked his glass against Nic's and took another gulp before pointing at the door.

'And, look, there is another reason. See those two?' They watched as Nic's grandson Michel walked out of the bar, hand in hand with Antonio's grand-daughter Gabriela. 'That lad better behave himself Nico'. Antonio winked at his comrade and they both chuckled.

Teresa retreated to the kitchen and soon waiters started to appear with dishes of food for every table as well as more wine. It was late into the evening when the last guests took their leave. Teresa and Jose felt that the day had gone better than they could have hoped. It was an auspicious start to their new enterprise.

The following day, Teresa invited her family to come over to the bar before it opened for a coffee and churros. They were all dressed more casually that morning as they walked up to the doors and rang the bell. Teresa ran to let them in and locked the door behind them before guiding them to a table away from the glass frontage. Maria noted that one of the barmen they had seen the previous day was there to make them all coffee. Teresa arrived a few minutes later with a tray of churros, chocolate sauce and some English tea for her mother. Teresa and the barman exchanged a look, a signal of some tacit agreement between them and then she introduced him to her family: 'So, I wanted you to meet Andreas,' she started and he nodded to her to encourage her to continue.

'We invited you this morning to let you know that Andreas and I are engaged.' Teresa pulled out a ring that she was wearing on a chain round her neck. They could all see that both Teresa and Andreas were really happy. Andreas was good looking but not in the typical Spanish way. He had the brown eyes and the tan but he was tall and his hair was a light brown, as if bleached by the sun.

They stood together arm in arm looking very comfortable exchanging smiles.

'That's wonderful and I am very happy for you…' Maria said before John continued.

'But isn't this a bit sudden. Shouldn't you wait until you are a bit more…established.' John looked at his wife and could see that she was not in complete agreement with him.

'I understand your concern, you don't really know me yet. Would it help if I told you something about myself?' Andreas asked.

'Yes, I would like that,' replied John.

'Yes, please do,' echoed Maria.

'So, my name is Andreas Perez i Oliveras and I only work in the bar at weekends to help my old schoolfriend Jose and, of course, to earn a little extra money. I am studying architecture at the University of Barcelona and I have another two years until I am qualified. Most likely we will wait until then before we get married. By that time, we hope that Teresa and Jose are making a success of their business.' He looked at Teresa at that point before continuing. 'I am really pleased to meet you at last and hope to see you one day soon in England. My parents have met Teresa as we have been seeing each other for many months. They have invited you to have dinner with them this evening at eight o'clock. I know you have a plane to catch tomorrow so they will understand if you decide that it is not convenient. My parents do not speak English very well. I will need to call them to let them know your decision.'

'Of course, we have taken the evening off so that we can join you. We can pick you up from your hotel at about seven o'clock. What were your plans for the rest of the day?' asked Teresa looking at her parents and her brother.

'I've got a plane to catch at 4, so I'll be making a move soon. Some of us have to be back at work tomorrow.' Rob said as if he was feeling sorry for himself. 'Oh, and congratulations sis' he added smiling.

'I wanted to take a walk down to the port and lay some flowers for my mother. It is something I like to do when I come here. My mother was killed by a bomb there.' Maria added the last bit by way of explanation to Andreas.

'Teresa told me. It's very sad and you were so young. I understand you named Teresa for your mother.'

'Yes. That's right.'

'My mother named me for her father who was from Austria. He was in the International Brigade and died during the Civil War when she was young. It's such an interesting coincidence - don't you think?'

'Yes, but not so unusual to be named for a grandparent surely. I am sorry for her loss but then so many died in that war, as we were reminded yesterday.' answered Maria looking at Andreas who nodded in agreement.

'I'll get more coffee. Would anyone else like one?' Andreas got up as he spoke. Perhaps he had done it to allow them to speak in private or perhaps he just drank a lot of coffee. The coffee machine was noisy and was far enough away for Maria and John to confer and decide if they would go to meet his parents. They stayed until Rob needed to leave and said his goodbyes. Rob got up, put an Elvis Costello tape in his Sony Walkman and placed the headphones over his ears. He threw a sports bag over his shoulder and walked towards the bus stop for the airport. Maria watched him walk away until he disappeared into the crowd.

Maria and John decided quite quickly that they should go to the dinner and let Teresa and Andreas know. Shortly afterwards, they left the bar to make their way to the port area and it was Teresa's turn to watch from the window. They knew roughly where they were going but every so often, Maria checked on the map that she carried in her pocket. They both enjoyed strolling around the city.

She stopped to buy some red flowers on the way and when they reached the spot where she normally threw them into the water, they sat down on a bench shaded under a tree.

'What did you make of that then?' asked John. 'It all seems to have happened so quickly. They are both young and haven't know each other that long.' John had trouble adjusting to the idea that his daughter was a grown adult.

'Yes, I was thinking the same thing' agreed Maria. 'It put me in mind of the day you came to visit Granny Vera at Blackthorn and she asked you, in her roundabout way, what your prospects were. Do you remember?'

'Oh yes. She could be quite scary for a little old lady couldn't she.' John laughed.

'Teresa does look very happy though, doesn't she?'

'She's doing what she always wanted to do: running a successful food business. I always thought she and Jose got on very well.' John looked shocked when Maria laughed.

'What are you saying. Surely you know Jose isn't interested in women.'

'Oh… No, I hadn't thought of that.' John felt a bit embarrassed.

'Honestly, John. Do you walk around with your eyes closed?'

'Maybe so. I wonder what this dinner will be like,' he said changing the subject. 'I hope we get to eat something before ten. You know I don't like dining late like they do here.'

'Andreas speaks English very well, doesn't he?'

'Yes, he does. I rather liked him. He seems to have his head screwed on.'

'You can see that they are in love. And she has always had a determination to make things work.'

They sat in silence for a while each in their own thoughts and then John nodded towards some benches by a low wall.

'Have you noticed those young men over there on those benches?' Maria looked over to where a group of five young black men were engaged in an animated discussion. There were a number of bags with their contents spilling over the pavement nearby and one of the men was rolling up a sleeping bag.

'Oh yes. They don't look Spanish do they? And it seems like they may have been sleeping rough.'

'I read in the paper that there are quite a few young Africans making their way through Spain to get to France and the UK. There are several conflict zones in Central and West Africa at the moment. And where there is war, there are refugees seeking safety.'

'It's so sad isn't it. When people have to leave their own country and seek a home elsewhere. I often think that I was one of the lucky ones.'

'Yes, you were. And I am thankful that I found you. I hope those young men find a good home somewhere like you did. Now, are you ready?'

John held his hand out to Maria who smiled as she took it in hers and got up from the bench. They walked to the quayside which was bathed in sunshine. There was a slight whiff of fish and a chug-chug coming from an incoming fishing boat. Maria gave half of the flowers to John and they threw them into the water and then stood together for a while, watching them bob away.

Printed in Great Britain
by Amazon

23447766R00208